THE GREAT MR. LLOYD

BRUCE FREEMAN

ARCHWAY
PUBLISHING

Archway Publishing books may be ordered through booksellers or by contacting:

Archway Publishing
1663 Liberty Drive
Bloomington, IN 47403
www.archwaypublishing.com
1 (888) 242-5904

ISBN: 978-1-4808-8705-3 (sc)
ISBN: 978-1-4808-8706-0 (e)

Library of Congress Control Number: 2020901213

Print information available on the last page.

Archway Publishing rev. date: 1/27/2020

First and foremost,
this book is for Kathy.
It is also for Ginny.

CHAPTER 1

That morning, Arthur Lloyd listened absently as Dorothy, his wife, addressed him in that stiff-backed way that she had. He paid attention not to what she was saying, but rather to how she arched her left eyebrow, presumably to give the point she was making more gravitas. She was pulling out all the stops. It was something about how Arthur needed to get past Celldesign, a lecture that had become a sort of morning ritual. He had done so, he wanted to say, but her mind was made-up. She did not know it, but decisions had been made, and Arthur's mind was centered on "the culmination," as he called it. And that led him back to his grandson, Spencer.

At other breakfasts on other mornings, Dorothy had gone over and over what she thought he owed, or, more precisely, didn't owe to Spencer. He could see that she still blamed Spencer for triggering the battles over Celldesign and the whole public dissection of the Lloyd family, a painful affair; but he was beyond that. He looked at her: intense eyes, hair pulled back so that it suggested ferocity—she had held up well, but she clearly missed the high perch that Arthur had occupied at Harvard for all those years. Now she saw him as "moping around" the apartment on Beacon Hill, a phrase she reserved for her greatest disdain. Spencer was a convenient target, if nothing else. But Arthur knew better.

Arthur had put together a plan that was quite skillful, neither obvious nor overbearing, something that would reach out to Spencer, that would overcome the damage to the bridge between them that had once existed.

He knew his grandson's habit of going for a run each morning. Five miles, like clockwork, and always with his phone in his pocket. It was the perfect time to send him a text, as he would be alone, outside the influence of others who would push him away, who might be hard and fast and unforgiving, who would advise him that the chasm Arthur had created could not be bridged. But running along the streets of Boston by himself, Spencer would react differently. That was the bet.

Spencer Lloyd was a Red Sox fan, one of the faithful, but he had never gotten closer than the cheap seats in the right-field bleachers. Arthur was well aware of that when he wrangled tickets from a colleague at Harvard for opening day. He knew that the prospect of seats right above the dugout, where they could see the players close-up, hear their chatter, and feel the optimism of a new season, would be rather enticing to Spencer—Arthur, on the other hand, was not a fan. To the contrary, he looked down on those who would idle away precious time watching grown men play what he regarded as an inconsequential game. The tickets were a pretext for Arthur, merely a means to an end. But that was the whole point.

Still, it was a tall order: the two of them had not spoken in several months, not since they had parted on the courthouse steps. A wall had come up between them; and also between Arthur and his legacy. And those walls seemed related in some way.

Arthur's text was minimalist:

Dear Spencer, I've managed to lay my hands on two tickets, opening day, good ones, above the Red Sox dugout. Would be pleased if you would join me. I hope you agree that we need to get back together. Best, Grandfather.

Arthur's bet paid off. Spencer texted back right away—agreeing to meet outside the Fenway gate at noon, an hour before the game started, so that they could get hot dogs and beer and watch batting practice.

Alone in his library, Arthur said under his breath, "Good," although he thought the prospect of a hot dog cooked in cloudy gray water to be appalling, and Spencer would have known that. *That should tell him something about how important this is,* Arthur thought.

Satisfied that his plan had been launched, Arthur turned from the desk in his study only to confront Dorothy standing silently in the doorway, straight and proper, a look of disapproval on her face, which brought him up short. "Damn it," he mumbled, loudly enough for her to hear but softy enough so that she could ignore it if she wished. She had been following him around the house ever since the court hearings, and he resented it. And it was worse when, like now, he had something that he was keeping from her.

But he didn't want her in on this. And at long last, he felt entitled to that.

He hurried unsteadily past her, but no words were exchanged. She gave him a sideways glance, and Arthur returned the favor, mumbling something to the effect that it was "insulting" as he brushed past her, feeling her eyes on the back of his neck as he made his way to the kitchen for another cup of coffee.

It tested his determination, but his plan was singular in the sense that it came from within him, the great Arthur Lloyd, and he would see it through.

Arthur knew that his days as a hero in the heady world of Boston were over. It had taken months after the court hearing for that to sink in, but by now it had. At first it troubled him, but he concluded that he was merely being vainglorious—something that Dorothy pointed out unsparingly, over and over. Perhaps that was the time when he had gotten beyond Celldesign—it was somewhat of a blur.

He kept his eyes on the coffee machine, making a show of concentrating on the first few drops from the coffeepot as they hit the bottom of his Harvard cup; it allowed him to sidestep Dorothy's gaze. He knew that if he were honest, he would have said something, something real, and perhaps even admitted to a sense of apprehension at the prospect of meeting Spencer at Fenway. Instead, he remained silent, defiant. Perhaps, in some abstract way, she had a right to know, but he had discovered that if he looked at the coffee long enough, she would vanish.

So, he thought with even greater resolve, he would put on "the uniform" with the rest of the throngs at Fenway: khaki pants, a BOSTON sweatshirt, and a Red Sox cap, its visor forward, as designed, although he knew that Spencer would wear his visor to the rear, a kind of statement for Spencer's generation. They would try to make small talk, and Spencer would watch the players—something he had liked to do since he was a child. But by the seventh inning stretch, Arthur would have to be listened to as he explained himself to his grandson. He thought of this as his MacArthur speech. And there had to be enough time for that.

He was quite sure of his purpose; there had been time enough to think it through—and it made sense at that level, the level of rational thought. It was the emotional part that worried him. Was he just a crazy old man? Wasn't that what Dorothy's arched eyebrow meant? He drifted with the steam rising from his coffee, staring out the window of his massive apartment overlooking Beacon Hill, thinking back to the Arthur Lloyd that he had been, towering above the crowd at six feet five inches, glaring behind his hawk-like nose, with his salt-and-pepper hair slicked straight back, and his voice disciplined by years of being interviewed. It was low and brooding, imparting a seriousness to each subject that he addressed. And now the subject was him. Was he just a latter-day *King Lear*, taking a final bow to his own crumbling vanity?

He sighed the way old men do, more of an exhaling of stale air, full of doubt, than an expression of youthful determination, yet he felt sure about Fenway and the lifeline it provided—Spencer had said 'yes' right away, hadn't he?

It was propitious that Arthur texted Spencer on one of his runs. The whole running business had started a few years earlier when Spencer, still in college at Tufts, joined the craze, which was Arthur's view of it. "Are you running toward something," Arthur had asked at the time, "or away from something?" He thought that was funny; such was his sense of humor. But he quickly moved on to the point: "How about running to Celldesign? Who knows? You might cross the goal line with us."

Arthur thought that Spencer had "gone off the reservation" when he rejected the admission into Harvard that Arthur had arranged, and went to Tufts instead. Deep down, Arthur took it personally. But joining Celldesign would, he'd thought, rectify that. Spencer would join the other employees who had been compensated largely with stock options, with an IPO on the horizon. "You'll walk into a small fortune," Arthur had exclaimed.

Not only that, but it would give Spencer something all youth seek—a chance to change the world.

Arthur was not blind; he knew that there had been a cost to his career. All the time away, traveling in Washington and abroad; all the time alone, writing; all the board involvements— he knew that these things had affected his role as both father and grandfather. Simply not enough time, and his priority had been his work. He had never apologized for that.

And in an odd way, fate had provided; after all, it was his chairmanship of the Board of Overseers of the CRISPR patent, held jointly by Harvard and MIT, that led directly to his role in founding, along with an exceptional student, the venture that became known as Celldesign. In short, Arthur saw to it that the company received the all-important license of the CRISPR technology, and that was the true start of it all.

Arthur remembered it vividly; that particular memory never faded with time. He would literally hear the knock on his faculty office door, and there would stand Mary Knightbridge, a perky, attractive, and brilliant student at Harvard Business School, holding a bottle of bubbly wine of some sort. It was an atrocious Portuguese, as he recalled, sold in a red clay container and likely the cheapest bottle on the shelf. Ostensibly, she wanted to congratulate him on his appointment as chairman of the Board of Overseers, although neither of them, in truth, understood the science behind it. But they were both businesspersons, sharp to see and seize an opportunity. Although Arthur subscribed to the open-door policy to which the business school faculty adhered for formal purposes, many of them, including Arthur, thought it was a waste of time—*their* time—and so they discouraged it as much as possible. But on that day, Arthur was lighthearted and self-congratulatory, due to his prestigious new appointment to the Board of Overseers, and he was unusually ready for a discussion with a student, especially a pretty, deferential one, who nevertheless had shown a particular clarity of vision in his class. She was one of those students who prompted Arthur to comment to himself, "There's a young woman who is going somewhere."

"It is a process," he'd told her after she had taken the chair opposite his desk. Arthur had screwed off the cap of the bottle, pouring the murky red fluid into two paper cups. "They call it 'gene editing,' but that gives it too much of a science fiction coloring for my taste. It really is a way to mimic how bad bacteria, virus-laden, are captured and stamped out by good bacteria. The virus-laden bacteria that might otherwise kill the cell are thus turned on and wiped out. Nice and neat."

Mary had pretended to be awed, careful to open her mouth just a bit, to keep her eyes fixed on the Great Man, but of course, she knew all of that. She made sure that the conversation turned to practical applications. "I have an admission, Mr. Lloyd," she said, putting a little smile on her thin but pretty face. "I was thinking about preparing a business plan for a start-up gene-editing company for my senior project." She paused for Arthur's reaction and, seeing him look down at some papers on his desk, went ahead to complete her thought. "And I'd like to try to persuade you to help me actually do it—change the world. In reality."

There was something in her voice—Arthur's head lifted to look at her, like a brown trout rising for a mayfly. *Audacious,* he thought, while directing a smile to his student. He wanted to see how far she had thought through her idea.

"Well," she said, "I'm thinking of a way where the gene that makes people susceptible to disease from shallow wells in developing countries—where the water can't always be purified—might be snipped out of the DNA strand and replaced with a gene that fights back. In other words, providing an immunity. Like a vaccination."

"Why don't you simply purify the water?"

"Because without a deep well, it is not possible to get truly clean water. Perhaps better, but not truly clean. And drilling rigs are not available and would never be allowed in that habitat anyway. Remember, thousands of years ago humans had the genetic structure to tolerate unclean water. We lost that along the way of civilization, but we did have it once. Why not again?"

"Won't you need a doctor to administer the enzyme?"

"I'm thinking more in terms of a patch, something simple to make and transport right to the site of the problem."

"I'm impressed," Arthur said in a tone intended to encourage her. "You've given this some thought, haven't you?"

"Why don't we call it Celldesign?" she asked, and Arthur nodded approval, but his mind was racing. Initial financing, product development, and sales all were predicated, Arthur knew, on the license. He knew he would have a hard sell to his Board of Overseers—and he did. He recalled how strained the negotiations were, with the accusations from some friends that he was serving two masters—a charge he considered himself above. In fact, he thought that the mere suggestion of a conflict was "abusive," as he put it. And no one wanted to be seen as abusive to Arthur Lloyd.

He smiled—that was when he was at the height of his powers.

With Dorothy out of the hallway, Arthur headed back to his library, which was where he went to be alone in a sense.

Alone with his memories. It was his private place, where his mind had been the clearest, but now was the place where he still saw his friends. He would sit in his old leather chair and stare at a bookcase festooned with framed photos, pictures of him on campus; or in Washington, standing next to the Secretary of Commerce; or next to a Justice of the Supreme Court; or in Boston with the Mayor; or next to Mary in front of the Celldesign offices just outside of the city. The record of his lifetime was there. Photographic depictions of the times and people of his life. But on that day, his mind was on a missing piece—not a single framed photo of Winston, his only son.

It was odd, Arthur thought, that reaching out for Spencer seemed almost compelled at some instinctual level, but not so with respect to Winston. Whatever Celldesign had meant, it had led his son and grandson to different places, from which they called to Arthur in different ways.

He remembered, with mixed feelings, how he had tried—he thought he had positioned Winston to thrive. But it turned out to be more complicated.

It was all in how he set up the financing of Celldesign, or so he thought. Who could argue about the rights of an initial investor, a risk-taker, the very engine of progress? Setting things up so that Winston had that role would, Arthur thought, give him stature by osmosis, that he otherwise lacked.

At the time, Mary had been telling Arthur more and more frequently that she needed the seed-money. They were already feeling the pinch. Celldesign was being held back; the venture was ready for office space, phones, a business development budget, the money needed to pay for the license, and, most important, salaries. Her "animal spirits" were being reined in; they were ready for the first round of financing.

Arthur saw it as an opportunity for Winston, which, he

knew, would strike Mary as a subtle but real change in the dynamics of the venture that the two of them had brought to that point. It would no longer be just the two of them.

Yet if Mary was offended in any way, she did not show it. Not that Arthur could discern. She merely asked that she be designated CEO, which Arthur was quite prepared to do anyway.

The fact was, however, that Arthur never looked at Winston as a threat to Mary. He did not bring Winston on board with any thought that Winston would compete with Mary; he did it for other, private reasons.

Winston was in the investment business, although his success rate was rather low—so low, in fact, that under ordinary circumstances, he would not even have qualified to be an investor in a start-up like Celldesign. Celldesign's seed money was as far beyond his grasp, as it was beyond Mary's reach. And that was Arthur's advantage.

Winston lived a contradiction: he suffered under the weight of Arthur's shadow, yet he did not have the courage to escape. Large and gregarious, Winston looked as if he were in constant conflict of some sort, not outwardly exerting himself, yet constantly perspiring. The back of his shirt was almost always stained and wet. His temples were dotted by droplets of sweat, and his upper lip glistened. He seemed destined to remain in that semi-comfortable area known as Arthur's shadow, not ever moving too far in any direction without Arthur's approval to do so.

Arthur, however, could not look at Winston's physical presence without a sense of regret. "Any two-bit psychologist," he would say to himself, "would look at Winston and deduce a famous and overbearing father." And that would send Arthur, the optimist, into an inward spiral, not exactly depressive (because how would that solve anything?) but reflective. That is when he thought of the time he had not spent at home.

Arthur was a man who taught economic principles, markets, competition, and Adam Smith's unseen hand, and, of course, he would have liked to have seen more initiative from Winston. But Winston was a special case, he told himself. Arthur was well aware that his own life had cast a shadow that would have engulfed almost anyone, and it certainly had engulfed Winston. "It wasn't a level playing field," Arthur would argue to others when examining Winston's track record. And Winston's inner life, to the extent it was accessible to Arthur, suggested the kind of quiet desperation that simply made Arthur sad, although at the same time, he thought it preposterous that one should feel guilty for being successful.

His son, Arthur would say, was "the nervous sort" and not as tall as Arthur, not as thin, not as commanding. Rather, Winston was average in most respects, except for his hair, which was reddish. He was balding, revealing a moist scalp that required frequent wiping with a handkerchief, and his eyes could be described as filmy, the kind of eyes that seem to result from one drink too many the night before. And that was often true.

He had all the advantage of legacy admissions, and thus listed both Harvard College and Harvard Law School on his résumé—always something Arthur worked into the conversation whenever the issue of what his son was doing came up. But Arthur was aware, as any parent would be, that his son was floundering. Practicing law had never been a serious consideration, so Winston had bounced around the securities industry, never finding a fit, each year losing more hair and watching his eyes sink back farther into his puffy face until they were barely visible.

Arthur simply could not watch Winston's life play out like that. So, he had a plan.

Arthur had become a wealthy man by that time in his life. The royalties from his books alone exceeded most peoples' income, and then there was Dorothy, heir to an Irish immigrant family that had amassed a fortune from banking and then secured their fortune by controlling local politics. It was she who owned their exquisite apartment on Beacon Hill, with private elevator, marble entry, heavy handmade chandeliers reputedly crafted by descendants of Paul Revere, and mahogany millwork, all overlooking Boston's most elegant street. Arthur decided to provide the seed money for Celldesign but with a catch: he would provide the seed money to Winston, who would, in turn, loan it to the company in exchange for a seat on the board, ostensibly to keep an eye on "his" investment.

Arthur was told that, legally, Winston was nothing more than a straw man, but Arthur considered that an uninformed position. The plan gave Winston a position of importance that he otherwise would not have been able to obtain. He was certain that, "this kind of thing was done all the time;" it was something that a founder was entitled to. With one stroke of a pen, it allowed Arthur to avoid the conflict of interest he would have had if he had invested directly in Celldesign, according to the attorney for the Board of Overseers, who insisted that Arthur's involvement in the company had to be untainted by personal financial interest. In short, Arthur had to be solely beholden to the licensor. Arthur was certain that nobody would question his intentions or his expertise. There would be nothing wrong, he was certain, with bringing in Winston, his son, who would act as Arthur directed.

Winston had little to say in the matter; it was presented

to him as a fait accompli that, to all appearances, was fine with him.

Arthur looked at it as nothing more than a business choice, which, of course, required the usual paperwork—a promissory note as well as a nondisclosure agreement to the effect that Arthur's actual financial involvement—ten million dollars—would remain between them and was not contingent on any specific conduct, although Arthur was confident that Winston would make the right business choice if a question ever arose; he always sought Arthur's advice.

With that, Winston left the financial firm for which he had been working (without much distinction) and set up a small office on Newbury Street in Back Bay, taking up the second floor of a brick building near the heart of old Boston, a few steps from the Boston Gardens and Swan Lake, and began keeping an eye on the family investment in Celldesign. From a psychological point of view, Winston needed a score. It wasn't much more complicated than that; he needed to bring one in, and as Celldesign began to move forward, he began to have some hope that it would finally happen, particularly when an IPO was talked about. Winston couldn't hold himself back. He began shopping at Louis of Boston, as his father did—the finest bespoke suits, custom shirts, handmade shoes imported from England. He began to look the part he anticipated, even though it was a part that he had not yet earned.

Arthur thought that his grand strategy had worked brilliantly. Mary and Winston settled into their designated roles, and Celldesign began manufacturing patches with the overseers' approval and exploring far-flung markets for sale and distribution. The state lab monitored the efficacy of the patch and was expected to soon issue a favorable finding, which in turn would pave the way for the heralded IPO. Arthur was

full of optimism. Celldesign was so very Boston, the inherent
superiority of the venture harking back to the days of the best
and the brightest.

Arthur was not "moping around" the apartment—he was
merely living in memory. As Arthur's head dropped back against
the familiar leather, he could feel Dorothy's eyes upon him. He
thought for a moment to lift himself up and say something, but
what was there left to say?

CHAPTER 2

After graduating from Tufts, Spencer entered the world of Celldesign, trusting that Arthur would make good on his promise of an opportunity to change the world. He was tall and trim, as one would expect from a runner. He went to work in khakis and boat shoes but no socks, even in the snow. His hair was never quite combed. His face exhibited a two-day stubble on one day, clean shaven the next. He appeared to everyone to be a happy-go-lucky young man who laughed easily at himself. He was a young man who really wanted to take a year after graduating to bum around Europe and find himself but then discovered that neither his father nor his grandfather would finance his travels. Instead, he was shown to a cubicle at the Celldesign building on Route 128. He thought it was just a matter of time before he'd save enough money to finance the Europe trip himself. He especially wanted to explore the beaches around Cannes.

There were whispers from the outset—nepotism, unqualified, unfair. Spencer could sense it. "It must be nice to be the founder's grandson," said the blonde MIT grad who was seated in the next cubicle.

"Listen," Spencer replied, "you've got it all wrong. I promise."

Companies like Celldesign did not have watercoolers for the employees to hang around; they had coffee stations. Keurig, fourteen flavors. It wasn't exactly that Spencer was un-welcome at the coffee station, but when he came by, everyone seemed to suddenly get busy. So, he stuck to his job description. He had taken and passed a course in statistics at Tufts, and Arthur suggested the Quality Control Department, focusing on data collection. It consisted of a small group of people who collected information on the patch, collated the results, and ultimately reported them to the state lab, which was a qualifying process for Celldesign to sell its securities to the public.

The company had targeted test markets for the patch, mostly in Africa and India. Spencer was responsible for data coming from a few villages in Kenya, a minimally engaging task, Spencer thought, dull, routine, monotonous. And he soon learned which markers in patch experience to look for and how that information should be grouped and charted in order to continue the company narrative about how successful the patch was in addressing waterborne illness.

But the picture changed. At first, Spencer sensed it vaguely, as if his computer screen were commenting, calling him back for another look, but he could not pinpoint what was disturbing him. He would look around the office, peering over at the blonde in the next cubicle, looking for any sign of disquiet on her face as she scanned her computer screen, but nothing was there. *Just me*, he thought. *I need to improve my focus.*

But improving his focus merely served to increase his sense of disquiet with the data, and he began to see a pattern. He thought the results that were reported to the state lab were being molded. Too many data points that did not fit Celldesign's preordained model were being tossed, and it didn't seem right. The picture one would glean from his charts, Spencer thought, was misleading.

But what if he was wrong? He was quite aware of his status as a *newbie*, as they termed it on the office floor, and was hesitant to make a false step. And now, he felt that eyes were upon him. All the cubicles, including his, had glass walls on three sides and were open on the fourth—transparency was a stated value of the company—and that became a sense of exposure, as if everyone around him knew what he was thinking. It was quite uncomfortable. He could have just graphed out the results and passed them on, but he hesitated. Could he let it slide by? Or should he rely on his superiors having accounted for what he was seeing?

As he saw data being tossed, day after day, Spencer felt something new—a mature, sober voice within. He had heard Arthur and Winston both speak about conscience, criticizing this or that public figure for not having a conscience or for ignoring his conscience, but he always thought of it himself as a vague notion that could await his middle age. Sitting there in his cubicle, his mind began to drift, but not in the happy-go-lucky way he was accustomed to—no images of beer and beaches. Instead, he wondered if all the data were deployed, then what would the model look like? Would it reflect the Celldesign narrative?

Although it was against company policy, he secretly took some printouts home and tried to plot them on a rough graph, first closing the blinds covering his kitchen window and turning off the overhead lights—it was all quite secretive. But the pattern would be obvious to anyone. The more data points he accepted, the more irregular the graph. That was not the narrative that the company was presenting to the state lab or the IPO community.

Who else knows? he wondered. Or was he out on a limb, all by himself?

For Spencer, as for everyone else at the company, Mary was the day-to-day face of Celldesign. And that gave Spencer some sense of comfort; he had known Mary since before the Celldesign days, when she was Arthur's favorite graduate student at Harvard Business School. She was like an older sister in some respects, though now powerful and busy. Still, his compass turned her way.

Spencer's immediate superior in data collection, Patty O'Donnell, did not seem right for the problem he faced. She was a confusing figure, rarely in the office, and when she was, she spent most of her time huddled with the CFO, Olga Numerovski. Patty was pretty, normally in pink, and wore her strawberry-blonde hair in a bun. With her deep-red lipstick, noticeable rouge, and a smile that seemed painted on, she was hardly someone to confide in, Spencer thought, especially about a serious matter.

Spencer's glass cubicle began to feel more and more claustrophobic. With each passing day, he felt a terrifying sense of imminent exposure, as if he were holding back secret knowledge of immense yet unknown importance, and he began sweating to the extent that his shirt seemed perpetually wet. Every time he looked up, someone seemed to be looking in. At his apartment, with its thankfully solid walls, he broke out his college statistics textbook and located the process called *eliding*. It was all a matter of degree. A small amount of data elimination (or eliding) was acceptable; a larger amount was not acceptable. He sensed that the amount of eliding of the data at Celldesign was out of control, but he was not sure of himself. It was something that gnawed at him each minute that he sat within his glass cubicle. But he had nowhere to go with it, except to family friend Mary. He never thought about going to Arthur. The only question was how to present it, and an email seemed to be the most restrained approach. He would be careful. Tact was required, of course. Mary had always seemed to be on his side. She would want him to do the right thing. She was almost family. She would protect him.

He made sure that nobody was paying any attention to him—he looked around and saw that everyone was glued to their computer screens. He took a breath and typed out an email to Mary.

> Hi, Mary. I've been wanting to thank you personally for this opportunity, but the time never seems right, and I don't want anything I do to seem inappropriate. I hope you don't mind this text. There is one other thing—I don't know if it is anything significant, but I think the data I am working on isn't being reported quite accurately. I've noticed an inordinate number of trials being discarded that could not be justified by the modeling and hope you can help me understand. Be happy to talk about it.

He pressed send and gave a sigh of relief. The blonde in the next cubicle looked over and gave him a smile, which he returned. *She thinks I'm hot*, he thought.

A copy of Spencer's email reached Arthur casually, a mere "cc" in a forwarded message from Mary to her confidant at the company, Olga Numerovski, asking Olga to "take care of this for me," with no allowance for the seriousness the email posed—an internal writing to question the data on which the IPO was to be predicated. During the time leading up to an IPO, any internal observation that suggested that the product quality was being misreported was a big deal, something that had to be investigated. If true, it would affect everything.

All of this hit Arthur immediately; he couldn't believe his eyes. He was rigid with concern yet kept telling himself that it couldn't possibly be true. Spencer could not possibly have seen a flaw that had escaped all the other quality control people, all the MIT grads, all the cubicles. It was preposterous, all a great misunderstanding, no truth to it. Everybody discarded obviously flawed data so that the analysis would express the real truth. It might sound paradoxical, but it was standard procedure.

Arthur could almost feel the weight of thousands of pages of SEC regulations that might become involved by dint of that simple email, all intended to assure that the truth—the whole truth—would be disclosed to investors. And Spencer had brought all that into play, all those regulations and everything they portended, intentionally or not. The lawyers would have to be alerted. It had temporarily gotten by Mary but, Arthur knew, only temporarily. It was like a strange and foreboding item had been placed at Celldesign's doorway that was the size and shape of an electronic bomb, which was to say, almost invisible. The chain of unintended consequences was too long to assess.

Arthur exhaled loudly, as people do when they are making a point of their exasperation. "Shit," he said, his mind fixed on Spencer's image. It was more than a mistake on Spencer's part. It was an assault against Celldesign. And what was more, it would put him at odds with Olga, who, he was sure, would react violently and set in motion a terrifying chain of events.

He had always been leery of Olga, who, although she was Mary's confidant, was also jarring in demeanor and appearance—a dark, furtive little woman who appeared one day with an MIT degree in statistics and Mary's blessing but who always seemed resentful and suspicious. It was as if she was holding something back, perhaps some unimaginable torture in Ukraine, where she had been raised. Mary had an odd connection to her; they had been roommates through graduate school, and as far as Arthur was aware, Olga was practically the only person with whom Mary seemed truly comfortable, so in that sense, it was not unusual for Mary to slough off Spencer's email on her trusted friend. But on the other hand, Arthur thought, everything was now in the balance, and holding the scales was a strange little figure from Ukraine.

Whatever synapses light up when written words reach the eye were firing away in Arthur's brain as he looked, again, at the words of the email: "I've noticed an inordinate number of trials being discarded that could not be justified by modeling," and "wondering if you could help me understand." *Why in writing?* Arthur moaned to himself. It was almost like a schoolchild raising his hand in class. But this was not a classroom, and Spencer failed to appreciate that—failed in a very large way. *Why not come to me first? If only he had done that.*

Spencer's email had put Arthur's handcrafted world in jeopardy. There would be an investigation, the IPO likely would be put off, the bankers would then start putting on pressure, and credibility would be lost, all due to a short, pointed email that was sent in the wrong way to the wrong person at the wrong time. It was something that Arthur could have controlled, if he had been given the chance. By pressing send, Spencer had inadvertently put in jeopardy everything Arthur stood for. Arthur surmised that Spencer could be fired for that alone, unless he quit first.

In that moment, Arthur's red-hot anger was directed at his grandson.

Arthur looked away from his computer screen and took a breath, going through the litany of possible excuses Spencer might put forth, including inexperience and good intentions. But there was not enough time to think it through to any extent, since the first domino would fall soon. It was foreseeable to Arthur that Olga would not control herself; she would resend what she would perceive as an attack on her, and it would bubble over. To her, it would amount to a questioning of her statistics reporting—something she had traveled across the globe at great peril to attain—all because of a wet-behind-the-ears, silver-spoon kid. Perhaps Mary could have contained it, but she had handed it off, delegated it, something Arthur had taught at Harvard—a lesson plan that suddenly looked incomplete.

Olga would lash out, he thought. She might even try to destroy Spencer; that much was undeniable. For if Spencer was right, then Olga's department, by definition, would have been involved in promoting a blatant fraud. And that could not be true, Arthur reasoned. There was too much going against it, too many eyes looking at the process, too much certainty that, in the end, such a scheme was irrational. Thus, it could not be, and Arthur's mind was settled.

Though the motivation was innocent, Spencer was in the wrong, and he must be man enough to take whatever came his way. He should apologize, Arthur concluded, and retract what he'd said. Admit the mistake. Yes, he would be fired because it was a big mistake, but then, at least he could move on.

Now pacing in his study, Arthur accepted the fact that he

could not intervene on Spencer's behalf. "There are limits," he muttered, "to what I can do." His mind suddenly was alert to the conflict-of-interest rules that he had taught for so many years. He did not have to wait long for the explosion to continue. Olga had no more discipline than Spencer when it came to pressing *send*. Her email was directed to Spencer, with Mary copied; it came to Arthur second-hand, again from Mary.

"I was shocked and flabbergasted," it began, "to be questioned by you, especially in front of the senior staff of this company. Your lack of judgment is catastrophic, and your email is totally unacceptable. You have no background in the kinds of statistics analysis we are performing. Except for your father's and grandfather's positions at the company, you would never have been hired in the first place. You not only misunderstand the statistics, but you also misunderstand the chain of command. As the junior-most employee in the entire company, you do not have the basis for contacting the president directly with an email. You owe it to the company to apologize to all concerned and ask for a transfer to a less sensitive department."

The first time Arthur read Olga's words, he nodded in silent acceptance. She was right; Spencer didn't know what he was doing. And he had put many things in jeopardy. Thank God that Olga didn't come right out and say that the company would have to disclose or report this incident to the state regulatory bodies.

But he read it a second time. It really was vicious, overkill, raising as many questions about the person who sent it, Olga, as it did about Spencer, who, Arthur thought, deserved being rebuked but not publicly destroyed. One thing had become clear, though: Spencer could not return to Celldesign.

Arthur reached for his phone to call Spencer, but a sense of caution stopped him. The threat to his own interests arose like flames in a firepit. Nepotism, conflict of interest, mismanagement, all suddenly had achieved an elevated place in his mind. He had much to protect, he thought, much to be cautious about. He put his phone down.

Mary had still not reached out to Arthur. He wondered if Mary had yet picked up on the potential devastation to the company she co-founded. Because things had changed—utterly or subtly, Arthur did not yet know, but they had changed.

In his cubicle, Spencer's thoughts were not logically arranged along a chain of future consequences, as Arthur's were. Instead, his brain seemed to be trembling as much as his body was in response to Olga's email. He had made a great mistake! The words on his computer screen began to blare in his mind like a fire alarm, calling attention to something terrible. He thought he might pass out. He would be fired ignominiously! This was horrible! Carefully, he looked around the office floor. Everybody was busy, as usual; nothing out of the ordinary, nobody seemed to know. He read the words on the screen again, their meaning clearer and clearer. Something needed to be done. He could not sit there and wait. Suppose Olga came marching down the hall, and everyone stopped and listened as he was humiliated publicly. Maybe Arthur would walk in—he could not bear that either.

He had to escape. There was still time, while everything looked normal. He grabbed some data printouts, just in case he might need evidence, and stuffed them in a manila folder. He headed toward the men's lavatory with no real plan, but just before opening the bathroom door, he instinctively made a right turn into the elevator. He was thankful it was empty because at that moment, one cross-eyed look and he would have lost all courage and broken down into a puddle.

In a moment, though, he was down on the main floor, eyed suspiciously by the security officer, who merely said hello and then looked back down at the crossword puzzle he was working on. Walking swiftly, Spencer made it to his car, and he was away, irretrievably.

CHAPTER 3

Arthur thrashed about in his bed that night, finally drawing a groggy rebuke from Dorothy.

"Arthur, what *is* it?" She spoke in a tone of annoyance more than concern. Arthur did not answer, seeking to avoid a lengthy discussion in the middle of the night what-ifs. And he remained in that zone of being half awake, half asleep, until the alarm on his clock radio finally went off at six. And when he stepped out of the shower and wiped the condensation from the bathroom mirror, he saw an anxious face staring back at him. "Coffee," he muttered, as if the caffeine would jolt him into an understanding of what had happened, and he hurried to the kitchen.

Arthur needed some alone time; the "Spencer problem" had many wrinkles and ramifications, not the least of which was to avoid the appearance of siding with Spencer, who seemed clearly in the wrong, against Celldesign, to which he owed his complete loyalty. He had to think it through. The IPO could not be upended; plus, he could not risk charges of nepotism. And of course, there was his relationship with his grandson. And in the background somewhere, what was Mary thinking?

The correct thing to do, he thought, would be to recuse

himself entirely, take no side at all, neither Spencer's nor Celldesign's. It would be a rude introduction to the real world for Spencer, he made his bed—let him sleep in it! Arthur was indignant, almost righteous as he considered what his grandson had done. But the other half of the equation bothered him— could he simply turn over Celldesign, the company he had created? How would it look if he were to put himself in such a passive posture? And worse, how would he explain himself to the Overseers? *A great deal of standing to lose*, he thought. *A terribly great deal for me to lose.*

He was getting impatient with himself. Time was of the essence, and he did not yet have a charted course. He felt Dorothy's eyes upon him; she had caused an unnecessary stir by bringing the newspaper, the *Boston Globe*, to the kitchen from the apartment door, where it was delivered each morning, and then by dramatically removing the paper from its plastic weather wrap as loudly as possible. He had not told her at that point about the email and Olga's response. Time to do so.

Arthur looked up and waited for Dorothy to pay attention. She feigned disinterest by snapping the paper open to the business section. Arthur took that as a signal to begin but was almost immediately interrupted as Dorothy's eyes widened, and she blurted out, "Good God," pointing to the lead article in the business section. The headline was, "Local Company's Data Questioned." Arthur looked at the byline: Patrick Garrigall.

Things had moved much more quickly than Arthur had anticipated.

Patrick Garrigall was a known commodity around Boston, generally, and to Arthur in particular, having held the economics desk at the *Globe* for over two decades. His habitually humorless, deadpan expression, combined with his rumpled Irish appearance (right down to the bushy dark eyebrows) gave people the sense that he was trustworthy, a reporter with classic journalistic ethics, another Murrow, but that was a mistake Arthur would never make. They had traveled in similar circles, and he felt that he knew exactly what motivated Garrigall—resentment. He was a man who had lived on the sidelines, watching others play the game, coveting all that the real players had gotten. Arthur was sure that Garrigall would do anything to even things out in his own mind. That is, for recognition, to finally stand on the same ground as the Brahmins, and all would know it—everyone has a quest, and that was his.

Arthur devoured Garrigall's article, which cited an "anonymous source" for the proposition that Celldesign was shaping, perhaps fraudulently, the data it was reporting to the state lab; in short, that the effectiveness of the patch was being misrepresented. Arthur raised his head to the ceiling when he read the next line: "The *Globe* has been provided with samples of the raw data and the data as reported to the state lab, and the alleged discrepancies appear obvious, even to the untrained eye."

Had Spencer taken proprietary information from Celldesign and given it to Garrigall?

"I said," Dorothy intoned, "how bad is it? In case you didn't hear the first time."

"This could be quite serious," Arthur said, in a tone midway between despair and anger. "All employees sign paperwork affirming that the data are proprietary, owned by Celldesign, and that any disclosure would irreparably harm the company and, as if that were not enough, amounts to theft. Garrigall is not talking about a schoolboy prank, Dorothy."

Arthur was stunned. If Spencer were responsible, matters had taken a quantum leap in the wrong direction.

Dorothy might not have had a background in business, but

she did have one in wealth. She knew the rules of the game instinctively—that whoever turned over proprietary information to the likes of Garrigall had committed a cardinal sin, the most serious of errors. It was unheard of to come between the business interests, the shareholders, the employees, the bankers, and their expected rewards. It would lead to a bounty being put on his head. As well it should! She looked up from the newspaper, pausing to let out a breath of air that seemed to expel the world as it existed only days before. "Spencer?" she asked, shaking her head as though she could drive away her apprehension by doing so.

Arthur merely said, "What other conclusion?"

"Why?"

And Arthur finished telling her about the exchange of emails.

At that time, Arthur had had a driver, Jimmy Quinn, a ne'er-do-well distant cousin of Dorothy's. Jimmy may have had his faults, but lack of promptness was not one of them. There might be a smell of stale beer about him, but, somehow, he would be on time. And, remarkably, he hadn't had a ticket, even for DUI, in more than a decade.

When Arthur came downstairs, Jimmy was waiting out front, his newspaper, the *Globe*, opened to the business section. "To the office, Mr. Lloyd?" he asked in a subdued tone, quietly closing the paper, as if that would chase away Garrigall's headline. Like most of Boston, he had read the article but only vaguely understood.

"No, Jimmy, I'm afraid we'll need to go to Winston's office first."

Arthur was not in the mood to address Jimmy's fears. He simply opened the rear car door and slid himself into the back seat.

Jimmy and Arthur had been together long enough for Jimmy to sense a problem and remain quiet. He reached down and turned off the car radio.

It was a short drive to Newbury Street. Without a word, Arthur hopped out and went up the stairs to the second floor, knowing that Jimmy would simply circle the block until his conference with Winston was finished.

Upstairs, Winston stared at Arthur when he walked in, nodding his head in the direction of an empty chair. Arthur sat and tossed the business section of the *Globe* onto Winston's mahogany desk. "And?" Winston said, his voice expressing false confidence, fake toughness.

"Don't give me that," Arthur replied more loudly than necessary. "How much do you know?"

"Undoubtedly less than you," Winston replied defensively, already having given up any kind of confrontational attitude.

"Well, what are you doing just sitting here?" Arthur said with an edge. "Garrigall didn't just dream up this story. There was a source, and it was Spencer—had to be."

"You're losing me," Winston said, sitting straight up, so Arthur walked him through Spencer's email exchange with Olga. Winston's expression remained impassive, but he turned ashen. "I wasn't aware," he said to no one in particular.

"Don't you two speak?" Arthur shouted.

"About as much as you and I do," Winston said.

On another occasion, they might have exploded at each other, but both recognized the gravity of the situation they were in.

"You sure it was him?" Winston said in a quieter voice.

"No, but he's the most likely candidate. Striking back. Against Olga. Never liked her. And now"—Arthur looked back up—"we've got Garrigall involved."

"And the state," Winston offered. "What if they start digging?"

"There's nothing to find. One thing is certain: we hired all the nerds on the planet. We've got the math covered. I'm sure of it. It's just the PR that's the problem for the company." He paused. "Celldesign wouldn't be the right place for Spencer long term, anyhow. Don't you agree? Let's get him out of there, back to school, whatever. Then it'll all just fade away."

Winston's face stiffened. Arthur saw that his attack on Spencer was taken as an insult. Winston said, "You're hurling charges around. Do you know the whole background?"

"I know enough," Arthur growled.

"No, you don't," Winston stood.

Arthur saw something in Winston's demeanor as he did so—a certain protectiveness. It would be catastrophic for Winston to turn on him.

Arthur sat, and Winston followed suit. They avoided each other's eyes and endured a moment's silence that seemed interminable, and then Winston said, "He's your grandson. You set him up in this job."

"For crying out loud, Winston. I know that. But I didn't escort him to Garrigall."

"True." He paused a moment and then asked, "Where do we go from here?"

"You realize that I'm in an awkward position, don't you?"

"So am I."

"Let me see what Mary says. You try to reach your son. And for God's sake, tell him to shut the damn hell up."

Arthur rambled downstairs, not in the mood for small talk.

He stood in the doorway of Winston's building and watched as Jimmy made a turn back onto Newbury to pick him up.

"Now to the office?" Jimmy asked, referring to Arthur's office in the economics building off Harvard Yard.

"Sorry, Jimmy," Arthur said, still distracted from his visit with Winston.

Jimmy waited a respectful few seconds, then said, "Ahhh ... that would be ..."

"Sorry. Out to 128," Arthur replied, referring to Celldesign's offices.

It was a twenty-minute drive, enough time for Arthur to go over the morning's developments. How would the information that Garrigall had reported be received by the investment community? What would be the implications?

All the while, Jimmy was quiet, except for his frequent glances into the rearview mirror.

When they reached the parking lot, Arthur rushed through security, walking directly to the elevators; they were used to his imperious attitude.. When Arthur reached Celldesign's floor, he walked through the cubicles, straight to Mary's office, waiting impatiently as she completed a phone call. Mary's desk was completely clean, as always—no files, no papers, no dust. Arthur deliberately put the *Globe* on top of the desk, opened to the business section. Mary glanced down as she was listening to the voice on the phone.

She finished the call and looked up. Then she got out of her seat and went over to close the door to her office. Turning, she said, "It's a big fucking problem, Arthur."

"That much I know," he replied.

"Are we drawing the same conclusions?" Mary asked. "He makes something up, puts it *in writing*, gets a reply he finds upsetting, and then goes to the press. Are we on the same page?" Her words were spat out, full of anger.

Arthur winced inwardly. He had known in a intellectual sort of way that Mary was no longer the student who approached him in his office with the idea for Celldesign; she was its CEO, the one responsible for the IPO on the horizon. "You skipped over Olga's asinine response," he replied, loading as much sarcasm into his voice as he could, but it was merely a defensive statement.

"Before we get to Olga, let me fill you in on one other little item," Mary retorted. "He stole a bunch of files."

"Wait a minute."

"No need to wait, Arthur. The facts are clear: he got upset and walked out, brazen as all hell, and before he left, he printed last month's data and put it in a file. Then, on camera, he waltzed out with the file under his arm." Mary stood in front of her desk, hands on hips.

Arthur wanted to ask why she had passed the email on to Olga. It was like letting an animal loose from a cage. But the room was too charged, the tension too thick.

"I've got to get that data back," Mary said. "It's ours. We own it. He signed an employment agreement acknowledging that. Do you understand? We've got to get it back."

She had never before spoken to Arthur in that manner. It was immediately obvious to them both, and her face suddenly softened. She put her right hand up to her forehead; then she said with a sigh, "You have to do this. You have to put the company first and get Spencer to give us back the files. It is your duty."

My duty? Arthur asked himself. For the second time, he thought of recusing himself. *Let the others work it out.* He felt the conflicts of interest as sharply as a knife between his ribs.

Mary took the opportunity to press on. "Arthur, look at me. The data need to be returned. Think of it this way: they are our lifeline. They cannot be in the hands of a self-seeking reporter, for God's sake! With all due respect, you brought him in; you got us here. Now you must secure our survival as a company."

Arthur felt his pulse beating; his chest was tight. He knew he had made a mistake in confronting Mary. "I came here to discuss Olga's email. We would never be in this position—"

"I'm fully aware of that. I will be dealing with Olga; you may rest assured."

He felt cornered. "We're moving too fast."

"Wrong," she replied. "Not fast enough. Since the *Globe* was delivered this morning, a few short hours ago, our lenders have called. And the investment bankers are going batshit. Who do you think I was on the phone with when you walked in?"

Arthur knew well how the bankers would react. He averted his eyes in an effort to steady himself.

"Arthur," she added as he fell deeper into thought, "there is one more thing, unfortunately. And you know how I hate to say this. I've known Spence since he was a child. I watched him grow up. But I cannot allow him to destroy us. We will be hiring a lawyer, a big name." She hesitated for effect. "He will be instructed to do what is necessary. I hope you can get control of Spence, like, right away. The lawyer is on a plane here right this minute."

"Anyone I know?"

"Charlie Apple. He'll be briefed, and then we will follow his advice. I'm sorry."

Apologizing before any steps were actually taken—there must have been a preliminary exchange that was serious enough to merit that.

And she's right, Arthur thought. *The best thing for Spencer would be to hand over the papers he stole and apologize. Maybe I could use my influence to avoid prosecution.*

Arthur left Mary's office, but he was unsettled, berating himself for slowness of response. She had raised her voice to him. And worse, she had taken unilateral action against his grandson. In twenty-four hours, the world had changed.

His head was spinning, but he had to maintain focus. Spencer was wrong about the data and very wrong to have taken the data, and inexcusably wrong to have turned the data over to Garrigall. Charlie Apple would make him pay a price.

Am I for *that or* against *it?* As he sat in his car, looking at the back of Jimmy's head, Arthur could not answer the question.

CHAPTER 4

When Spencer read the *Globe* headline, he realized the gravity of his situation in its full dimension, and it sent a chill down his spine. Until that moment, events seemed to have carried him along—Olga's attack, coming to him from out of the blue; his hasty departure (but what alternative did he truly have?); and his call to Patrick Garrigall, all lined up like dominos. But now, he found himself one step away from being the headline himself. Who wouldn't be able to infer that he, Spencer Lloyd, grandson of the company founder, son of a board member, was the anonymous source for the story?

As soon as he finished reading Garrigall's article, he checked the blinds and locks on each window. Why hadn't he heard from someone—anyone? He realized that the reason was that he had somehow walked over an invisible but very important line—it was right there in his employment agreement; "proprietary information."

His mind raced. He remembered the word *criminal*. Was jail a possibility? Garrigall never told him about that!

He needed to take inventory. He could not make any more mistakes. All of a sudden, his future was in the balance.

As a child, he'd never been in trouble and always tried to

follow the rules. It was the Lloyd family way; one could not risk embarrassing Arthur. The mere step of leaving the company without giving any official notice was a big enough departure for him, but the notion that he had committed a crime never crossed his mind. He just knew that he could not be in a place where Olga was above him, as he was sure to his core that she would ultimately take him down if she had the opportunity.

He could feel her hatred of him, not just in the words of her email, but in the looks she had given him since he joined the company, especially whenever Arthur was around. There was always a look in her eyes, suspicion, resentment, something that could only be felt, like hot or cold. He was sure that she would have shot him dead if she could have.

Having been born and raised in Boston, however, he was familiar with the *Globe*, the city's leading daily newspaper. One of his beer-drinking buddies from Tufts had gotten himself a job with the newspaper and now worked under a man named Pat Garrigall in the business section. Halfway home, the thought jumped into Spencer's consciousness—he could at least prove what he had observed by showing the data to someone like Garrigall, whom he assumed to be a seasoned reporter with a nose for the truth, something like Woodward and Bernstein. The manila file was a backup; he felt sure that the data would tell the story. He smiled; it was prescient of him, and he felt better. He thought at the time that he'd done the right thing, even though it all happened so quickly.

Although he was also counting on Arthur to back him up— after all, blood was thicker than water—the file would help if Arthur questioned why he'd left Celldesign.

Calling Garrigall was natural. And Garrigall had said he'd protect Spencer's identity, hadn't he? Talking to the *Globe* was merely a way to restate his email. Surely it was appropriate to double-check the data reporting, wasn't it? Why would any company be upset about that? They should have been glad that he took his job that seriously.

"The folly of all assumptions," he said to himself, his hands cradling his head.

He kept looking at the manila file, which was staring back at him like a malicious intruder. Had he observed the right data? Was he right to have said anything? He wasn't sure about his knowledge of statistics, and Olga was an expert. Doubts began to crowd in. He needed to speak to someone, and his father came to mind. *But wait a minute*, he told himself. *Think this through.* He had seen Winston and Mary together on several occasions; she always appeared in control. What could Spencer expect Winston to do? He held the title of chairman of the board, and that carried a litany of responsibilities to the company.

It seemed to be of no use. Anyone who could help him was tied to the company. "You're alone in this," he mumbled.

And Charles Apple, the man Celldesign hired to destroy Spencer, had not yet landed in Boston.

Arthur was worried about old Charlie Apple, as everyone called him. Mary indicated that Apple would have free rein to, in her words, "handle the situation." It sounded to Arthur like the instructions given to a special operations squad, heading out into the night in some far-off war zone. But how could he intervene? On whose behalf?

Arthur expected old Charlie to land with a plan in hand and thus was not surprised when he got Charlie's text, calling for a meeting in the "war room" that had been set up for him in the building on 128.

"Arthur, old buddy, how the hell are you?" Charlie said, extending his hand.

Arthur was wary but friendly, having sat on the dais at Harvard Law School when old Charlie gave two of his entertaining speeches to the students.

Arthur knew all about old Charlie, whose law firm was in Virginia, just outside DC, but his practice was national in scope. He'd picked Washington as its headquarters mostly because, at fifty-five, still vibrant, with long white hair and a golden tongue, he had become the silver fox, and despite his relatively short height and round girth, the ladies in DC were available to him, married or not. "It's the greatest perk in the world," he would brag to his close friends.

He had gotten Mary's call the day before, a referral from an old classmate at Yale Law, which he'd attended after graduating from Tulane in New Orleans, paying his tuition by working days at an insurance adjuster's office. He would send a surrogate to his classes to take notes (which he read in his spare time), yet he graduated first in his class and then went back south—but only as far as DC, where he thought the action would be—and started his own firm. He hung around the criminal courts, trying to drum up paying clients, handling the dregs of the criminal court system as often as he could—all the drunk driving and domestic abuse cases that tended to show up each Monday, the most important day of the week for him; anything for a fee. He had developed a slight drawl, just right for northern Virginia, as he was convinced that the simplicity of the Southern vocabulary was an aid to both clear thought and good communication with the common man. Almost everyone called him "old Charlie" because of his avuncular way of speaking. And, of course, there was that mane of white hair, most of which consisted of plugs.

"Have you been briefed?" Arthur asked.

Old Charlie nodded. "Got a memo from Olga, here," he said, gesturing in her direction. The room was quiet. Arthur, Mary, and Olga were each focused on Charlie, who got right down to business. "He's a kid. We'll scare the piss out of him and see what he has to say then. I'm guessing he's at home, shaking like a rabbit in a snake pit. Sorry to be so abrupt, old buddy," he said, looking at Arthur.

As old Charlie's brown eyes bore into him, Arthur recalled one of the talks old Charlie had given to the Harvard Law students years earlier on how he would treat most cases in the same way—find the soft spot and exploit it for all he could. It was something he'd learned from standing in front of all those juries in District of Columbia criminal courts, juries that often didn't like his clients and had already voted in their hearts to convict before old Charlie even opened his mouth. He learned to see it in their eyes, and if he saw "that look," he knew it was time for a plea bargain. But if he saw something else, a glimmer of an opening, he would strike like the snake he was paid to be. As Arthur recalled that story, he looked into old Charlie's eyes and understood the question that was about to come; it was the reason Arthur had been asked to the meeting.

Old Charlie put it right out there. "Arthur, you're in a tough spot. I feel for you, buddy; I really do. But you got yourself into a pickle here. Hell, you're standing in the shoes of a fiduciary—founder, chair of the Overseers, and pullin' all the strings behind Winston. Oh, I know all about the phony 'family investment.' I'm assuming that you're going to abide by your legal duty to this company. I'm just stating what you already know—you have to be loyal solely to the company, not to your family, not to Spencer. Undivided loyalty. That is the law. You know that, and we expect that." Old Charlie made it seem like a pronouncement from on high.

"Don't insult me, Charlie," Arthur replied impatiently. He felt something and turned toward Olga. She was glowering at him, her black eyes reflecting the overhead lights in the war room and appearing to throw sparks his way.

But before Arthur could say anything more, Mary spoke. "Charlie, how is a person supposed to do that? Shouldn't Arthur simply step back, away from anything involving Spencer?"

Old Charlie looked as if he were considering Mary's suggestion but only for a moment. "Mary," he said with that fake Southern drawl, "we've got some plans for that young man that his grandfather could help with."

Arthur was incensed. They were talking about him as though he were not even in the room. *So he wants me to do the dirty work*, he thought.

Old Charlie continued staring at Arthur, seemingly looking into Arthur's soul. He asked, "Have you spoken to Spencer since his email?"

"No. I didn't dare."

"Because of the appearance of conflict?"

Arthur nodded, wondering where the conversation was going.

"Well, we're going to need him to renounce his email, say he was wrong, and ask for forgiveness."

"Is that all?" Arthur said sardonically.

"The way I look at it, it's your moral and legal duty. Otherwise, one might ask whose side you're on, old buddy."

"Are you threatening me?" Arthur demanded.

Old Charlie demurred. "No, no," he said in his softest voice.

But facts are facts, Arthur thought. It was obvious that old Charlie had done just that.

The following morning was rainy, but the *Globe* arrived on time. Turning to the business section, Arthur saw the headline: "Celldesign Hires Attorney." And Garrigall went on and on about the famous Charlie Apple, his past exploits and famous cases, laying the groundwork for the implication that the Celldesign saga was just beginning. Why else did they need to import legal talent like old Charlie in a city like Boston?

This one had not been written with Spencer's help. No, this one was the product of a new source but one who was obvious to the cagey old Arthur: Mary. She had been told, Arthur rightly surmised, to gain control of the public narrative, and she was trying to do so in the most direct way possible. Naturally, old Charlie would think that by merely mentioning his name, they had achieved that goal.

This information was the beginning of the attack on Spencer, Arthur knew. And he knew that Garrigall would play it for all it was worth, which is what one would expect from such a bitter, middle-aged man, a man whose life was perfectly depicted by his rumpled trousers and scuffed shoes—the epitome of the little man but one who nevertheless got himself into the position to affect real lives. And Spencer's life had just been placed in his crosshairs.

Still, Arthur dared not reach out to Spencer. Old Charlie's voice was ringing in his ears.

Arthur re-folded the newspaper and called down to the doorman, to tell Jimmy to bring the car around; Arthur would be waiting. He would spend the day in his faculty office—that would give him time to think it all through.

Garrigall had not yet begun reporting on the Lloyd family, but Arthur knew that it was only a matter of time. He could not let Garrigall get started on the family—misquoting, taking things out of context. He could destroy the Lloyds, and by the time the truth was uncovered, it would be too late.

It would be a test, Arthur thought, *he had to outflank Charlie and Mary on one side while outflanking Garrigall on the other. Where to start?*

He remained sure that Spencer was wrong on the data issue. How could it be otherwise? Did the junior-most staff person see something that all the other geeks missed? Why, the question almost answered itself.

And on top of being wrong, there was the matter of being impetuous, going straight to Mary—and in writing, no less! Not following channels at all.

There was a price to be paid by Spencer. But it should end there. Celldesign should not destroy a young man—Spencer or anyone else—out of spite or to defend a principle that was not actually at risk. It was an unworthy goal, one designed to feather the cap of one person: old Charlie. But Mary was the CEO. She had the full legal right to hire Apple and to follow his recommendations.

As Arthur stood under his umbrella in the drizzle, waiting for Jimmy to bring the car around, his cell phone rang. It was old Charlie. They were scheduling a press conference for that afternoon, following up on Garrigall's headlines, and Arthur was expected to be there.

They were moving faster than Arthur had anticipated.

In fairness, Charlie had told him, "It will be rough on Spencer, but he's young and will recover. Celldesign, on the other hand, is facing its moment of truth."

"Why do you want me there?"

"Atmospherics."

"What? What are you talking about?"

"Listen, I've got a lot of things going on. I can't hold your hand, Arthur. Just be there. It's your duty."

Charlie laid a heavy emphasis on the word *duty*.

It quickly dawned on Arthur—this was to be step one in the destruction of Spencer. *They would start to capture the narrative today. That is what a press conference is all about.* Arthur would be there to stand with the management team behind Apple as he attacked Spencer, to make it seem that there was a unified position. But it was one thing to be part of a strategy of renunciation—a withdrawal of mistaken, even false claims—and quite another to destroy Spencer and embarrass the Lloyd family name while doing so. Apple cared not a whit about the Lloyd name. He'd toss it in the garbage along with Spencer's future without a second thought.

They're using me, Arthur said to himself. "Well, two can play at this game. I'll go, but not for the reason old Charlie wants me there. I'll go as a double agent of sorts."

As Arthur stood waiting, feeling the kind of special caution that arises in the face of danger, Jimmy brought the car around, and Arthur could see immediately that it had been a tough night.

"How goes it, James?" Arthur said in a rendition of an Irish brogue.

"Good, sir. Where do we go this fine day?"

"I'm due at Celldesign," Arthur said. "Big day."

"Hope you don't mind me askin', sir, but will Mr. Spencer be okay?"

He's passed on from childhood, Arthur thought. *It's a world of consequences for him now, just as it is for the rest of us. He has passed the point where someone else will look out for him. He must protect himself now.*

Celldesign's building on 128 had a small conference room, and that is where they'd set up the press conference. Mary, Olga, Arthur, and a few other senior staff were there, all cleaned and shined, providing a show of strength. But old Charlie Apple was center stage. Classic—blue suit, white shirt, red tie. White hair trimmed that morning by a private barber. He was ready to go. He stepped up to the microphone. Arthur stood behind him with the others. There were two cameramen and half a dozen reporters, including Pat Garrigall in a worn blue and grey plaid sport jacket. His hair was matted down from a baseball cap he'd worn but now had tucked in his back pocket. His eyes crinkled at the corners, suggesting that the scene was providing him with a bit of entertainment. He seemed to pay particular attention to Arthur—their eyes met several times. Frequently enough that it gave Arthur pause. *Does he know something,* Arthur wondered. *He seems too cocky.*

Old Charlie was as polished as his reputation. "I'm afraid I must notify you all today of yet another example of how a disgruntled employee can go unilaterally to the press and cause a great deal of harm to one of the great business stories in America, out of pure spite. It happened the other day to Celldesign, and it's been reported in the *Boston Globe*, a fine newspaper. The young man in question was recently hired and has precious little knowledge or experience in reporting test results for tech companies, like we have here. He got a little reprimand from his superiors and quit in a huff, walking out with papers and documents belonging to his employer. The next thing we know, he's on the phone to the *Globe* and hands over the papers, even though they were chock-full of proprietary information. And that, my friends, is a crime. In case there is any question, we have formally terminated him and look forward to getting back on track for our next projected round of financing. In the meantime, I am announcing that we are filing suit against this employee, seeking damages and an injunction. That suit will be filed today here in Boston. Thank you."

Charlie started to walk off the dais, but Garrigall shouted out a question. "Mr. Apple, some of the data printouts seem to raise questions about Celldesign's truthfulness in the reporting process. Are you completely discounting the possibility that inconsistent results have been systematically eliminated from the reports filed with the state?"

The room quieted suddenly. Garrigall, the little man in scuffed shoes, stood defiantly in front of old Charlie, who turned and approached the microphone. "If I may point out, sir," Charlie intoned, "the man is a common thief. Do you normally accept the word of a common thief? That data is owned by my client. It is proprietary and should not have been removed. Really, it should have been turned over to the authorities when *you* received it. Not only is it stolen property, but you would need to evaluate the information in context before concluding that anything was wrong. By accepting these materials at face value, you have gravely and unfairly harmed my client." Old Charlie finished with a flourish and was again trying to leave the dais when Garrigall asked another question.

"Is it true that the employee is a member of the Lloyd family, and if so, why would he harm the company his family is so tight with?"

Old Charlie turned again back to the microphone. "Because the young man, as I pointed out, has some obvious problems. We probably shouldn't have been so good-natured when he was hired. You'll see from his record that he wasn't quite up to our usual standards."

With that, old Charlie turned and made a point of looking at Arthur, who was standing behind the dais. The glance was lost on no one. The inference was that the grandfather agreed with the company against the grandson. Arthur's eyes narrowed, but he remained silent.

Garrigall was like a dog with a bone. He shouted up to Arthur. "Mr. Lloyd, do you agree with that characterization?"

"Pat, Spencer is my grandson," Arthur replied. "The Lloyd family has earned, I think, a certain respect. He's a good young man. However, I will say that I have full confidence in the way that the Celldesign data have been reported. We will clear all this up and move ahead with our business plan."

"Have you been in touch with him since this incident?"

"No, I have not."

"And why would that be?"

As Garrigall smiled in that malicious way he had, old Charlie stood walked over, grabbed hold of Arthur's arm and pulled him toward the set-up room, smiling broadly the whole time. Once in the set-up room, Arthur saw old Charlie glower at him.

"I thought we were not going to make any speeches, except mine!" old Charlie said as soon as the door closed. He was clearly irritated.

"Did I say something off-script?" Arthur asked in an innocent tone.

Old Charlie was about to reply, but Olga could not contain herself. "Fantastic, I think. Fantastic," she said in her Eastern European accent. "We really got our side across. 'Common thief.' Exactly!" Her eyes seared everyone as she looked around the room. There was a sense of victory in her voice. Her enthusiasm pacified old Charlie, who began smiling broadly. His teeth, a winter white, dominated his face.

Arthur was glad that a confrontation had been avoided, but

he was concerned about Garrigall's aggressiveness. It was too confident. *What*, Arthur wondered, *does he have?*

When the congratulations exhausted themselves, old Charlie turned serious. "I have to know, here and now, that we are all on the same team. I'm not going to ask for a pledge— wouldn't do any good anyway. I am going to ask that you all dig deep. If you can't be totally with us, say so now. There must be no further leaks or forays off-script."

Nobody responded, but it was clear that the last part of what Charlie said was a rebuke of Arthur, which he expected. He was quite unconcerned, except for one thing. Olga suddenly seemed to have become troubled at something. Arthur attributed it to her unfamiliarity with the press in the United States, yet he would remain uncomfortable, for quite a time, with the image of Olga fidgeting in the war room as old Charlie brought up the topic of loyalty. There was something unnatural about her demeanor, as if she were struggling to keep a secret.

Arthur evaluated: old Charlie's star had risen. He commanded the room and laid out a plan. Of course, a lawsuit would be filed against Spencer. It was the leverage that would, he thought, get Spencer to "renounce" his actions, to say that he had been mistaken, that he hadn't understood the statistics. At the same time, old Charlie promised an "expert" he had used in many cases, who would write a report, defending the statistics model that Celldesign had used. They would go public with that, and hopefully, it would all end there without unreasonable damage to Celldesign's name.

The meeting ended with everyone agreeing that Spencer must renounce his email. No-one agreed more strongly than Olga or more softly than Arthur.

Arthur made sure he was home in front of the television for the nightly news; the press conference was scheduled to be on. Dorothy joined him, sitting quietly, holding the frame of her reading glasses against her lips, striking a pensive pose.

"You can't deny that Spencer deserves some sort of comeuppance, Arthur," she said.

He nodded slightly, which was as much of a concession as he would give.

"And you do have a responsibility to others in the picture, notably your friends on the Overseers."

Again, Arthur nodded agreement.

"And there is the matter of the Lloyd family name. All in all, I thought your performance was quite fine," she said with a sniff, "but Charles Apple will want to stay relevant, and the only real way for him to do that, as far as I can see, is to go after Spencer." She paused. "Whether it is overkill or not is quite beside the point. I wonder if young Spencer realizes that. He's never seemed too deep to me, you know? And you still think that it would be inappropriate for you to reach out and talk to him? Why is that?"

"It would be seen as consorting with the enemy," Arthur said ruefully.

"Hmph! And you say that I am imprisoned by appearances," she said with a false giggle: "Hah!"

Arthur lifted his glass of scotch, stiffened his face, and spoke slowly. "Dorothy, I believe Spencer must renounce. He hasn't a leg to stand on."

Dorothy straightened her back, a gesture that indicated she was getting bored. "Undoubtedly."

CHAPTER 5

Spencer was still looking blankly at his television, trying to understand what had just happened, when Garrigall called.

After the usual salutations, Garrigall said, "Listen, I've kept our deal. I haven't disclosed your identity, but those guys are coming after you—and hard."

Spencer waited to respond, wanting to know more about where Garrigall was headed with his questions. His mind was still on the coverage of his grandfather, standing there on the dais.

"Just came from the press conference they held with the lawyer," Garrigall said. "I think it was on TV. Did you catch it?"

"Yeah, I saw it."

"They're suing you, man."

"Who is 'they'?"

"Celldesign. Aren't you upset? Do you have any comment?"

"Of course I'm upset. This is all coming at me pretty fast. I don't think I did anything wrong."

"Hey, man, that was your grandfather standing up there, you know. Your flesh and blood, supposedly."

"What do you want me to say, man? All I can say is, he's

my grandfather. He'll have an explanation." Spencer's voice conveyed his uncertainty; it was quiet, apologetic, sad.

Garrigall must have sensed all that because he said, "You got anything you want to say for the record?" But his voice was just a beat too fast, a bit too insistent, and it raised a warning signal to Spencer.

"I didn't really steal anything," Spencer said with a firmness that Garrigall caught. "There was no theft. I was just taking precautions so that I could defend myself. And lucky I did."

Spencer opened the *Globe* the following day to the headline he now expected: "Celldesign Charges Employee with Theft of Trade Secrets." Garrigall included Spencer's statement that he was merely defending himself, but the article broadly cited Mary, who had prepared and made available a press release that was polished and smooth and cited legal precedents to the effect that Spencer had, in fact, committed a crime.

Garrigall's article went on to say that there were a growing number of calls to Celldesign from investors and banks, worried about what might happen. Would the state lab reopen the file on Celldesign? Just why were some test results thrown out?

It was all well beyond what Spencer had anticipated, and he realized that he had been *terribly* naïve, but the last few days had also given him an opportunity to reflect. Suppose he was right about the data being faulty? Nobody seemed to even consider that, yet it seemed to Spencer that it had become the most important question in the world.

Spencer was trying to face up to a new and terrifying set of issues, different in nature and impact from anything that he had ever dealt with before. He had managed to get himself into the position of threatening his parents' financial position and his grandfather's legacy, all in one fell swoop. The image of old Charlie Apple chased him constantly. The press conference, the newspaper headlines, the troubling charges of criminality, the loss of privacy—it was all new, all unwelcome.

But at the bottom of it, he'd seen what he'd seen. And there was something right about that, but also something incomplete.

He had an apartment in Chestnut Hill, near the train station and the Boston College campus. The apartment, a one-bedroom, was all he could afford with a starting salary, and now he didn't even have that. There were empty pizza boxes on the floor and several empty beer bottles in the sink. There was a faint odor of garbage that had lingered too long.

So on that morning, after reading Garrigall's article, Spencer headed north to the B. C. campus. He was looking for a coffee shop where he would not be recognized.

Gizmo's was located on the edge of campus on Commonwealth Avenue. Spencer fit right in. It was almost full of students, all in shorts and T-shirts with slogans. He found a small table with a barstool and sat, feeling invisible. Perfect. He hardly noticed at first when a young woman server impatiently asked for his order.

The server was dark and thin, with eyes that curved down at the outer edge, recalling a young Joan Baez. Spencer felt her impatience, and he wanted to hurry.

"I guess egg and cheese and coffee," he said, noting her slim figure.

"You guess?" she said, as if it were a quiz.

"Yes, er, no. Egg and cheese. That would be great."

She turned and headed back to the cooking station. It seemed as if he had not even had time to scan the room before she returned with his order. As she walked to his table, the movement of her hips caught his downward-glancing eye.

She saw that, and as she placed the plate with the sandwich and the cup of coffee down, she stopped to ask, "You go to school here?"

"I graduated from Tufts over a year ago."

"You working in the area?" she asked.

"I was," he said. Then, he decided to be honest and forthright. "Out of work at this time." After another awkward pause, he added, "As of recently. Very recently."

She didn't seem to mind the answer, and she appeared to be waiting for him to reciprocate by asking her a question. "So, I guess you do?" he asked. "I mean, go to school here?"

"No," she said, still smiling. "I live around here with my dad. He teaches here." Then, after a moment, as if she were weighing whether to complete her thought, she added, "I go to school in Cambridge. MIT."

Spencer could feel all the color drain from his face. She reacted by bringing her hands to her hips and assuming a stance, one foot in front of the other and glared at him. "Is that a problem?"

Spencer backed off, raising his hands off the table slightly. "No, it's not that; nothing to do with MIT. That's not right either. It does have to do with MIT. But not directly. It's kind of hard to explain." He looked at her sheepishly.

It took a few seconds, but she finally smiled. "I get off in one hour and ten minutes, if you want to wait and explain yourself."

So, he did.

They walked westerly on Allston Street, past four-story brick buildings filled with students and faculty. She listened almost the whole while. It was pure relief for Spencer. As confession is supposed to be. He brought her up to the point where Charlie Apple was hired, and she stopped walking.

"This is where I live," she explained. She tilted her head toward the building. "Divorce. Two teachers. Also complicated." And she turned to walk up the steps of the brownstone apartment building. As she put the key in the door, she looked back and saw Spencer standing there.

Not knowing what else to do, he waved at her. He thought it was goodbye.

But she said, "By the way, I'm Pamela. I'll be at Gizmo's tomorrow as well."

Spencer walked into Gizmo's at nine thirty the following morning. He looked about, expecting to see Pamela, but she was nowhere to be seen. Spencer's smile turned into an impassive mask. He had felt a welcome sense of semi-normalcy after seeing Pamela the day before but now thought that he had been fooling himself. Someone to his right asked if he would like to be seated, which he declined with some annoyance.

"I'm waiting for someone," he said.

He turned to face the door, intending to leave, and he found himself looking down at Pamela's face.

She reached for his arm. "I have to take the train to Cambridge. You want to come?"

Spencer shrugged. "I have nothing better to do."

As they walked to the train, Pamela asked, "Were you about to leave Gizmo's?"

"Yeah, I guess."

"I was just in the back, getting my stuff together. You aren't known for your confidence, are you?"

"I used to be," Spencer said, "but things are a little weird right now."

As the train bounced along, Pamela looked around, apparently making sure they had some privacy. She leaned toward him and said, "I saw that press conference on TV last night. That was your grandfather in the back, right? Wow. That must have freaked you out. Did you really steal that stuff? You don't seem like a thief."

Spencer was nonplussed. There were a lot of questions on the table. "I didn't steal anything. At least, I don't think I did. And yeah, seeing my grandfather there was tough."

Pamela considered his answers, then said, "Not enough detail; just like a guy. So what did you actually do with that data?"

Spencer wondered how cautious he should be. After all, he had just met her, and now she was asking him, essentially, if he had committed a crime. *You can't be too cautious in this world, right?* But if he said he couldn't talk about it, he would blow up any chance to form a relationship with her. He looked over at her Joan Baez face; his option was either to trust her or walk away alone.

The train bounced along.

"I took it, er … them. The data. Not sure why; it was like an instinct. Somewhere down deep I sensed that I might need it, er … them. It's what my email was all about. It was a perfect example of what I was seeing. Without some proof, how would anyone believe me? And I knew Olga was out there. So I looked down, and a manila file was in my hands. Things are getting murkier in hindsight. It's supposed to be the other way around, isn't it? So there—you can leave if you want."

"You think it was the right thing to do?"

"Doesn't look too hopeful, does it? Already cost me a grandfather."

"Tell me all about it."

They reached a point just off campus where there was a stone retaining wall, and they sat, interspersed among three or four other couples enjoying a spring breeze. Spencer told Pamela all about Celldesign, how it was formed, what its mission was. He expanded on the Lloyd family connection and how he had gotten his job because of the family influence. Then he reached the point in the narrative where he'd pressed send, and everything changed in a millisecond—but differently than he'd expected. "You know the rest."

"Have you thought about giving the papers back and just looking for another job?"

"All the time. Maybe I should. But it wouldn't solve Celldesign's problem. They're reporting the data wrong. The patch is not really working, not like they said it was. Maybe it works here and there, but that's not the narrative. Can I just walk away from that like it didn't exist?"

"Are you one of those guys who's out to change the world?" she asked warily.

"I'm really not. I'm no hero."

"Good, because I'm not looking for a hero." Pamela put her hand atop his. She watched him smile. It was a different smile from what she had seen before—a "killer smile," she would later say—relaxed and open and honest and trusting, and she leaned over and kissed him.

When Arthur saw that it was old Charlie on caller ID, he answered warily.

"Arthur," old Charlie growled, "I've got to know if you're on board or not."

It seemed to Arthur that old Charlie asked that same question just about every time they spoke. "Get to the point, Charlie."

"Do you agree that young Spencer has to renounce fully? Yes or no."

"Charlie, I agree with that."

"Good! Because I have an idea. I heard you say that you haven't reached out to Spencer since the email because of legitimate concerns about how it would look. I'd have done the same. But you'd like to patch it up with him, wouldn't you? I thought so. How about having the young man over for steaks and beer some night? Just the two of you. To talk it out?"

"What's the kicker, Charlie?"

Apple laughed. "The kicker is that we'll have some papers drawn up and delivered to your place that'll make it easy for him. He can sign and then go on a vacation somewhere. And we save the company."

Dorothy liked cocktails at five and dinner at six. Without variation. As he stirred his scotch and water, Arthur announced the plan to have Spencer for dinner and to take the opportunity to persuade him to "do the right thing."

"Which 'thing' is that, dear?" Dorothy asked.

"Renounce," Arthur said firmly. "It is my moral duty as grandfather, *and* it is my fiduciary duty as founder of Celldesign to get this done. It is the only way for me to fulfill all my duties. It is something I must try to get done, if I can."

"Arthur, I adore Spencer; you know that. I just wish he would grow up. He's like a perpetual adolescent."

"There is one other detail. Charlie Apple spoke to me about this, and he wants us to have some papers on hand for Spencer to sign, if we get that far. He views it as a settlement before Spencer hires a lawyer."

"Sign?"

Arthur cleared his throat. "Yes ... legal papers."

Dorothy straightened her back. "Am I to understand that the real purpose of our dinner with Spencer is to approach him with the idea of renouncing his email in a quiet and relaxed setting, with people he trusts—family—and to have legal papers on hand to seal the deal?"

"In all honesty, Dorothy, you are glossing over the main point. It will all happen in our home, under our control—my control. I won't do anything inappropriate; surely you know that. And the alternative is head-to-head litigation with Charlie Apple, and we'll all be dragged into it. At least, I will. The Lloyd name will never be the same."

"Still, Arthur, there is an unmistakable air of deceit about it."

"No. It's in the boy's best interests."

"But you're maneuvering around Spencer. Isn't that the problem with all deceit?"

"You yourself just called him hopelessly adolescent. Am I supposed to sit back and watch him—an adolescent—get cut to ribbons by a man like Charlie Apple?"

"No. But perhaps this isn't the right way to go about it."

"Dorothy, it's not the right or wrong way; it's the way ahead. Look, I think Apple will stop at nothing. It's in our interests, as well as Spencer's, to contain the problem."

They looked at each other from across the dining room table, their difference of opinion hanging in the air like the smell of the roast Dorothy had prepared. As she handed Arthur his plate, she added, "You realize, I'm sure, that you are biting off quite a bit."

Arthur accepted his plate with a disdainful look that was intended to reassert his superiority, but in truth, Dorothy's points had given him pause, as usual. But he was committed, and he would handle what needed to be done, as he always had.

Spencer's first thought when he answered the phone and heard Arthur's voice was that perhaps his nightmare was over. Perhaps his grandfather had decided to set it all straight, to press reset and bring everything back to where it was, back where he could be an adolescent again, back before he had hurt anyone, back when he had a family and a job and a future. And when Arthur brought up a steak-and-beer dinner for that evening, he was almost overcome with relief. His only comment was, "Is Dad coming?"

This was not part of the plan, and it caught Arthur by surprise. To avoid raising suspicions, Arthur replied immediately, "Sure, I'll invite him too."

It was a bit of a curveball. Arthur had misgivings about Winston's stability, especially in a fast-moving, fluid situation such as the one at hand. *Winston has virtually disappeared since it all hit the fan,* Arthur thought. He'd been frightened away when old Charlie called him and lectured him about the damages he could face if he breached his fiduciary duty. How would he react when the topic of the evening was broached? Why, Arthur didn't even know if Winston had agreed about the wisdom of renouncing. It was a judgment call. Arthur would have Winston over but would not tell Winston about the real purpose of the evening. *I'll explain it as a family night,* Arthur thought, *steaks and beer, and I won't mention the papers that will be there, waiting to be signed. I'll handle it as it arises.*

Nor did Arthur tell old Charlie that Winston would be there. After all, the evening was to be under Arthur's control; that was why he'd agreed to it. Blanketed by such blissful optimism, Arthur went about preparations—ordering steaks from the butcher down the street, checking on his supply of craft beer (for Spencer).

But old Charlie and Mary had something up their sleeves. About an hour before Spencer and Winston were due, two young lawyers with old Charlie's firm stood in suit and tie at Arthur's threshold, looked him in the eye, and one said, "We're delivering the affidavits. Mr. Apple said you'd understand."

Arthur's jaw dropped. Suddenly, old Charlie's plan had a different feel. Arthur hadn't expected *affidavits*—but what else could such "papers" be? Arthur reached for the affidavits and quickly read them over as all three stood awkwardly in the doorway. *These papers are not what old Charlie represented to me,* Arthur thought, his face darkening. They went farther, not merely saying that Spencer had acted hastily, not merely that he had no scientific basis to say that the data were being manipulated, but all the way to admitting that he had committed a crime by removing data from the premises.

He looked down at the eager faces of the two young lawyers. "These aren't the right papers. Did Mr. Apple look them over?"

One of the young lawyers said, "We were just given them and told to come over here and that you would know."

"But you are asking not simply for renouncement but for admission of criminal guilt. For God's sake, he could go to jail," Arthur said, his eyes frantic. But the moment was upon him, something had to be done. He wanted the lawyers away, off his premises, vanished into the night. "You have accomplished your mission and are free to go. Mr. Apple can call me if he would like to discuss it."

One of the lawyers said, "I'm sorry, sir, but we can't do that. We were told to be inconspicuous but to witness and notarize Spencer Lloyd's signature. Otherwise, it would be useless in any legal proceeding."

One of the lawyers reached out and took back the papers Arthur was holding.

The two sides stood facing each other; the moment was rife with tension. Arthur quickly calculated. He could call the doorman and have them forcibly removed, but the implications of that were troubling. He eyed the two young men; their gaze was steadfast. *What am I doing here if not to obtain renouncement?*

There was more to consider. Turning away the lawyers at this point could put him in a bad light. Perhaps in and of itself a breach of fiduciary duty. All of a sudden, everything seemed to be at stake. *At least get them inside the apartment*, he thought.

He looked gravely at them and asked, "Are you carrying any recording devices?"

They each said no.

But Arthur did not believe them.

It's all wrong, he thought. *I must play both sides against the middle.* He showed them to a spare bedroom, asked if they wanted refreshments, and—smiling, his voice lowered—told them that they must not leave until he called them. They nodded in acquiescence. He emphasized, "Everything depends on that," and they nodded seriously.

But he had no intention whatsoever of calling them out of the spare bedroom. The papers had gone too far; Arthur blamed himself for leaving the details to old Charlie. Yet he remained convinced that if Spencer saw the logic behind renouncement, there would be no need for an affidavit. He could send the lawyers home and deal with old Charlie later. "God damn lawyers," Arthur said as he closed the bedroom door and walked into the library to await his son and grandson.

The way Spencer understood it, the dinner had the best of purposes—to reopen the lines of communication, to patch up any lingering anger, to forgive and forget. He intended to apologize, not for alerting the company to the data-reporting issue (because with each day, he had increasing confidence in his observation) but for doing so in such an abrupt fashion.

It had been a long time since all three of them had been together. Spencer thought it to be better than a holiday, better than Thanksgiving or Fourth of July, almost as good as Christmas—an opportunity to erase the haunting image of Arthur, arms folded, on the dais at the press conference, appearing to all the world to be against him. Spencer had felt abandoned, yet now there was an opportunity to make all that right. For a moment, as he greeted Arthur's doorman, Spencer felt like a member of a family again—reconnected.

Spencer arrived first; Winston followed within a matter of minutes. Each was predictably dressed—Spencer in jeans and boat shoes; Winston in Zegna slacks and highly polished loafers. But as much as Spencer tried to dismiss the feeling, it was inescapable: Celldesign was in the air.

Drinks were poured, scotch for Arthur and Winston, a local IPA for Spencer. The three men smiled but circled each other. Spencer noted that Winston seemed a bit distracted; Arthur seemed a bit rattled. It had been the first meeting with all three of them since Spencer's email. Spencer proposed a toast—"To the Lloyds"—and they touched glasses.

Talk drifted to the New York strip steaks awaiting them, with Arthur commenting extensively on how he had wrangled them from a butcher shop just down the street that supplied all the better restaurants in town. "They are perfectly marbled," he said.

Spencer had promised himself that he would not raise any issue relating to Celldesign, and he kept that pledge. Surprisingly, it was Winston who first brought up the subject, albeit in an off-hand way. Trying to inject some humor, Winston said to Spencer, "Your mother wants to know why it's all men here tonight. She was complaining that when she's invited, it's hot dogs, but when it's the men, it's New York strip."

Arthur thought he saw an opening. "We must talk and reach an agreement to do what is best for the family. This seemed like a good way to accomplish that."

Spencer thought Winston looked pained as he creased his brow and turned his head down, looking at the floor, as if to find guidance there. After waiting a moment to give his father the next opportunity to speak, Spencer then turned to Arthur and said, "The problem is, I know what I saw."

"Fiddlesticks," Arthur replied testily. "You don't have the slightest idea how those data are evaluated and reported. You jumped the gun!"

Nerves were raw. Winston looked at the other two, moving his head back and forth.

"Grandfather, I thought this was supposed to be a nice evening. A reconciliation of sorts. Instead, you sound like Olga."

Arthur took offense. "And what if I do? A PhD from

MIT. My Lord, Spence, the good name of the Lloyds is being tarnished. And you can rectify that."

"Okay, I get it." Spencer's voice was subdued. "We'll find out in the end. If I'm wrong, I'll apologize. I'll admit it."

"No, damn it, the end is too far away. You're talking about forces beyond your control. The business world. Every day that this thing hangs over our heads, Celldesign loses credibility with the markets. It can't go on much longer. Just look at your father, Spence. His future is tied up with the company." He took a deep breath. "With all due respect, you're being unreasonable. You should listen to what I'm saying. My God, your father looks like he's having a stroke. His Celldesign—my Celldesign, our futures—are in your hands, and I'm afraid you don't even know what it is you've done."

With a growing determination, a feeling that surprised even him, Spencer said, "And what is it that I've done, other than tell the truth of what I saw?"

Winston squirmed but did not speak; he kept his eyes on the floor.

Spencer noticed Winston, even as Arthur did not.

Arthur said, "That's my point, Spencer. 'The truth of what I saw' is deeper than you know. Truth is a slippery old thing. All we were doing was providing more reliable information, not less reliable. It's like your golf handicap. You limit the really bad holes because it would skew the overall score. It's a common statistics procedure. Look at it that way, why don't you?"

Spencer's eyes went back repeatedly to Winston, but he stood stoically. "What are you asking of me?" Spencer said in a wary voice, as he turned toward Arthur.

Arthur said somewhat loudly, "Simple. You should renounce your email. Take responsibility for what you've done. Be a man about it. Like getting a bad tooth pulled. All be over shortly."

And at that moment, without warning, the two well-dressed young men came marching into the library from the guest bedroom.

Winston dropped his glass on the wooden floor, where it crashed with an enormous sound and split into a million slivers of glass, sending scotch across the floor and onto his highly polished shoes.

Arthur looked in the direction of the two men. "What the hell are you doing?"

Spencer tried to make sense of what he was seeing as the two men approached him. They walked across the floor, avoiding the scotch, holding papers out to him and smiling as if their actions were the most common thing in the world.

Spencer quickly concluded that the men were not thieves—at least, not the usual kind of thieves—but something was terribly off base about it all. One of the men had managed to put several papers in Spencer's hands. Spencer looked at the top of the page: CELLDESIGN, INC. v. SPENCER LLOYD.

"What the hell is wrong with you?" Arthur demanded, hovering over the two men, his eyebrows moving up and down involuntarily.

Winston appeared ready to faint. Spencer reached out to take hold of his arm. With Spencer's hands on his arm, Winston shouted, "Get out! Get out now!" And he kept shouting it.

One of the men was right in Spencer's face, saying something about Spencer being "under oath" and something else about "renouncing his legal position and claims." Then Spencer looked at Winston again, who had regained his footing and had turned to Arthur, eyes wide in disbelief. He kept repeating the phrase "a trap" several times.

Spencer's eyes flashed toward Arthur, who was shaking his head. One of the young men, having become aware that something had gone wrong, was on his cell phone. Spencer heard him say, "Mr. Apple." It was chaos. Utter chaos. And that is when Spencer left, almost at a run, taking the fire stairs down instead of the elevator because he thought that they might stop it and capture him between floors, as improbable as that sounded, and that led him breathlessly into the night air on Beacon Hill. The Charles River faced him like the Jordan.

As he hurried away from Arthur's building, Spencer had a sense that someone was looking at him, in the way most people will suddenly stop what they are doing, instinctively look in a different direction and see someone staring at them. Spencer did the same; he stopped to look around, sure that he would see someone looking his way, but there was no one. So, he hurried along, as he needed to get away from his grandfather's home; he needed distance.

He walked quickly in a westerly direction, instinctively heading for the train station, which would have taken him home, but before he got there, he stopped again. Where, exactly, was he going? Back to his empty apartment? Would they follow him there? He had to get away from Arthur's, but he felt boxed-in. The sidewalk was bustling with people who had to walk around Spencer's solitary figure, usually casting a nasty glance backward, as if to say, "Move it!"

Spencer responded by stepping off the sidewalk; he remembered that he had Pamela's cell number in his contacts, and he pressed send. And she answered.

"Sorry to bother you," he said.

"No bother," she replied in a hushed voice.

"Sounds like maybe I am bothering you," Spencer replied to Pamela's lowered voice.

"I'm at the library," she said quietly.

"Really?" Spencer asked. "At MIT?"

"Mm-hm. How did it go tonight?"

"Well, I'm standing out here in the middle of the block, shaking, with nowhere to go, and no prospects except jail. Other than that, everything seems okay."

"We're about equidistant from the Mass Ave bridge. I can meet you in the middle in about fifteen minutes."

Spencer saw her silhouette waiting for him as he made his way up the pedestrian walkway on the bridge. It was mid-June, and the light stayed longer at this time of year. He could see her clearly, and then he was next to her, and she kissed him, and he began talking, telling her everything that had happened, as runners, walkers, and bikers streamed by and looked at the two of them as if they were actors shooting a movie, like *Love Story*.

She listened as he spoke. Her Joan Baez eyes tilted ever so slightly downward at the corners, which, he thought, was probably how she looked when upset, perhaps just before crying.

Pamela's mouth dropped open in astonishment as he described the two young men with legal papers. "They were hiding in a bedroom?" she asked. "Is that even legal? Can they do that? Shouldn't they be disbarred or something?"

"They were doing what they were told to do," Spencer replied. "They were playing me."

"Who?" Pamela asked.

"All of them. Well, maybe not my father. His look of shock was genuine."

Pamela took his arm, and they walked off the bridge toward the Back Bay train station.

"I went there looking to make peace, and here I am," Spencer said.

Pamela's look of shock was replaced by a sober expression. "If you were to renounce what you said in your email, just to make peace with your grandfather, it would ultimately not be a good enough reason. It wouldn't work, and what's worse, at the same time you'd become culpable for whatever happened as a result. Why doesn't Arthur see that?" She looked at him to see if it was all right to continue, since she was attacking his family, and it was. "From what you've said, it sounds like Olga is discarding outlier data but way too much. Everything is a matter of degree, isn't it? I'm thinking that what she has done is, like, securities fraud. And she knows it, somewhere deep down. What you did instinctively was right."

As they were about to board the train to Chestnut Hill, the stop for her apartment, she suggested that they divert course to his apartment. "It's probably not the right night for you to meet my dad."

Spencer nodded in agreement.

Then she added, "You're lucky your dad was there."

As he watched Spencer's back disappear down the fire stairway, Arthur was furious with everyone involved, including himself. It had been a catastrophe. One of the young attorneys was still on the phone with old Charlie Apple, trying to explain what had happened. Arthur walked over and took the phone from the young man's hand.

"Damn it all, Charlie!" Arthur roared, as if his voice had to carry all the way out to Route 128 without enhancement. "This was the most ill-conceived strategy imaginable! And your two lawyers here led the way. They were like a couple of storm troopers, breaking in at just the wrong moment. Did you have anything to do with that?"

Old Charlie ignored the question and instead said, "Jesus, Arthur, what the hell was Winston doing there? Sounds like he screwed it all up."

"Fuck off, Charlie. Listen, Winston was the conscience of the evening."

Old Charlie resorted to the last line of defense for an attorney. "You are the client, Arthur. You could have overridden me at any time. Listen: we tried something, and it didn't work out."

"You bet it didn't," Arthur said. "And now what? He'll never agree to renounce or withdraw or cooperate or anything. Would you? Charlie, tonight was a disaster. Like taking an ax where a scalpel is required." Arthur heard nothing on the other end of the phone, so he handed it back to the young attorney and turned to Winston. "I'm sorry," he said as he ran his hand lightly over the top of his combed-back hair, assuring himself that it was back in place. "I lost it." He stood erect and reached to put his hand on Winston's shoulder. "I understand what you did, telling Spencer to get out. That damned Charlie—bad plan, terrible plan."

Winston broke in. "He's my son."

"Yes, of course."

"No, Dad, listen to me. He's my son."

It was the first time in Arthur's memory that Winston had lectured him. It felt odd to them both, but Arthur had no retort.

Arthur pulled his royal-blue sweater down around his hips and smoothed out the front. He stood before Winston in a way for which he was not prepared. He had been humbled. And instead of taking a giant step to resolve the emerging battles, he had done the opposite, and there was a crushing weight to that. He spoke in Winston's direction, but the words were meant mainly for himself. "We cannot be expected to be supermen. No court would say we violated our duty to the company. We are fiduciaries, yes, but not supermen."

Winston shook his head. "Why didn't you tell me about this elaborate charade? Why was I left in the dark?"

Arthur came back to the moment, spitting out his answer. "Because I had to make choices with no time on the clock. Apple says one thing; you say another. There are competing demands! A choice had to be made. At the moment. And the choice I made was right at bottom—Spencer should admit he was wrong, and we go from there. But he would not listen, and ... and ... it was all a huge mistake, okay? Nobody won tonight. And I regret it, okay?"

Winston looked embarrassed.

Arthur realized that that look was directed at him. *Composure*, he thought. He must compose himself. The night had been a total loss in every substantive way, but more important, he must compose himself.

He put his hand back on Winston's shoulder and guided him into the study, stopping at the wet bar for two glasses of scotch. The lighting in the study was controlled by a motion sensor, so that as people walked in, the overhead lights that illuminated the giant bookcase went on automatically. Arthur was very proud of it. All the framed photos of his colleagues that adorned the bookshelves were lit up. Arthur unfolded his six-foot-five frame into the leather chair that had become "his" over the years. He pointed Winston to the companion chair, arranged not to face each other but at an angle, so that each had a sideways view of the other. Arthur found that arrangement better for talking.

"I'm sorry if I said anything intemperate," Arthur said, finally. "I'm getting old, you know." And he told Winston the whole story of how the dinner had been planned.

Winston took a drink, seeming to savor the scotch, warm and friendly. "A fine mess," he said, which Arthur had to acknowledge. But then Winston returned to his concern. "Spencer's going to have legal expenses. He can't be exposed to Apple without a weapon of his own. That was proven tonight."

"We can't just fund an effort to thwart the company to which we've each sworn to be loyal."

"But he's our flesh and blood."

"We're not rehashing the Old Testament here. We're trying to save this venture, which I promoted, from a lynching slowly played out in the press, something that would take our money and shred our reputations. To do that, we must enlist Spencer's cooperation. He owes us that much."

"I always told him to stand up for what he believes."

"Winston, we can't be doctrinaire. Now is not the time. There are realities! You want to lose the entire investment?"

Winston looked down without speaking.

"I didn't think so," Arthur said, slapping Winston's knee lightly. It was intended as a gesture of two comrades involved in the same game. Straightening up, Arthur pronounced, "Spencer will simply have to bear the consequences of his decisions. He can still come over to our side. We need to maintain that incentive. All he has to do is call. Then, and only then, will we get him out of the legal mess he's gotten himself into at our expense. Agreed?"

Winston nodded without looking up. "No more fiascos," he said with utter resignation.

"We'll need backbone." Arthur raised his glass. "It's a fine line we must walk."

Arthur's eyes widened as he looked over the business section of the *Globe* on the following day. "Garrigall's like a junkyard dog," he muttered. The headline was, "State Lab to Investigate Celldesign." Apparently, Garrigall had developed a source inside the state bureaucracy, which was the journalist's stock in trade.

Garrigall pointed out that Celldesign used the so-called scatter-plot statistics approach, where the number of people who reacted as expected were plotted, as well as those who had an adverse reaction after using the patch, which was a perfectly valid model. His source confirmed that the data points would be expected to form a pattern, falling within a box, graphically—a square, with few if any outliers or abnormal data points. The box would then support the theory, and the outliers would be elided, or dropped, from the graph, supposedly following guidelines for the presentation of such data. These reports were intended to form a scientific basis that would ultimately justify the sale of the patch to the public—unless there were too many outliers. And that was one of the things that the state lab would check; they would look over all the data, including the outlier data points, to see if there was a true pattern or a false one. The review would take several weeks.

In the interim, Celldesign's credibility was in tatters.

As Arthur read, lines of concern formed across his forehead. That was what Spencer said he'd observed—too many outlier data points; people who got sick despite the patch, who were not reported at all. For the first time, a deep concern about the data crept into Arthur's mind, and he thought of Olga. He recalled her zeal when Apple went after Spencer's credibility, her mouse-like dark eyes reveling in the attack. Was it too much to be merely an expression of her loyalty to Celldesign? Was there something more at play?

He would keep an eye on the state lab and on Olga. Had he been wrong to rely on all the MIT grads? Was that not enough assurance? *Good Lord*, he thought, *the Lloyd name will be decimated.* He could afford no more mistakes.

Arthur reached Mary, and they agreed to meet, just the two of them, at her new condo. It was the only place for Mary to give Arthur her full attention, away from the phone ringing off the hook with nervous investors, finance bankers, and investment bankers, all of whom were relying upon the IPO for their pot of gold.

Mary had recently purchased a penthouse in a new high-rise building on Boston Harbor, facing south over the ocean. It was tall and sleek, all reflective glass, which she paid for by means of a bridge loan, anticipating the IPO cash would arrive soon. The building had a doorman—a diminutive man in uniform, including a top hat that obscured his face, almost leaving it in shadow, which added to the building's menacing aura.

The doorman rang Arthur upstairs to the second-highest floor, after looking him up and down, undoubtedly wondering what hanky-panky the old fellow was up to.

Arthur did not notice the man's scrutiny. He was preoccupied with trying to make sense of Celldesign's problem.

Mary met him at the door with her usual panache—a smile, a kiss on the cheek, an inviting hand leading him into her space. Arthur had not been there before. There was an absence of anything personal within the four walls—no photos, no art, no furniture except for a couch that looked like it had been retrieved from a consignment store and a straight-backed chair that looked new but uncomfortable.

It was a sterile space. Mary seemed to be aware of that fact; she blushed when she invited him in. "I don't even have a coffee maker," she said, "but the doorman is a doll, and he'll scoot over to Starbucks if you'd like something."

Arthur almost accepted, but he wanted to get down to business. They recapped what had happened at the dinner and agreed that the details of that evening must remain totally sealed, completely leakproof," or Garrigall would get on to it, and a story would destabilize things even further. Mary's facial expression—a blank nod intended to substitute for *of course*—betrayed their joint understanding that Arthur would insist on sealing off the inner workings of his family.

Arthur moved closer to her, and said, "Let's go with a different approach. How about taking the S.O.B. out for lunch?"

They both knew that Garrigall was the ultimate creature of the press, a man who would subtly repay any news that was slipped his way, news he could break; it was the unspoken exchange when dealing with the media. It often happened, Arthur knew, over lunch at the fabled Parker House. Garrigall was sure to accept, and perhaps the encounter would pay dividends in terms of shaping the narrative coming from the *Globe*. He would hear their side, face-to-face, in a memorable setting—ground zero for the power elite.

"Maybe we can ply him with Dover sole and a tidbit of news," Arthur said. "He'll feel like the big man he has always wanted to be."

Mary had brought her right hand to her chin. She thought a moment and shrugged. "I guess it would be low risk."

They talked further about the lunch idea, and Arthur was about to excuse himself and go back to his office on campus, but for one more detail that bothered him. "Did you see today's *Globe?*" he asked. When Mary nodded, Arthur continued. "He's doing his homework. That part on statistics was pretty good."

He waited for Mary to answer the implied question: *Is there any chance that the data we're excluding is creating a misleading picture—that the patch actually is not performing as well as those data would suggest?* Arthur paused, waiting for reassurance, but none came.

Mary assumed a faraway look, a look that spoke to Arthur of distance. For a moment, it seemed as if she was going to say something consequential, truthful, honest, which was the way they had interacted during the building of the company. But after a pause, she merely said, "I'm sure we're okay, if that's what you're asking." And thus, she had taken a step that would have been unthinkable even a month ago; she had dissembled. Lied to his face.

It was just a little seed of doubt. *Just a dot on the landscape*, Arthur thought, *but the dots are beginning to add up.*

As he left the building, after nodding to the diminutive doorman, Arthur felt a chill on his neck. He twirled around, almost falling, to see who was there—but there was nobody to be seen. "Am I paranoid?" Arthur asked himself. He looked up, trying to see the window on the seventeenth floor, but it was too high. "Maybe it's Mary," he said, unconvinced.

Garrigall made Arthur's skin crawl, but he knew well enough that he had to swallow his feelings and fawn over him under these circumstances. The little man jumped at Arthur's invitation to lunch. He seemed especially delighted when Arthur suggested the Parker House. Arthur knew what the dynamics of their relationship were—that he was coming down to Garrigall's level—but Garrigall knew that too.

For the moment, Pat Garrigall, with his pock-marked skin, receding hairline, and Land's End wardrobe, was in the driver's seat. It was what the lunch was all about. And he intended to ride that for all it was worth. For the Boston business community, including Arthur, Garrigall was a known commodity, a reporter who often looked at the people he covered with a barely concealed sense of resentment. Arthur had double-checked the story: when Garrigall came out of South Boston and was accepted to Dartmouth, where he got high grades in economics, graduated with honors, and stayed on for an additional two years at the Tuck School, much was expected of him. But he made the mistake (as it turned out to be; at the time, he was praised to the heavens) of going into journalism rather that joining a banking firm on State Street. That was why he especially enjoyed lunches at the expense of a news source that wanted something from him at the Parker House, lunches that were otherwise out of his reach, yet were enjoyed on a regular basis by those he openly regarded as inferior—young MBAs who knew half of what Garrigall did yet made ten times the money.

But Arthur was restrained in his criticism; after all, he was doing the same thing. He was there to use Garrigall, just as Garrigall was using him. Each knew the game; each consented to it; each hoped to benefit from it. In short, it was business playing out in Boston. And with the backdrop of the elegant Parker House, the allure would be too great for Garrigall to object on principle.

Mary was dressed in a smart black-and-white pantsuit;

Arthur in a blue blazer with a red bow tie. Both were known by the waitstaff. Garrigall came by at twelve thirty, dressed in khakis and a seedy, worn, brown wool blazer, quite inappropriate for the summer months. The maître d' discreetly offered him a yellow striped tie from the coat closet.

There were a few jokes, a bit of inane chatter, and then they ordered—Dover sole all round (the Parker House was famous for it) and three glasses of Chablis, French, premier cru.

Arthur took the lead. "Our discussion is off the record," he stressed, "but we have some news for you."

All was going well. Mary described how strong Celldesign's people were, all MIT and Harvard, a board composed of the best and the brightest, the shapers of America in the last half century. "How credible is it, really, that the statistics reports would be wrong and that it would be discovered by someone like Spencer?" She turned to Arthur and put a hand on his shoulder, as if to say, "No offense."

Arthur took none.

Garrigall seemed to be basking, looking about to confirm that he was actually in the company of the real business stars in Boston. The Parker House was the best setting for that: white tablecloths, sparkling glassware, waiters in suits, but most of all, the long tradition. It was where Brahmins had gathered and spoken and shaped Boston and beyond for decades.

Arthur watched as Mary leaned toward Garrigall and said softly, "Of course, we're disappointed that we've been questioned in this way, publicly, when we've been so careful at each step. And our product is so important to humankind. Nevertheless, we are hiring a statistics firm, an independent one, to double-check our reports. And we'll correct whatever we have to—if we have to."

"That's for attribution," Arthur said, watching carefully as

Garrigall pursed his lips and nodded—not the response Arthur was looking for.

Arthur expected to catch Mary's eye, but she seemed oblivious, continuing to pitch Celldesign's virtues, when Garrigall, in Arthur's view, had signaled some skepticism.

Negative vibes, Arthur thought.

"So, there is really nothing for anyone to worry about," Mary said. "It all sadly stems from an inexperienced, perhaps well-meaning young man we hired as a courtesy to his grandfather and who is now in well over his head."

Garrigall seemed to take it all in as he lingered over his lunch, although he finished his glass of Chablis in short order and nodded when the waiter asked if he wished for another. He looked at Mary. "A thief. I think that's what you called him."

Mary looked at Arthur, then back at Garrigall. "Yes, but that was Charlie Apple. Our attorney. We have to protect our company. I'm sure you agree."

"I don't know. He's just a kid. If he turns out to be right, who would be the criminal then?"

As the second glass of Chablis arrived, Garrigall asked Mary about the bank debt that had been undertaken after the initial seed money and whether Celldesign would be in default if the IPO were delayed.

Mary acknowledged that it would.

Garrigall nodded and went back to his sole. "Here's a hypothetical, nothing more: if Celldesign's statistics were improperly presented, would that fact shut down sales? Specifically, would the patch's trial runs be discontinued?"

"That might be true," Mary conceded.

"Good deal of pressure on the data coming out right, huh?"

Arthur saw what was happening and made a point of looking at his watch, as if signaling the end of lunch.

Garrigall, however, continued, clearly enjoying the conversation. "We're hearing rumors that Celldesign had an *envoy*, for lack of a better word, on staff who did nothing except escort the data to the state lab. Can you comment?"

This caught Arthur quite by surprise, and his face flushed involuntarily with anger. Turning, he noticed that Mary seemed ready to respond. *Do they know something?* he thought.

Mary took a breath. "Pat, we have many people on payroll. I'm not familiar with the person you're describing, but that sounds like a conspiracy theory, doesn't it? We *know* that this technology works, and in the long run, we will do what we have to do to jump every hurdle so we can get on with the business at hand and change the world. Folks should focus on the long run, rather than these minor statistical blips."

Garrigall replied, "Who was it who said, 'In the long run, we are all dead'?"

Arthur said involuntarily, "Keynes. But Pat, you must give credit where it is due. Celldesign has a chance to be a great company. Look at the people on the board. These are serious people who will not be thrown off the horse easily."

Garrigall's voice was purposefully unctuous. "Arthur, I'm merely writing a story."

Arthur leaned toward Garrigall. "You never *merely* write anything, Pat. You have extensive influence in this town. And you've always been fair, observed the lines. Why the change now?"

Garrigall smiled wryly.

Arthur waited.

Garrigall looked over at the table to his right, at which an actor, who had once played a president in an acclaimed movie, sat surrounded by young men in suits. Garrigall seemed to be feeding off the atmosphere. He then said, "How are things with your grandson?"

Arthur stiffened. Garrigall had gone off limits. "Quite fine. I love my grandson. That's for the record."

"What about off the record? Is this email business coming between the two of you?"

Arthur harkened back to an earlier time, when journalists— real journalists, not the phony, resentful kind like Garrigall— would respect certain boundaries. Like with Kennedy and even Johnson. Arthur now knew for certain what he had feared: that Garrigall believed that the story involved at least two layers—the Celldesign business and the Lloyd family—and he punctuated the underlying conflict by sitting there like a cheap Buddha, arms folded across his full stomach, a light smile on his face.

"Come on, Arthur; that's the real story here. You can't avoid it. You have two mistresses, don't you? Don't you have to make a choice about where to place your loyalty? Whether to save the company you founded or the family you sired. My readers want to know."

"Pat, I am going to trust that you will realize that exploiting my family does you a disservice."

Mary ran her hand through her hair and looked out over the dining room. Arthur turned to make eye contact with the waiter. *Time for the check.*

Jimmy drove Arthur and Mary back to 128; the car was basically silent all the way. Arthur was more certain than ever that the *narrative*, as old Charlie liked to call it, was running away from them. One glance at Mary confirmed that she felt the same. She was slumped against the back-seat window, as if the lunch had taken everything out of her. Arthur went away from the Parker House sensing the strength of the enemy, which he had seen, dimly, for the first time as Garrigall devoured his Dover sole and basked in the light of the rich and famous all around him and asked the two of them questions that required better answers than those they'd given. He already surmised that Garrigall had his sights on a Pulitzer. But now he had a glimpse of how Garrigall might be able to get one.

CHAPTER 6

Spencer listened as Pamela called her father and simply told him that she would be out for the night. He shouldn't worry. That was their agreement. The simplicity of the trust between them struck Spencer; the contrast with his own situation was unavoidable.

They had reached his apartment and were sitting over two bottles of beer. Pamela wanted to know everything about the dinner, and Spencer needed to put the experience in words, rather than to simply absorb it, like a boxer absorbs a body blow. They talked as the sun set and his windows darkened, trying to make sense of the dinner, as they called it. What had happened? Who was behind it?

That night was so odd that he was not sure about his own perceptions of it. It was hard to make sense of the images, his father's panic, his grandfather's anger.

To Spencer, it felt like his grandfather had become a stranger. "He has it all," Spencer answered when Pamela asked about Arthur's motivation. "He has money, success, respect. He's approaching eighty years old and lacks nothing." Spencer shook his head.

"*Nothing* is not the answer," she said. "He lacks something—something important—because it is all so sad."

With each date, Pamela had become more vocal. She was skeptical about Celldesign—the enthusiasm, the idealism, seemed unreal. And she was convinced that Celldesign was misusing the scatter-plot statistics model. She did not understand, however—because the misuse was so obvious to her—why it had been undiscovered for so long. And more to the point: "Why is it that Arthur still acts as if the data were right?"

They finished the beer and philosophy and retired to Spencer's bedroom, as naturally as if they had been lovers for years.

That night was long and he had trouble sleeping, but he loved watching her dream—her eyelids moving, indicating REM sleep, deep and far away, and he wondered if he was in those dreams or if they were too gentle for him to be included.

Spencer ran most mornings and always on Saturdays, jogging around the pond in Allston, near Fenway, hoping to clear his head. While he was out, Pamela showered and dressed and made a pot of coffee. Spencer was not an especially neat person; his apartment was always littered with empty things—beer bottles, take-out food containers, plastic bags that he thought about recycling but ultimately would throw away. There were a few rock-concert murals that had been thumbtacked to the wall, their ends now curling a bit. Previously read newspapers were stacked near the kitchen cabinets. And a few photographs, cheaply framed, showed his family or friends. He maintained that he was quite popular before the Celldesign mess, and the photos were proof of that. He was always smiling broadly, his arm around someone—his mother, an old girlfriend, and, in one case, his father (on one side) and his grandfather (on the other).

Spencer came back holding a paper bag with milk and cornflakes. They sat down to eat breakfast but were interrupted when someone banged on the front door. Based on the timing alone, Spencer ventured a guess. "I'm betting that's my mom." He watched the blood drain from Pamela's face.

Spencer's mother was insistent—*knock, knock, knock*. He stood, shrugged his shoulders at Pamela, and went to let her in.

"Spencer, I've been worried sick," she said, admonishing him in tone but smiling. She was quite handsome, fiftyish, brown hair, elegantly dressed, sunglasses perched on top of her head, and a large leather handbag attached to her left forearm. She grabbed Spencer in a hug, and then she glanced into the kitchen area, where Pamela was sitting.

She cleared her throat, turned Spencer loose, and, reaching out, said, "Hi, I'm Mandy, Spencer's mom."

Spencer watched as Pamela stood and offered her hand to Mandy. Although each was smiling, Spencer already knew Pamela's genuine smile, and her expression at that time was nervous and shy, sort of pouty. Pamela ran her hands over her torn jeans and T-shirt that read "Born Wild." She appeared to be in the middle of an apology for the way she looked when Mandy, in her blustering way, said, "Oh, honey, I just *wish* that I could wear tight jeans and a T-shirt. There was a time!"

Mandy's comment caused Spencer to blush, but it made Pamela laugh. Mandy went ahead and hopped up on the Formica countertop, her feet dangling over the side. She ran her right hand through her wavy hair and said, "So go ahead—eat." Only she said it in her native Brooklyn accent, and it came out as, "Ga'hed—eat."

Spencer knew what was coming. Mandy turned her eyes toward him and pointed to the empty chair and his bowl of cornflakes, all in the same sweeping gesture. Spencer sat, and

Mandy started. "So I heard a version of what happened on steak night, and I haven't slept a wink. I'm not letting this go until I know everything. So, come on." She waved her arms like a traffic cop.

Dangerous territory, Spencer thought. *Better to keep it short.* "Look," he said, "it's complicated, but there were lawyers there; they had papers."

"But you didn't sign anything, thank God?" It was articulated as a question, and Spencer shook his head.

"No, but honestly, it seemed like a big screw-up. Grandpa was mad at the lawyers, Dad was mad at Grandpa, and I just skipped out."

"It must have been terrible for you."

"I'm becoming an escape artist."

"What? And then you just happened to meet …"

"Pamela," said Pamela.

"Afterward?"

"No," Spencer said, "we met … a while ago."

"I'll make some more coffee." Mandy grabbed the now-empty coffeepot that had been on the table.

Spencer shrugged as if to say he had no way to stop her. He watched while Mandy opened each cabinet door until she struck gold and found the "Mr. Coffee" machine she had been looking for.

Spencer loved his mother; he thought she was warm and vivacious and irreverent and fun. As the three of them sat in the kitchen with coffee, though, he regretted that he had not told Pamela that his mother did not see Arthur the way almost everyone else did. She did not see a great man. She did not get wrapped up in his outward achievements. All that was secondary to her. She would never forgive him for his impact on Winston.

Spencer had seen her explode and rail against Arthur from time to time; he knew how it built up and how it felt, like storm clouds gathering. And this was one of those times. So it did not surprise him when she started in.

"That conniving little fish. The hypocrite! Always talking about the search for truth, lording it over us all, and here you are, doing precisely that—what he has preached—and he turns on you. Who else could have been so manipulative as to set a trap for his grandson?"

Spencer focused on Pamela, watching her face, her posture for any reaction. Would she conclude that he had a dysfunctional family? Would it disqualify him and end their relationship? He began to feel sweaty and nauseated, like he had been hit with motion sickness.

Mandy's words called him back. "All members of that little club," she was saying. "How many times have we all been to that mausoleum he calls a library, and he springs *his plan* on us. How he wants things to go. So that he can tell those octogenarian friends of his how he solved these problems. That's how they all stay together, you know. Controlling people—that's the glue. At first, the stage is the world. Then they age, and the stage becomes their families. A little group of former shapers of the world, aging now—and not gracefully, by the way—hanging on to their collective self-images with their bony fingers."

Pamela said, "Maybe I should go."

Spencer did not want that, but before he could gather himself, Mandy replied with a wan smile, "No, no, dear. I'm just blowing off steam—to the embarrassment of my son. I apologize. Like every family, we have some … issues." She laughed at herself, and Spencer began to feel better.

Arthur and Mandy had never gotten along, and hearing her diatribe brought back unpleasant memories for

Spencer—holidays when she and Arthur battled over anything from politics to education—but at bottom, it was always about Winston and the effects of living in Arthur's shadow. Spencer could see both sides but tended to support his mother, simply because it seemed like an unfair fight. But he would never engage in a "discussion" directly with his grandfather; he knew enough to avoid that. Usually, his bedroom was close, and he would escape there.

A part of him, an ever-smaller part, wanted to do the same now. Or at least change the topic of conversation. He found that the best he could do was to say, "I'm a little worried about my legal position."

Mandy could not hold back. "You're not the only one! I haven't slept a wink. I know it—I just know that he's behind Apple's strategy. He could stop it if he wanted. The founder? Come on, he could take it in another direction, but not him. Not the great man. And he won't give a nickel. We've tried. All the money in the world, and he'll only talk some trash about him and Winston breaching their fiduciary duty or something. We're drowning; his grandson is drowning, and he's all about moral superiority."

Spencer winced inside, recalling Arthur when challenged, how deftly he could defend his positions. Mandy had exhausted herself. But the subject was on the table. Spencer began to sweat again, and he rubbed his forehead. "I'm not even sure that I understand what I'll be charged with. Or if I'll be charged with anything criminal, or if it'll all be civil. And they've hired some heavy dudes to come after me—not to be ignored."

Pamela's face suddenly looked awkward; Spencer got the impression, for the first time, that she might be holding something back. Her hands were in her lap, and she was bent forward so that her forehead was hovering above the table. But he thought he should give it time, rather than insist that she tell him what was on her mind.

Instead, he turned toward his mother, who seemed lost in thought, a memory, perhaps, of a slight by Arthur, a defense of Arthur by Winston, or perhaps the residue of years spent in Arthur's shadow.

Out of that momentary awkwardness, Pamela said, "I know a lawyer. He's just a friend." She turned her eyes toward Spencer. "We met a few years ago. He graduated from law school and everything. He has a job downtown. He might be able to help. Or at least tell us where to go for help. He speaks street jive sometimes but mostly when he's nervous. Underneath, he's brilliant and courteous and kind."

Spencer saw it in her eyes. "Sounds like quite a catch," he said.

Pamela blushed, lifting her chin, a subtle expression of belligerence that was not lost on Spencer.

Pamela arranged for the two of them to meet with Alan Brown after work at a local watering hole off Boylston Street. Brown was there, with a beer in front of him, when they arrived. Pamela had told Spencer what to expect—a short, muscular, light-skinned black man with a receding hairline. Brown had arrived in Boston about ten years earlier, when he was recruited to Boston College on a football scholarship from the backwaters of Jacksonville, Florida. Football did not work out, so he went into pre-law and then to NYU Law School in New York. But he longed to return to Boston and jumped at the chance to take a clerkship after NYU with the presiding judge of the Second Circuit Court of Appeals, which sat downtown.

He had recently become an associate with a small firm. He also had been involved with Pamela for over a year, although they'd broken up several months earlier.

Spencer compared their facial expressions and judged that Pamela had been the active party in the breakup; Brown had merely accepted it. It was written on his face when he looked at her, and when they exchanged glances, there was the smokiness of former intimacy, the restraint of lingering pain. Spencer had his guard up; the situation seemed to have tilted from merely awkward to something more.

As Alan said hello to Pamela, he reached for her hand, which she subtly withdrew, pointing to Spencer to introduce him.

Obviously disappointed, Alan said, "Umm, so … not really sure why we're here."

Spencer could see that Pamela was unsure about what she had done in setting up the meeting. She kept her hands under the table and looked about the room, as if there might be someone she knew. Her eyes glistened a touch—but only a touch.

"It's really a favor to me," Spencer said. "I've gotten myself into some trouble, and I could use some help—in the sense of general legal guidance. I don't expect to be able to hire you or anything. I don't know; maybe this was a bad idea."

Alan said, "Well, we're here. Talk to me."

Spencer then went over the entire scenario, handing over wrinkled copies of the papers he had received, which Alan read silently. Once Spencer had finished, some twenty minutes later, Alan sat back and said, "Wow, you got a big-ass lawyer out hunting for your scalp. You sure y'all want to stay around these parts?"

He evidently meant it as a kind of joke, but it was not funny to Spencer, who said, "All I did was report some crap that I saw going on—"

"Whoa, whoa, there," Alan interrupted. "That's not all you did."

Spencer sat near the front edge of his chair in anticipation of standing up and leaving. His frustration broke through. "Okay, I get it. I do appreciate your time—"

"Hey, bro, you got a funny way of showing it."

Spencer saw Pamela's eyes close and stay shut for an extra beat.

Alan continued in his adopted and often exaggerated street accent. "Let me try to paint the picture for y'all. They suing you in federal court for a bunch of stuff—theft of trade secrets, breach of employment contract, defamation. A whole bunch of shit. They want an injunction stopping you from doing anything they don't like. They say that the business might be knocked to the ground. They want millions of dollars in damages that you obviously don't have, or you wouldn't be dining in an establishment of this, er, quality. And it looks like you did all the shit they're claiming." He paused for effect, raising his right eyebrow slightly, and then said, "On the other hand, dude, they want this thing to just slip away quietly. That's what they want. So they can continue with their IPO, which—if you're right—is a fraud."

Spencer said, "Apparently, if I'm right, it still doesn't get me anywhere."

Alan twisted his face into a look of false shock. "You mean you not interested in doing the public good?"

From Spencer's point of view, Alan seemed to be enjoying the way he was able to toy with him. Spencer looked over at Pamela. That seemed to prompt Alan again.

"If, man—if you right, it does get you something. It gets you a new label. Instead of thief, you become a *whistleblower*. And that's a big deal. It turns the tables; they owe you money.

And one other thing, if you're interested. They'd be on the hook for your attorneys' fees." Alan sat back, curling his lower lip.

Spencer and Pamela looked at each other and then, in unison, looked at Alan. They ordered sandwiches and another round of beers. Spencer reached for Pamela's hand under the table and squeezed it. It was like the answer to a prayer, if he'd heard Alan correctly—the subtle offer to exchange desperately needed legal advice for payment of whistleblower counsel fees.

Spencer felt that something had changed. *Odd*, he thought, *it was just a word. Whistleblower.* It didn't change what he did or why he'd done did it, which was certainly not to protect the public interest. But it was a word of some weight. He hadn't thought of himself as a whistleblower. Hell, Charlie Apple had called him a disgruntled employee and a thief. But whistleblower—that added a new dimension to everything, as whistleblowers were quite different from thieves. Everyone knew that. And that grin on Alan's face suggested that he actually believed that Spencer was in that category.

There was one other aspect—the path that had rather suddenly emerged in front of him was all about standing up. And not standing up to just anyone. It meant that he, Spencer, could stand up to all the force of Celldesign, from old Charlie to Mary and to his grandfather, the great Arthur Lloyd. Something that felt right and wrong simultaneously.

"Do we have a deal?" Spencer asked.

"I'll run it by my firm, but I think it'll be okay. It's the first case I've brought in, man. Can't wait to write to Apple and say hi."

CHAPTER 7

Arthur had already heard it directly from old Charlie Apple by the time Winston called. He had received his own set of the papers that Alan Brown had filed with the court, so everyone knew that Spencer had gotten himself a lawyer—and that he was making out a whistleblower case against Celldesign. Shaking his head in disbelief, Arthur thought, *the stakes are rising*.

At the end of the day, could both his grandson and his company survive?

"The other shoe has dropped," Winston said in the tentative way he would when dealing with Arthur.

"Yes, I've heard," Arthur said impatiently.

"I can foresee the banks calling our loans if they think we will be tied up in years of litigation," Winston said.

"Unlikely," said Arthur. "All they'd get would be some desks and chairs. The license for the technology would be automatically revoked, and without that and without the markets that Mary has developed, there would be nothing left, no assets."

"How can you be so sure that the license would be revoked?"

"Because, Winston, I am the chairman of the Board

of Overseers, and we are in charge of licensing the patent. Therefore, I am in position to do that."

"And what of Spencer? What if everyone is right, and the data are okay? He can't be a whistleblower then, right? What happens to a failed whistleblower?"

"Winston, we can only hope that he's getting solid legal advice. Losing a high-stakes lawsuit carries—well, let's say one would pay a price. But he's a man now. Let's hope that he isn't being talked into something by his lawyer."

Arthur was trying to be optimistic; he had always done that with Winston, in hopes that he would bring him out of the doldrums. Arthur knew that the options were closing. And he knew the effect on Winston, who seemed burdened to the breaking point by the prospect of losing his entire investment and failing again. The Celldesign IPO represented a passage for Winston, a long-awaited step out of Arthur's shadow. The importance of the IPO to his psyche could hardly be overstated.

And now, Spencer, his son, had placed himself clearly on the other side for all the world to see—and speculate about.

"We will continue to control the license," Arthur repeated firmly. "That is assured. The problem now is that we must stop the way in which our lenders and investors get bombarded every day with news that would shake up anyone. The bonds of friendship won't hold if it continues."

"But Mary is the one who's taking us down that path, mainly by trying to discredit and ruin Spencer. That's the lead news story, isn't it? Why don't you call her off?"

"It's not that easy," Arthur said. "Spencer didn't have to go out and hire a lawyer, either."

"He's just a kid, Dad. My son, your grandson. You've got to concede that he's entitled to a lawyer. For God's sake, you're suing him."

"One must consider the risks," Arthur said soberly. His voice took on a weariness; he suddenly felt his age. Another headline was around the corner, with more pressure on the company, more pressure on him. *In a way,* he thought, *Spencer can wait it out longer than Celldesign can. Time is on his side, now.* Surely Mary would know that. *It's the last thing I want,* Arthur thought, amid a new and deeper concern, *a public spectacle.*

Arthur could have written the headline himself; that was how perfectly he'd anticipated it. It read, "Whistleblower Claim Filed in Celldesign Case," with a second line in smaller type that read, "Grandson versus Grandfather?"

Arthur wondered wearily if somebody had dreamed up an algorithm that predicted the market effect on a start-up company of each additional negative headline.

This time, there were no references to unidentified sources; the material came largely from Alan Brown's court filing on behalf of Spencer. As a matter of course, Alan had to emphasize the whistleblower part; that was how he intended to get paid. But the word assumed that Celldesign had done something wrong.

To add to the list, Garrigall, the cagey old reporter, took another step that Arthur had not anticipated: he had called Winston. It was on the pretext (in Arthur's point of view) of reaching a Celldesign board member for comment on the latest development, but it was really a trap.

"The *Globe* reached Celldesign board members for comment," the article reported, "but we did not receive any specific denials of the new allegations." That would have been bad enough, but Garrigall went one step further. "Board member Winston Lloyd is the father of Spencer Lloyd, the alleged whistleblower."

Fencing with the likes of Pat Garrigall was not, to Arthur' knowledge, playing to Winston's strength. Winston would have been nearly panicked. Arthur could imagine him sweating through his shirt as Garrigall toyed with him. *"We're following a lead, Mr. Lloyd, that's all. Perfectly legitimate. After all, you are the young man's father. Rather awkward, isn't it?"*

Arthur did not have the heart to call Winston and tell him not to deal with Garrigall. He would take it as a reprimand, and Lord knew, he'd had enough of that in his life. Besides, it was Garrigall who should have been reprimanded. "He knew better."

Celldesign was becoming all-consuming to Arthur. He had failed to find a solution, and his frustration with that fact began to occupy him day and night. On cue, Celldesign's investment bankers had begun calling after every headline—they had concluded that the company's value in an IPO, even if they were fortunate enough to get clearance from the regulators, had at least halved, and soon the prospect of an IPO would vanish altogether. "Markets need to *believe,*" they said, "and that isn't happening right now."

Like the investment bankers, Arthur had spent his life following markets. They were sounding an alarm, and perhaps their discomfort went deeper than Spencer's email.

Arthur phoned down for Jimmy and, once inside the car, told him to head for 128 on the pretext of meeting with Mary. In reality, he wanted to bump into Olga Numerovski, whose image had begun crossing his mind incessantly, waking and sleeping.

Celldesign's troubles, after all, arose from her department. Perhaps she had been overlooked.

Whenever he thought of her, he became suspicious. It was a natural reaction, like sneezing when dust was in the air. He tried not to be persuaded by her appearance—the short hair that looked like she cut it herself; her nails bitten down to the pink; her odd dress style, always with something yellow. Yet when he tried to limit his focus to her behavior, he realized he didn't have much to go on. She seemed intent on her work, dedicated. She had gotten good reviews, and she and Mary were tight. But he saw something in her that was crying out. He saw it in the movement of her eyebrows, in a quick glance when she averted her eyes. It didn't seem to be shyness. He thought perhaps she was hiding something. Initially, he thought it might have something to do with her personal history or her immigration status. But just as likely, it was something else.

Arthur walked into the building where Celldesign's offices were located and brushed by the security desk without a second glance, as he always did. It was not unusual for him to arrive unannounced, and he was easily recognizable. There was always a murmur on the office floor when he was there. He walked directly toward Mary's office and saw through the glass partition that she was on the phone—had to be one of the commercial bankers or investment bankers, given the latest Garrigall article. Arthur gestured that he would be going down the hall, and Mary signaled okay.

Olga's door was closed—unusual because Mary had an open-door policy that applied to everyone. Arthur opened the door without knocking.

Olga was on her cell phone and, at the same time, was making notes on a laptop, not company-issued. She looked startled as the door opened and seemed about to reprimand the person on the other side.

Arthur caught her eye and thought he saw a flash of panic, like one would see in the eyes of a child caught stealing a candy bar. She abruptly ended the call and closed the laptop. Her black eyes bored into his. "Hello. I wasn't expecting it to be you."

"Yes, sorry, just came by to take the temperature of things in light of the barrage from the press. Are you holding up okay?" He pointed to a chair opposite her desk—both standard issue, no frills—and Olga nodded. As he sat, Arthur remarked to himself that she had switched gears almost seamlessly.

Her eyes lost the desperation he thought he'd seen at first and became almost open—but not quite. She even smiled when she described how the calls were cascading in, as if it were humorous—how all the bankers were fearful that their positions were at risk, how she had tried to reassure them—but Arthur thought her speech was a little too fast.

As she spoke, Arthur only half listened. His thoughts drifted back to the early days when Mary first had told him about "this friend" of hers who was graduating from MIT and had nowhere to go except back to Ukraine and who would be perfect for what they termed the "bean-counter" role. As Arthur sat there, he watched Olga fidget. She kept touching the laptop, as if she wanted it to disappear entirely. And he realized that he knew very little about the person opposite from him, a person whose role within the company had grown and who now had a certain amount of power.

"Are we solid on the data?" Arthur asked.

Those eyes again, so dark. "The data will stand up," she replied.

Looking closely, more so than he had ever done before,

Arthur saw small beads of perspiration above her upper lip. As if on cue, she casually raised a finger and mopped the area, on the pretext that she was considering deeply his question, although he suspected she was not.

A masterful performance.

Garrigall must never get to her, Arthur thought as he excused himself and walked back toward Mary's office. He looked back to see—yes, Olga had immediately closed her office door.

Mary had ended her call by that time and was waiting for Arthur.

"Let's get a coffee downstairs," Arthur said, referring to the cafeteria two floors below. Once they were seated, with Styrofoam cups in front of them, he said, "In next year's curriculum, I am devoting an entire week to the business crisis."

It was intended as humor, but Mary merely smiled and said that the commercial banks were talking about calling for more collateral, with the ultimate object being an *assignment* of the patent, rather than a *license* to use the technology, which could be revoked at any time.

Arthur shook his head. "Won't happen. I won't even vote for that."

"I know," said Mary wearily. "I know."

"Are you comfortable with our comptroller?"

"That comes from out of the blue," Mary said, feigning surprise.

Given their current situation, Arthur regarded her answer as evasive; it was a way of responding without answering. He looked at her, but she glanced away, as if there were something else on her mind.

Finally, she said, "Yes, I'm comfortable with her."

Was that assurance? Arthur wondered. "Okay, then, tell me about her. Married? Lives with someone? Where?"

Mary sipped her coffee. She looked wary, suggesting she resented being questioned like that. "Okay, Arthur," she said brusquely. "Olga was my roommate in school. We lived in the basement of a house on Sherman Street in Cambridge. We've shared everything ever since. Olga had a tough childhood in Ukraine. Her father is one of the millions who simply disappeared one night. She never saw him again. Celldesign is her life, her entire life. She's highly motivated, MIT-smart, what else?"

Arthur felt the strength in Mary's voice. On the surface, she had assured him about the data, in her way. But he felt something had been left hanging, and before he could question her further, she changed the subject.

"There is another issue," she said. "I feel that Winston has a visible conflict of interest. If it were anyone else, I would ask him to step off the board entirely, but I will make an exception and ask Winston to temporarily step down. We're getting questions. Especially since Spencer got a lawyer—and then the Garrigall article. People assume Winston had something to do with it. And that would put him on both sides of the fence. Can't have it."

Arthur considered the issue for a moment. He had been afraid of this; it was not part of his plan. But then again, he could not insulate Winston forever. "Yes, you're right. You'll tell him?"

Mary took a gulp of air. "Yes, I suppose so," she said quietly. Then, almost as an afterthought, she added, "If you prefer."

"I do," he said. "And you need to keep in mind that I will have to report to the Overseers. And soon. There will be questions. They will want representations. We need to be as pure as Caesar's wife. It is quite serious."

CHAPTER 8

A lan Brown's law firm was in the Prudential Building downtown, the one with the famous problem with defective windows that blew out in heavy winds back in the seventies.

Spencer went over to see Alan after reading Garrigall's latest article, feeling guilty in the moral sense and lost in the legal sense. He noted that Alan was clearly a junior member of the firm—no corner office for him; rather, a cubicle reminiscent of Spencer's cubicle at Celldesign.

"It's clear from the *Globe* article," Spencer said to Alan after being shown in by a receptionist, "that just by filing a defense, the company has taken a hit."

"Investors are nervous by definition," Alan replied. "Besides, you didn't start this."

"In a way, I did."

"You're splitting hairs. They were the first to file a lawsuit. Remember: they were really bullying you."

"Let's wipe the slate clean. No sophistry. Shouldn't I just do what they're asking and renounce—I think that's the word— renounce my original email, and give my father and grandfather what they're asking for? Am I being unreasonable if I don't do that?"

Alan sat back in his chair. "You think the slate we dealing with gets clean just by waving your hand in front of it?"

"Be clearer, man."

"Okay," said Alan. "Can you wipe away what you saw? Forget the technical terms and the stats lingo. Throwing out the data that don't fit in the box is bullshit, man. 'Excessive data,' my aunt Harriet. You been telling me you saw what was going on. Cooking the books, man. You ready to take that back, which means you're going to say you were lying?"

Spencer shrugged, then nodded and said, "'Excessive' is the point. That was my interpretation. That's what I'm worried about."

"You're ready to say you didn't see that? You're ready for them to then go out in the public market and say, 'Hey, we were just joking. Everything is okay. See? The boy says so. Go ahead and buy our stock.' Then the patch don't work, and people will be coming back to you, looking for answers. Guess what they're going to say. They'll say, 'What'd you do that for? You defrauded me as well.'"

Spencer slumped his six-foot-four frame in the chair, the same posture Arthur would frequently adopt in contemplative moments. "What are you telling me?" he asked.

"Depends on what you're asking," Alan retorted. "If you're asking me if you can just walk this back, I'm saying it's too late. In for a penny, in for a pound, man."

Alan was being flippant, appearing to enjoy the give-and-take, but his motives were suspicious.

And Spencer was not used to conflict of this nature. Of course, he did not want to be any part of a fraud on the public, but his own family was asking him to do this—to renounce. He wondered if everyone reached a point where they said no to their parents and grandparents, the people who sacrificed for them, stood behind them, raised them. He looked at Alan. "Are you saying that I am part of the fraud if I renounce?"

"'Fraid so, man. The short answer is that you became involved when you saw what you saw. You can't run away from that shit."

It was still late summer, and much of Boston was at the Vineyard or the Cape or Nantucket, but Spencer didn't have the money for a trip, and Pamela was on scholarship and working at Gizmo's, so she took classes year-round. Spencer walked from the Prudential all the way over the Charles, sat himself on a bench outside one of the MIT engineering buildings, and waited for her, thinking that he was in the middle of a giant and unfair catch-22.

Throughout his childhood, Spencer thought of himself as being somewhat inconsequential, and he had been okay with that (having seen what happened to his father, who resisted). It went with the territory as Arthur Lloyd's grandson. But that seemed to have changed right under his nose, without his consent. As he sat there on campus, below a spreading oak, with the breezes off the Charles in his face, he realized that he had passed a certain line. It was a line defined by nebulous words like *responsibility* or *duty*.

At that moment, Pamela walked over and stood in front of him. "Should we walk to your apartment?" It was not a question; rather, it was polite and coquettish. It was what Spencer was living for. He smiled and stood.

That night, after Pamela had gone back to her father's apartment, Spencer called home, and Mandy answered. They had developed a routine that they both understood; when caller ID showed that Spencer was calling, Mandy would answer, put the phone on speaker, and pretend Winston was unavailable. Mandy would have to come up with a white lie, as she called it (something she'd learned as a girl in Brooklyn) about why Winston did not get on the phone. "Your father's busy in the library," she would say. Or "Your father's in the shower." It was a matter of keeping up appearances, but Spencer knew what the truth was: Winston didn't know what to say; he could no longer contain his anxiety and had begun to drink heavily.

On that night, Mandy slipped up. She said, "Your father's working on some board issue, honey; he'll call back."

Spencer could hear Winston's voice as soon as she said that. Judging by the sound of his voice, Winston was standing next to Mandy when he exploded, "No! I'm not on the board anymore! Remember?"

"What?" Spencer said immediately.

Silence. Spencer sensed that Winston had walked away, leaving Mandy alone with the phone.

"Apparently, they dropped him from the board at Celldesign," she whispered, confirming the picture in Spencer's mind of what was happening. "They claim it's a conflict of interest. You know—*because*. I wasn't supposed to say anything. Now you'll both be mad at me."

But it wasn't anger that Spencer felt; it was a kind of remorse. Winston's position on the Celldesign board was important to him, and his removal, even for perfectly legitimate reasons, was a blow to an already unstable man—and Spencer felt responsible.

At the same time, he had another thought, one that would not have occurred to him merely a few months ago. He wondered if that was precisely what old Charlie was banking on.

To Spencer, it was important every night—but especially that night—for Pamela to stay beside him in his bed, curled atop his left arm, rather than race off back to her father's apartment. That was the time when he felt most free, most able to speak, to wonder and speculate—but safely, at the right emotional distance—when it was just the two of them, still warm.

"What should I do?"

"You're telling the truth," she said. "And you're not doing it for personal gain or anything like that. That's what people are supposed to do. All these duties that Arthur keeps harping about are designed to get people to do just that." She lifted her head from his shoulder and caught his eyes. "It's kind of ironic," she said, pursing her lips, then brushing her hair back with her hand.

Spencer did not pick up the signal. "Pam, the one thing that's been confirmed—and it came from Arthur—is that 'truth' is a complex thing. Granted, there is the objective, narrow truth, assuming the state lab agrees, that they are eliding too much. Technically, that would make my email true, and I would win my case. But it is also true that winning my case would make me a loser because that would harm those I love most. I feel like Yosarian in *Catch-22*."

After lowering her head to her pillow, Pamela tried to turn the conversation in a slightly new direction. "Was your grandfather always this way?"

Spencer laughed. "I'm afraid so. His life was always logical. I doubt he ever got himself into a bad spot, certainly nothing like me. He was always a scary figure. You kind of knew that you weren't getting up to his level, so it became irrelevant. My great-grandparents were immigrants, and a lot of that generation seemed fixated on achievement. My theory," he said with a

smirk, "is that the following generations get successively softer
until all the ambition that once was there has turned to dust."

"If you've kind of accepted all that, why is it so important
now that you do this renouncing thing and basically try to pull
their bacon out of the fire?"

Spencer pulled his pillow up against the wall behind the
bed and sat up. "I guess because they need me to do it. You
know, family."

"And you would tell a falsehood that will ultimately get
picked up just because you're in the same family?"

Spencer did not reply.

"Why not let the process work its way out, let Alan do his
thing, and otherwise start a new chapter in life?" she asked.

As the two of them left Spencer's apartment the following
morning, Pamela turned and scanned the area.

"What's up?" he asked.

"I just felt the hairs stand up on the back of my neck, as if
we're being watched." She gave him a kiss and walked toward
the train station, with a look back at him and a wave.

The next day, after returning from his morning run, Spencer
flipped through the *Globe* on the kitchen table as he went
about his breakfast routine, but something caught his eye as the
sections of the paper unfolded. "Holy shit," he muttered as he
saw the headline in the business section: "Celldesign Employee
Reported to Have Left Town—Whereabouts Unknown."

He didn't know what to make of it, but it was suspicious.
He had heard that Patty O'Donnell had come over to Celldesign
from the state lab, and that her relationship was "valuable," but
he'd thought nothing of it. She was always out of the office,

entertaining someone, somewhere. He remembered because
she was reputed to have an in with the Red Sox, as she was able
to get mezzanine seats whenever she wanted.

He recalled that she also seemed close to Olga.

He read on. Garrigall reported that Patty had left Celldesign,
left Boston, and had changed her phone information. As
Garrigall reported it, he had developed "sources" inside the
state lab, one of whom called him out of concern for Patty,
saying that she had "up and left" Boston entirely.

Anyone would think that the picture could be incriminating,
Spencer mused. Why would the liaison between Celldesign and
its regulator, the state lab, suddenly disappear in the middle of
the investigation, unless she had something to hide? It occurred
to him—but only vaguely—that the article seemed to support
his version of events.

The article went on to quote old Charlie Apple, who insisted
that the *Globe* was jumping to conclusions. "There must be
a hundred reasons why a young, single employee of this or
any other company might move away from Boston without
prior notice. Boyfriend problems, credit card debt problems, a
better job offer. Perhaps she's gone to Silicon Valley, perhaps to
New York. But the rank speculation that her whereabouts has
something to do with the data-reporting case is irresponsible."

Perhaps, but Spencer knew by that time that old Charlie Apple
would say almost anything if it was to his client's advantage.

All this information, including the subtle inconsistencies,
seemed terribly important to Spencer, and so he called Pamela
to discuss it with her. He was surprised to learn that she had
not read the paper. As he went on about the article, he could
hear something in her breathing. She did not speak, did not
interrupt. Instead, there was a kind of hesitation he could feel
through the phone.

And that is when she told him. "Spencer, you're such a sweet guy, but I think we're moving a little too fast. You need someone who is maybe a little older. I just can't wake up every day, wondering what the press is going to say about you—or when they are going to get to me. It's just more than I can shoulder right now."

Spencer was stunned, silent.

"So maybe we should take a little time and then see," she said.

More silence.

"And you deserve to know this from me—I'm seeing Alan Brown again."

After several awkward seconds, Spencer realized that he needed to say something, though he had no idea what that should be. He mumbled, "Okay. See you around, I guess." He thought he heard something. Was she crying? As he pressed the end button, he wondered aloud, "Why?" A single word consisting of many questions.

He looked down at the floor and saw his running shoes where he had left them, under the table. He felt that more running might help; he needed something. The closeness that he had developed with Pamela seemed a bitter hoax as he plodded down Commonwealth Avenue, avoiding walkers and bikers. As he ran east, the building where Alan Brown worked came into view. How was it possible that Alan had come back into the picture? "Can you even do that when you're someone's lawyer?" Spencer asked himself as he kept running, plodding through the downtown streets. "Probably not," he answered aloud, unaware of the looks on the faces he passed. "It's probably prohibited by one code or another." Unconsciously, he picked up his pace and found himself standing in front of Brown's office building, his hair a mess, sweating from the run.

Security would not let him up to Alan's office; Brown had to come down to the lobby to vouch for Spencer. Which was just as well, as Spencer could not restrain himself. "Don't you have ethics or something that tell you not to screw over a client?" he said.

"What are you talking about, man?"

"Why do I have to hear it from Pamela? You're seeing her again, right?"

Alan straightened himself up and said simply, "Yes."

Somehow, it was the confirmation that caught Spencer off guard. He moved toward Alan, towering over him, but he had no words.

Alan stood his ground. "Listen, man. I just kept thinking about her after you two came to my office, and I couldn't get her out of my head, professional ethics notwithstanding. Hey, I'm not immune. Having a set of ethical rules does not separate me from humanity. We saw each other one night. I'm sorry."

Spencer knew what it was like to love Pamela; he knew that the two of them shared that. He had turned to walk away, having achieved nothing, when Alan called out, "I wanted to talk to you about this Patty person, but maybe this isn't the best time."

Spencer kept walking with Pamela on his mind and not a further thought about Patty O'Donnell. He had heard what she did at Celldesign also described as "being a runner," but it was not what he did, and that was all he cared about as he began his anguished, lonely jog home.

CHAPTER 9

Arthur knew what would come next; he was resigned to it. It came with a ping announcing an email on his personal computer in the library. He hurried to his desk. Sure enough, it was a message from the vice chair of the Board of Overseers, Monroe Benjamin, setting a meeting for that afternoon at one o'clock at his home in Wellesley, about a half hour west of the city. The subject was stated simply as "Celldesign—recent events."

Few confrontations concerned Arthur, but that was one of them. The Board of Overseers—a group of nine glittering men and women, whose names were familiar to anyone who kept up with the news. They ranged from former cabinet members to heads of major corporations to noted scientists to former leaders of the military. It was a diverse group that was connected by two things: impressive achievements in their youth and the markings of age.

These were senior people in every sense of the word. And how Arthur loved breathing the same rarified air! He was one of them; that was who he was in a very basic way. It was a matter of immense pride and satisfaction. In many ways, it was his identity.

Monroe Benjamin was the epitome of the group. A West Point graduate and former four-star general who had led troops in Korea and then went on to the Defense Department, he was barely five foot nine, but he stood ramrod straight, even as he entered his eighties. Yet the evidence of age was visible. Each time Arthur saw him, another bandage covered a spot on his bald head, where a growth of some sort likely had been biopsied recently. Monroe commanded the respect of everyone in every room he happened to be in. At the time, he held an emeritus position at the Kennedy Center.

Monroe greeted Arthur at the door of his brick Georgian home, set back from the road in an affluent neighborhood dotted with old deciduous trees, mostly sugar maple and oak. His handshake was self-consciously strong, and he pointed Arthur's way into the living room, which as almost aglow with the patina of antique side tables and commodes, the formality of lush draperies, the luxury of overstuffed chairs.

Arthur noted that the board members were all seated with half-full cups of coffee or half-drained bottles of water, which told him that they had convened earlier, undoubtedly to adopt a game plan, without telling him. But he understood that, given the press coverage. A less tolerant group might already have removed him.

Arthur stood, waiting for Monroe to indicate how they would proceed.

"Arthur," said Monroe, "I hope you don't take offense, but in view of your family involvement with the Celldesign company, we thought that the vice chair—that I—should moderate."

"Of course, Monroe."

"You certainly have your hands full with that reporter for the *Globe*."

One could hear a pin drop.

"And we all have children and grandchildren—and in my case, great-grandchildren," Monroe said, "so we know how *trying* that can be. But we have a duty, don't we? An overarching duty that we all took an oath to uphold. A duty that affects far more people than the relatively small group consisting of our immediate family. And we must rely on you to inform us of what we need to know, in order that we all discharge our respective duties properly."

Monroe remained at attention during the entirety of his comments, but then, as he finished, he sat.

And Arthur stood alone. "I will tell you all I know." And he did so, starting with Spencer's email and continuing through Patty O'Donnell's disappearance.

One of the board members said in a conciliatory tone, "You must be exhausted. Come and sit." He offered a spot on the sofa along the far wall, facing the rest of the room.

Arthur thanked him, walked quickly to the sofa, and sat.

Monroe directed his next comment to Robert Birtsch, a former lawyer at one of Boston's most prestigious law firms and, at one point, a prosecutor. "Where does that leave us, Bob?"

"We can revoke our license to Celldesign at will, so we won't get trapped in something unseemly. But when this O'Donnell woman took off—well, that's what we used to call 'consciousness of guilt.' It looks to me like she's trying to run away from a problem. Speaking for myself, I suspect she provided an old-fashioned escort service for those data reports."

Arthur looked around the room; eight faces were looking at him. He realized that the situation was more serious than he had anticipated. This was a group that was most sensitive to appearances.

"I understand what you are saying, Bob," Arthur answered quickly. "But we mustn't be hasty. How would it look if we pulled the license now because we suspect some sort of misbehavior without proof of that and without giving due accord to all the interests that would be affected? I think Mary is up to the task. You all know her. She shares our deepest connection; she's one of us. Remember that pulling the license at this juncture would sink the ship and cause a good deal of financial pain among the banks, of which we all, I believe, sit on the boards, and thus unintentionally harm friends of ours. Having said that, it is true that the *Globe* is all over this story, and the reporter, Garrigall, thinks he's on his way to a Pulitzer. But the balance of risk suggests to me that we hold course. At least for now."

"You make a good point, Arthur," Birtsch replied, "but please remember that we all believe that any given family unit—including yours, I'm afraid—is a relatively small interest compared to what we were appointed to do."

The prospect of inadvertently bringing unwanted light upon themselves and their banking relationships—and on the way things were done in Boston—was not lost on the group.

Someone asked, "What is Mary's plan?"

They had all met with and approved of Mary when the license was first granted, except for two new members, who were replacements. Her standing was still high.

Arthur felt that he had been given a reprieve. He expected that before he'd arrived, the group had discussed a far more extensive reaction, perhaps including removing him, Arthur Lloyd, from the board, as punishment for a bad choice made seven years ago.

"I was on my way to see her when Monroe called. Why don't I complete that task and then report back?"

Bob Birtsch broke the silence. "Just keep in mind, my friend, the paramount interest we all have, individually and collectively, is to do the right thing. We are not like any ordinary board. That is not why we were chosen. We have earned our way here, and we all want to keep all of that intact. You must keep that in mind and act accordingly."

A servant appeared in the entryway from the formal living room, where they were all seated, to the kitchen, standing as inconspicuously as possible, but he leaned in ever so slightly, awaiting word of what to do.

Monroe saw him and said to the group, "Coffee or tea? William, here, is at your service."

Jimmy was standing next to the car with his right elbow on the roof, his hand cupping his chin, looking desolate. When he saw Arthur come out of Monroe's house, he opened the rear door for him, then hurried around to the driver's side and got the car started. "Where to?" he asked.

Arthur replied tersely, "One twenty-eight." The meeting with the overseers had tired him. He put his head back to rest; it was a twenty-minute drive.

When they arrived, Arthur walked in without giving Jimmy instructions. He went directly to Mary's office, hand signaling for her to get off the phone. She pressed *end*, and Arthur reprised the Overseers' meeting.

"Before they called, I was headed here to ask you about this O'Donnell person who was the *Globe*'s latest headline." He stared at her, waiting for a response.

Mary took a breath. "I know. Bad timing, to say the least." She appeared fidgety, looking over Arthur's shoulder, rather than in his eyes.

There's something more here, he thought. She was not being candid with him. It was something he could no longer afford. "You seem uncomfortable," he said.

She lowered her eyes, and Arthur took that as the beginning of an admission.

"Where is Patty?" Arthur demanded.

"Nobody knows," Mary replied, exhaling.

"When was she hired?"

"Several months ago, as close as I can figure."

"What do you mean, 'as close as I can figure'?"

"Olga made the hire," Mary finally said. "I didn't know."

Arthur looked up, exasperated. "What was she hired to do?" he asked incredulously.

Mary stared at him but did not answer. It was in the air between them; Patty's hiring was just as Garrigall had described. No words were necessary.

Arthur sat back in his chair and looked up at the ceiling. If Mary had wished to correct the unmistakable impression she had created, that would have been the right moment. But there was nothing to correct. Arthur had to accept that Garrigall had reported the Patty story accurately.

Arthur assessed the situation. His foremost duty was as an Overseer; he needed to repeat that, it gave him direction. And Celldesign would be ruined if the Overseers turned against the company. It could happen in a flash; the license could be revoked at any time and for any reason or no reason.

And if he were removed from the Overseers, it would be a public humiliation, and go deep into his soul.

He came to a decision on the spot; he would no longer coddle Mary or the company she had been molding. Too much had gone on behind his back, and that would have to change. He pressed forward. "You know as well as I how this looks. We need answers! We have Overseers! I have come to suspect Olga of being involved. She was in charge of the data procurement and reporting, and this O'Donnell woman dealt with her, apparently behind your back. We need Olga to come clean. As of now, she looks like she's hiding something, and that is the one thing we cannot have."

"You don't know that," Mary replied, raising her voice slightly, seemingly maintaining control.

Now angered, Arthur said, "Well, I know a couple of things. Why would you hire Patty, unless you needed to grease the wheels? Why would Patty be missing in action unless she were hiding her complicity? Mary, we cannot ignore the signs."

"Let's talk, then, about Spencer," Mary shot back. "That's where it all really started."

"Spencer is irrelevant at this point."

"Do you have a conflict of interest?"

It was out in the open. Accusations had been made. Dangerous territory.

"Whatever I have or don't have, you will have to live with. I need to report to the Overseers, and if they are not satisfied, they will revoke the license and Celldesign will be history. Give up your loyalty to Olga; she's not worth it! And don't talk to me about Spencer. If it weren't for Olga's reply to him, we wouldn't be sitting here, an inch from destruction."

Mary was clearly taken back. She lashed out. "I'm sorry to say this, Arthur, but I think we stay with Charlie's plan and go after Spencer's credibility, which is really the same as the credibility of his email. I'm the CEO, and that is my decision."

Arthur looked at her with a mixture of sadness and anger. "You know not what you do," he said.

Arthur was curious about the email he'd received from old Charlie Apple, along with everybody else in the "management control group." Apparently, Alan Brown had filed a subpoena; in short, Alan was demanding to see all the electronic communications from the Celldesign management team that related in any way to Spencer's email, and he was entitled to do so. To old Charlie, this was routine, to be expected, even though it frustrated him, as it would string out the case until after Spencer's claim was verified or rejected by the state lab. He made no secret of the fact that he thought that was Brown's real objective.

But those were the rules of the game. Old Charlie alerted all who were covered by the subpoena of their responsibility to save and turn over their electronic records.

Arthur was as interested in seeing those materials as Alan was. Olga had been identified as part of the control group, and his suspicions were growing. He figured that she would drag her feet if she had something to hide.

The picture of Olga in her office with the door shut, phone in hand, private laptop in front of her, was forged in his mind. Arthur set out to make sure Olga complied with the discovery rules. He didn't want to come out with his suspicions unless there was more of a basis. But he was not above prodding old Charlie, who had set up a war room at the offices on 128 to comply with the discovery and was there most of the time.

Arthur could hear it in old Charlie's voice—that false exhaustion heard when one is being tiresome. But Arthur had to follow this lead, and old Charlie, in his best exhausted voice, finally agreed to check on Olga's compliance. Arthur felt patronized. Old Charlie did not share Arthur's suspicions about Olga—not surprising, for Olga was one of Charlie's biggest supporters—and he seemed to think that Arthur was checking on him.

"You want to come out to 128 and make sure I'm doin' this right, old buddy?" Charlie said.

Arthur jumped at the chance. "I'll explain myself later, Charlie, but I'll be there in half an hour."

The two of them marched down the hall to Olga's office, not a word passing between them. Old Charlie had not alerted Olga, in accordance with Arthur's request.

"Hey, gorgeous," Charlie said in a mock Southern drawl as they walked into Olga's office. "Listen, I really need your electronic files so that we can comply with the subpoena and get this thing moving. Time is of the essence, or they'll delay us to death."

Olga was expressionless as old Charlie stood over her, except for a peculiar shine in her coal-black eyes. Arthur stayed near the doorway, watching.

Charlie said, "Any problem? 'Cause if there is a problem, I need to know about it."

Olga managed to ask, "All? What about personal stuff?"

"Yeah, all. No exceptions. Let us know if there's something really personal. We'll review it all and claim privilege or whatever if needed. But the courts are serious about *all* the information being gathered."

Olga remained expression-less, her gaze steady, her face pale. Several seconds went by.

"And while we're at it," Charlie said, "I've got to produce Patty's electronic files as well. Who has her computer?"

Olga raised her hand, like a child in a classroom, without speaking.

"Can I have it?" Charlie asked, becoming annoyed.

Olga froze.

Charlie asked again, his mind involuntarily harking back to the early days in criminal court; one did not forget those lessons. "Where is it? I want to take it with me."

Olga bent and reached for the third drawer on the right side of her faux-wood desk, her eyes seemingly connected to the drawer pull. She put her hand on the pull and looked at Charlie, one more time, silently beseeching him to do something, say something. The nonverbal conversation was undeniable. Then she reached into the drawer and pulled out an iPad, which old Charlie grabbed, perhaps a bit too aggressively, as Olga looked as if she'd been betrayed.

Old Charlie repeated to her firmly that he wanted her materials by the end of the day, and he and Arthur headed back to the war room.

"What are your instincts telling you?" Arthur asked.

"Didn't like her demeanor. Didn't like it one little bit. If she were my client, I'd be workin' on a plea bargain right about now. Yes, sir, I surely would."

Arthur saw Charlie draw himself back inward. The room was filled with silence; for his part, Arthur was adding up the likely damage if Olga and Patty were coloring the data—or worse. He assumed old Charlie was doing the same. The room was noiseless.

Arthur said, "Look, all I want is to see what's on those computers. Olga's *and* Patty's. Do I have your word that I will?"

"You have my word."

Arthur felt instinctively that a turning point was approaching, one way or the other. On his way out, he stopped (unusually) at the security desk and asked the officer to check the security cameras for the Celldesign offices.

The security cameras in the Celldesign office caught it all on tape. When Arthur and old Charlie left her office, Olga's face became softer, yet impassive, and her eyes went immediately to the security camera that had been installed just outside her office. Arthur watched as her face seemed to age years in a moment. Arthur would soon find out why: Patty's laptop documented in reports to Olga that inducements had been given to state lab personnel on the understanding that the Celldesign data was coming around, that the elided data points could be explained away. Patty's job was not technological; it was to grease the wheels at the state lab. And when they got Olga's electronic discovery, they would see the rest of the story. The guilt was written on Olga's face as she looked up a second time at the security camera; it was an extended look, almost a stare. Arthur thought she seemed far away at that moment, calculating something, but he had no idea what was going through Olga's mind.

He watched as she went to her computer and deleted everything she could. She put her laptop in her Coach handbag and walked out, forgetting her phone, which Arthur had seen her tuck away in the top right drawer of her desk.

The police investigation filled in the rest. Olga drove out of the parking lot, stopped at a hardware store about two miles west, just off 128, and bought a two-quart container of antifreeze. She then continued west in her prized yellow BMW 525 series until she reached a motel in Ashford, west of Worcester, a nondescript brick building off the Mass Pike, probably popular with truckers and secretive locals engaged in trysts.

She signed in as Georgia O'Keefe and paid in cash. No questions were asked. Arthur wondered about the choice of Georgia O'Keefe, but concluded that her paintings of New

Mexico bighorn sheep skulls might have something to do with it. She seemed to be apologizing for a vast error, in which she went down one wrong path after another and at the end was unable to find her way back.

The manager found her two days later, huddled on the floor in the fetal position, having finished one full quart of antifreeze and having clearly suffered immensely. A trucker in the next room said he thought he heard something, perhaps sobbing, but he didn't think it was any of his business.

She must have wanted it that way, Arthur thought when he read the reports. He went over all the details as he tried to imagine her sense of hopelessness. It was a shock but only for a while. Arthur had to move ahead. A report was due to the Overseers.

Garrigall had his sources, even Arthur had to concede that. The morning edition carried the headline, "Celldesign Comptroller Likely a Suicide." Garrigall made the fairly obvious point that Olga's suicide reflected a consciousness of guilt. As did Patty's departure in the dead of night. But there was a deeper version of that, one that captured Arthur's imagination, the more thought he gave to it. He could not escape the ritualistic quality of Olga's behavior: cleaning her computer, seeking an anonymous place, securing her own death in an intentionally painful manner, leaving no note. The technique spoke for itself. Like a samurai. There was a quality of ancient culture in her choices. She had failed, and she had atoned. Her curled-up body was found lying in the blood she'd regurgitated as the antifreeze ate through the walls of her intestines. The agony must have been intended to purify.

What were her last thoughts? Arthur asked himself. *Was she speaking to her God or perhaps to Mary? What strength,* he thought, *to plan it and then go through with it.* There must have been many moments when she could have called 911 and escaped death. Garrigall reported with a false sense of concern that it probably took the whole of a day for her to die.

CHAPTER 10

Dorothy's brother, Rodney, had headed up the consortium of banks that provided the second round of financing for Celldesign. Arthur had always gotten along with Rodney, who had taken over Back Bay Savings Bank from his father, who, in turn, had assumed control from his father—a model of family succession, smooth and quiet, tight-knit, specializing in trusts and other means of perpetuating wealth. Financing a start-up company out on Route 128 was not, to say the least, bread-and-butter business for staid and straight Back Bay Savings Bank, but he was family. And he was Arthur Lloyd.

Arthur had expected a worried call from Rodney as well, but he thought that he could manage his brother-in-law more readily than he could manage the Overseers.

Rodney's voice was unmistakable; he had a slightly effeminate lisp and, perhaps for that reason, usually spoke in a hushed tone. Arthur heard him on the phone with Dorothy when she was in the laundry, and he was still grumbling about Garrigall in the kitchen—she had put on the speaker function.

"Dottie," he said when she picked up, "what the blast is going on with Celldesign?"

Arthur came over to listen.

"By God," Rodney continued, barely waiting for an answer to his question, "the banking regulators could be on their way over this minute. They don't give notice, you know. And they would be within their rights to make us write down these loans now. Dottie, that would hit our bottom line and tank the stock price. You know," he added pointedly, "the stock that you and Arthur live off of." Which, of course, was an exaggeration born of near panic.

He paused, seemingly to catch his breath, and added, "For God's sake, this has now become sensational. The tabloids will pick it up. It will smear us all! And just who was this horrid little girl? How did she become comptroller? I'm just beside myself. For God's sake, it's costing the bank money. Do you understand that? Money. That's not what we are in business for."

Dorothy glanced at Arthur and said, "Rodney, as usual you are blowing everything out of proportion. You know that neither I nor Arthur have any control over Mary's choice of personnel. What am I supposed to do? I thought all this mess would be over long ago; that Mary would take care of it, and the ship would right itself. Then these ghastly articles in the *Globe*—"

"Father would never have been compromised by someone like this Olga."

"Rodney, Father is dead."

"That's not the point."

"Then what is?"

Rodney explained, "There are people in the bank who already think we should call the loans. The lawyers, to start with. At the first whiff of trouble, they always want out."

"Precisely."

"That's not the point, Dottie. The only reason we went into these loans was because of the people behind the scenes, especially the Overseers. We *relied* on their reputations, that they would never allow any messiness to get anywhere near any of us. Now with all these tawdry stories coming out—I mean, suicide in a motel? Antifreeze? Seriously? That type of thing erodes the confidence that is our lifeblood. How many times did Daddy say, 'They give us their money so that they have nothing to worry over. Hence, their money must be with the right people in the right place'? Why, it's obvious. It would not be, shall we say, consistent if our name should come up when the press is covering a fraud. There would be *questions.* Dottie, it could cost my job."

Dorothy was about to quibble, if for no other reason than to fence with Rodney, but she stopped. Arthur shrugged his shoulders, as if to say, *"We're trying to contain this, but events are not cooperating."*

After a pause, Dorothy continued. "Rodney, if you have any real suggestions, please speak up."

"Dottie, you know better than that. You grew up with Daddy, just as I did. We're not on the front lines; that's for the heroes. We're bankers, and we only want our money paid back. No opinion on how you do it, only that you do it. We don't like problems that creep up on us, and that's what we've got here. A problem that has snuck up on us. And it must be taken care of."

Arthur acknowledged Dorothy as she looked up from the phone to Arthur's face, looming above hers.

"I'm rather taken back at your callousness, Rodney," she said. "I'll tell Arthur you called. I'm sure he'll want to discuss your concerns. We'll certainly expect you at Arthur's party. I think it might be just the tonic to turn things around and make everyone happy again."

Dorothy had been planning an eightieth birthday party for Arthur for many months, to be held at their expansive apartment on Beacon Hill. They discussed cancellation, given the Celldesign conundrum, but Arthur concluded that cancellation would give the wrong message. "We must convey a sense that we are on top of things," he said.

The party had been intended to reinforce the Lloyd name in the social register of Boston. At least, that was the intent when the party was first discussed, months before. Arthur had approved of each invitation. All the Brahmins would be invited, all the regulars at the Parker House and the opera house, certain media and society editors, the tenured faculty at Harvard, the bankers, including Rodney's board, and even a few retired athletes—but only the elite.

There was enough brain power on the guest list that security was hired to check for explosives at the front door where the valet staff would be. Such was the world they lived in.

The cars began to roll up just before six—limos, Mercedes 550s, Bentleys. Dorothy had secured a valet parking service. While it was not black tie, the gentlemen wore jackets, and the ladies, evening gowns. It started out as a golden evening. The invited guests filled the entire apartment, as young women in black-and-white uniforms passed canapes, and young men in white shirts and black bow ties offered glasses of Dom Perignon champagne. It was a glittering event, and it seemed to be reflected in Arthur's eyes. He stood at the entry to his library, wearing a white dinner coat and holding a glass of champagne, with Dorothy at his side, greeting all who came to congratulate him and keeping an eye on the groupings of his guests.

Rodney seemed pleased; he whispered that it was "quite a show of wealth. That's very good, you know. It relaxes bankers."

Mary was there in a blue evening dress, showing a décolletage for the mature gentlemen to stare at. Dorothy had sent invitations months earlier; it would have raised suspicions to make any last-minute changes. "It is simply not done in polite society," Dorothy had said. Arthur watched as she gravitated slowly toward the members of the Overseers, particularly Monroe Benjamin. Arthur watched as she ingratiated herself with Monroe, touching his sleeve, nodding, laughing.

Old Charlie was also working the room. He had called Arthur directly for an invitation, and Arthur felt it appropriate to oblige; it sealed the impression that the "Celldesign people" were unified, in spite of the fact that the opposite was increasingly true. "Keeping up appearances," Dorothy had said. Arthur watched as old Charlie made his way around the room, introducing himself to the Harvard Law faculty members there, undoubtedly fishing for new business or praise for handling old cases.

If Mary looked cool, calm, and collected, Winston did not. Arthur noted that he appeared to have gained several pounds over the past weeks, so that his jacket no longer fit properly. He had to leave it unbuttoned, which alone set him apart from the other, well-tailored gentlemen. He was scheduled to give the toast and was obviously nervous, his red-and-gray hair matting down on an Indian summer night.

As the evening wore on, though, Arthur could see eyes turning his way, then quickly turning away—a sure sign that those people were talking about him. He surmised that it was his "situation" that was being whispered about—Celldesign's turmoil, Patty's departure, Olga's suicide—somewhat scandalous, especially among the upper crust of Boston, and therefore irresistible. *Schadenfreude*—a trait Arthur had long thought to be hiding inside most everyone.

Olga's suicide was as present as if she had risen from the dead and attended herself.

A pianist that Dorothy had hired was playing a piano brought in for the occasion—"Fly Me to the Moon" by Bart Howard. One could almost hear Tony Bennett singing the lyrics. Someone said, half in jest, that he was surprised Bennett himself was not there. But the upbeat lyrics seemed out of place.

An incongruous figure—not guest, not staff—was the society-page writer for the *Globe*, who walked around in khakis and a sweater, taking pictures, some of which were to appear in the Sunday edition. Arthur noted that he was having no trouble at all getting guests to smile for a picture.

The sun began to set, and the west-facing windows brought in the golds and yellows of the autumn sky, but hardly anyone seemed to notice. Canapes continued to be served, the bartender in the living room continued to pour, and impressions continued to be made or confirmed. The tensions surrounding Celldesign were not understood, except in the vaguest sense. And yet, Arthur thought there was something irresistible about upper-crust gaiety, evening gowns and champagne, hobnobbing with icons of success, something terribly attractive, so attractive that the suicide of a Ukrainian girl seemed little more than a sad footnote. There was a growing sense of camaraderie. On that night, the Lloyds' apartment was the place to be.

It came time for the toast, and Winston nervously tapped his glass. It was not loud enough to command attention, so Rodney followed it up with his own tapping, and the room quieted almost immediately. Arthur stood just behind Winston.

"Ladies and gentlemen," Winston began, "I want to thank you all for coming. In case we haven't met, I am Winston Lloyd. You all know that this is a birthday party for my father and your friend, Arthur. We are celebrating eighty years! And a man who rose from an immigrant family in Brooklyn to Beacon Hill. Just look around his library at the pictures depicting his assent. He was responsible, along with many of you in this room, for steering this great country around the shoals of history to the great seas on which we now sail. It was not always easy, but he always came through for his beloved Harvard, his beloved country, and his beloved family. He is one of the great men, those whose duty to history, really, directed their lives and safeguarded the rest of us through periods of war and peace, prosperity and loss. Eighty more years might be a trifle optimistic, and Arthur is ever the realist, but there are obviously many years ahead when we will all cherish his company and advice. Please raise your glass with me to honor my father, Arthur Lloyd, on the occasion of his eightieth birthday."

There was a great roar as everyone raised their glasses in unison and shouted, "To Arthur!"

It all seemed to be going wonderfully to Arthur, who held his glass high and beamed at the recognition.

And it was at that very moment that the elevator opened, and Spencer walked in. He looked like he didn't belong—blue blazer over a gray T-shirt, golf slacks, and boat shoes—but everyone seemed to know who he was. Arthur's face sagged, and he lowered his glass. But it was a propitious moment, as the guests had already begun to sing "Happy Birthday," and that overcame some of the awkwardness.

But Spencer had not been invited. Arthur had talked it over with Dorothy and decided it would be too risky. Who knew what could happen? Nobody else was aware that Spencer had not been invited, just the family.

Arthur watched Spencer join in song, smiling just enough to appear that he was enjoying himself. But there was an awkwardness that could not be denied. He had crashed his grandfather's eightieth birthday party, surprising even himself.

Almost everyone in the room read the *Globe* religiously and seemed to know about Spencer's email and the travails of Celldesign that followed, judging by the glances that Arthur saw being exchanged.

Arthur took it all in. It had been a difficult decision not to invite his grandson, and he had gone back and forth in his mind over it; in the end, it was wrong time, wrong place. There was too much just below the surface for them all to be together at a public event, which is what Arthur's birthday party was intended to be. Yet there he was, crashing the party, boat shoes and no socks, standing awkwardly across the room, heading his way.

Arthur looked carefully Spencer's way, doing his best to appear as if Spencer were expected. *At least he's not drunk,* Arthur thought as he exchanged a glance with Dorothy, who seemed mortified.

Arthur watched as Spencer made his way through the crowd towards him. *Does he know what he's doing? Will there be a scene?* Yet he navigated the foyer quite nicely, making small talk with the guests, who seemed to enjoy the fact that he was not wearing socks.

But all was not positive. Arthur sensed that Celldesign had become a greater topic of conversation; he saw guests point Spencer's way and whisper.

Then Mandy (of all people) took charge of the moment, rushing over to Spencer and hugging him. "We're so glad to see you," she exclaimed, loud enough for everyone to hear, obviously trying to counteract the mounting buzz about Celldesign.

"How altogether odd," one guest was heard to say. "Delicious," said another, known for her mean-spiritedness.

Mandy took Spencer's arm and walked him around the room—somewhat defiantly, Arthur thought—introducing him to those who were outside Celldesign's ambit—professors at Harvard, a retired professional athlete—avoiding the bankers and, especially, Mary.

Finally, Mandy and Spencer made their way around to Arthur. Spencer said sheepishly, "Happy birthday, Grandfather." He then shook Winston's hand and said, "Sorry I missed your toast, Dad."

Stepping back and glancing at the both, he added, "I just had to be here."

Arthur acknowledged Spencer with a smile but still had not spoken when Mary, who was holding her third glass of champagne, laughed at nothing in particular and said, in a voice loud enough to carry around the room, "Perhaps another toast is in order, one with an apology. What a lovely birthday present that would be!"

Arthur winced; she couldn't let it go. Spencer was, to her, still the enemy, the preferred enemy, the origin of all that had gone bad, the beating heart of Celldesign's unraveling.

Before Arthur could say something that would deescalate the tension, Mary continued. "Your presence is curious," she added.

Arthur saw Winston look down at his shoes and keep his eyes there. Three generations of Lloyds stood in silence in the middle of a cacophony of clinking glasses, cocktail conversation, and a piano. It was the first time they were together since the Dinner.

Spencer spoke first. He said, in a quieter voice than Mary's, "I'm not here to disrupt anything."

Arthur looked at him. "Thank you, Spencer," he said in a non-committal voice, turning his cheek a degree or two to his left, then asked, "How did you manage to get in?"

Spencer smiled in a sheepish way, and said, "Don't blame the doorman. He didn't know what to do when I said I was your grandson."

Winston's eyes remained downcast, giving the impression of deep inner turmoil. But Mary was still close enough to be part of the conversation. "You seem to have a knack for bad timing," she said, as Old Charlie pushed his way through the crowd, heading her way, a false smile on his face.

"Look, I'm not here to talk business," Spencer said. "Can you understand that?" He paused, then added, "Haven't we all learned something from the news of the last few days?"

Arthur said, "Tomorrow. Any words we might speak tonight could be misinterpreted."

Spencer replied, "True." Then, "I'll leave if you prefer."

"Of course."

"I really just wanted to drop off my present to you."

He offered Arthur a square shaped object in wrapping paper, which Arthur removed and handed to Winston awkwardly. The object was a framed photo of Spencer walking off the lacrosse field two years earlier, when Tufts had played Harvard.

"We lost," he said.

Mary stood to the right of Arthur and followed the discussion, her eyes upon Spencer. She glanced up and down with such ferocious contempt that Mandy stepped to her left, coming in between the two of them. For a moment, it seemed that something physical would break out. Rodney and Dorothy looked helplessly at each other in the mezzanine. Winston continued to stare at his feet. The rest of the party, however, regained its rhythm, although in the background, the topic of conversation seemed to involve suicide.

Dorothy saw to it that more drinks were poured, and it was announced that the carving station was open, featuring chateaubriand, in hopes that the evening would move on.

The piano player picked up the cue and played "What a Swell Party" from *High Society*.

Arthur raised his chin in order to address the limited group that had immediately surrounded him. "I want to thank you all for coming, and I hope you will enjoy the chateaubriand that Dorothy is—over there, pointing to. And I just want to add that although my chronological age implies that it has been a long road to this point, my mind keeps telling me to look ahead, and I feel fully invigorated to continue into that darkness known as the future and do as much good as I can, so that perhaps in twenty years, we can all meet again for another party, for which I will actually qualify as old. For now, however, that is not the case."

Everyone laughed; it seemed that the party had returned to gaiety.

Most guests began moving toward the serving table, but Mary stood still. There was a sense of determination about her. She hissed, "You've got blood on your hands."

Spencer turned quickly to face her directly. Obviously, she was talking about Olga. He replied, "Somebody working for Celldesign filed all those false reports, not I."

"How dare you? The reports were not false! Incomplete. Perhaps. At most. The jury is still out. We will change the world."

"Are you suggesting that I am responsible for Olga's suicide? What about you, Mary? What do you see when you look in the mirror? She did it for you, didn't she?"

Arthur joined his son, Winston, in looking down at his shoes.

The piano player began "You're the Top" by Cole Porter, with an anxious look on his face.

Arthur saw old Charlie grab hold of Mary's arm, and tears were visible on her cheeks.

The golden evening had lost its glitter.

Later that night, after all the guests had left and Dorothy, exhausted, had gone to her bedroom, Arthur retired to the library, too wound up to sleep. One might expect that Arthur would have enjoyed the afterglow of being in the limelight, the center of attention. Normally, that would have been true but not tonight. At the end of the evening, alone in his library, looking back, he felt unsettled. He poured another scotch and unfolded his frame slowly into his favorite chair, as he had for years. *Eighty*, he thought. *The footsteps are at the door.*

He replayed the evening in his mind. His colleagues—they knew him, he knew them; they had accomplished a lot, things that would endure. He looked up, as he loved to do, at the framed pictures set on the shelves of his bookcase, pictures of Arthur and many of the men and women who had toasted him earlier that night. They had a hand in shaping the world, and he was part of that. But that was the past, sadly.

His eyes lingered over the framed pictures, each capturing a triumphant moment. He thought back, remembering not just the moment but the context—the odds they'd faced, what they'd overcome. And then his mind raced back to the evening, their faces now old, frail, not like they had been when they had the energy, the ideas, the pure will. They had occupied the commanding heights—that was his world but one must move on.

His eye caught a flicker of light, a reflection from the faux silver frame Spencer had chosen for his photo. *One could question his judgment,* Arthur thought, *certainly not politically correct. And he has a good deal to answer for.* He glanced again at the framed photo and said, "Yes, Harvard did win, as I recall."

His eye drifted to his bookcase, the framed photo of Mary standing next to the offices on 128, a smile on her face. *What a confrontation,* he thought, harking back to the exchange between the two of them earlier in the evening.

But he was tired of confrontation. *If only it could be avoided.*

Hearing Dorothy make a sound in her bed, perhaps as she turned over, perhaps an unsettling memory of the evening she had planned for so long, he thought, *how furious she must have been with Spencer. Crashing the party; getting into it with Mary, of all people, in front of the chateaubriand, the whole emerging story of Celldesign spotlighted for all to see.* Arthur smiled, he felt better for some reason, perhaps because Spencer had held his own. But his eyelids were heavy. It had been a long and strenuous day. *Perhaps it will be clear tomorrow. Yes, tomorrow.*

CHAPTER 11

Spencer heard the ring and spotted the caller ID: Pamela. He was almost unable to press the answer button. Since she'd broken things off, he'd thought of her constantly—her thin figure, the dark eyes, flowing hair, her smell in the morning, her smile at the breakfast table. He thought his relationship with Pamela was another casualty of Celldesign, which seemed to have become a shattering force in his young life.

"Hello," he answered. It was early morning, and his voice was thick.

"Still asleep?" she asked.

Spencer made a sound in acknowledgement.

"Thought so. You haven't heard, right?"

"Ah, no. Heard what?"

"It's kind of good news, yet bad news. Some of both. Can't really take comfort yet—"

He made another sound, blowing air out his nostrils in a sort of verbal smile. "Glad to see you haven't changed."

"The state lab report is coming out. The *Globe* got an advance copy. You were right. Data was mishandled and that screwed up the conclusions. The patch doesn't work, at least not in the sense of being approved for widespread use. It works

sometimes but not enough. They ordered a recall. Alan says
you won."

Pamela spoke the last sentence in a different voice, lower,
tentative, apologetic.

"Are you with him?"

Silence, then, "No."

Spencer was wide awake at that point, sitting upright,
looking around his small bedroom as if there were an answer
in one of the corners. He felt oddly anticlimactic. One waits,
imagining what the words will sound like, what words will
be chosen, how it will feel. Then the moment comes, and
the emotions are different, and it is not at all a moment of
celebration. Rather, it felt more like a different level of doubt—
bittersweet. Was it worth it? Did it matter at the end of the
day? Was he right to the world but still wrong to his father and
grandfather?

He quickly came back to Pamela. He wanted nothing more
than to see her, hold her, talk with her, but that part of his life
also had seemingly passed. He said, "Thank you."

There was a hesitant sound at the other end of the phone.
Perhaps Pamela wanted more as well; perhaps it was Spencer's
imagination. The circumstances were askew, and neither of
them knew what to say.

He put on sweatpants and a sweatshirt, as the summer had
retreated. It was New England autumn, leaves turning colors,
brisk air. He left the apartment, ran to a street vendor nearby,
and bought a copy of the *Globe*, a coffee, and a hard roll with
butter and ran home.

Garrigall's headline read, "State Lab to Reject Data." The
second line, in smaller type, read, "Whistleblower Case Gains
Steam."

The article did not pull punches. Filing data in that manner could be fraudulent. There was an element of intent implicit in the degree to which data were elided. A conscious mind was shaping the numbers so that they would express a different result, a hoped-for result, not the reality of the test results—and that obviously would have misled investors but for Spencer's email.

Spencer returned home to his shabby apartment and ate his roll alone, recalling how much different it had been when Pamela had sat with him, even without a word being spoken. It was different, full, and alive. His voice mail began filling up. Garrigall wanted a comment and left a message in his best "old buddy" voice. Alan asked tersely that he return the call. Mandy, his mother, called from her car. She was proud that he had stood his ground, but they needed to talk about his father. Nothing from Arthur.

Spencer didn't feel like talking to any of them. It was all so anticlimactic. So, he showered and went up the street to Gizmo's, on a hunch.

As he walked in, he scanned the room. It was hard to miss Pamela's sad eyes as she took breakfast orders at a table near the rear of the room. Spencer quickly grabbed an open two-top. She saw and sauntered over, signaling to another waitress that she would take Spencer's table, obviously happy to see him.

She said, "I can get you something, and if you eat slowly, I get out of here in forty-five minutes. Maybe you could walk me to class."

As they walked through Allston and then over into Cambridge, they talked about what would happen next.

"It's now too late to renounce what I did. Doesn't matter anymore. Probably never did matter."

"And Arthur?"

He began to tell her about Arthur's birthday party, when she interrupted in a surprised tone, "Were you invited?"

"No. But I thought I should have been, so it wasn't a real crash job. Anyway, I felt led there by some instinct."

Her eyes widened, and she managed to say, "Whoa."

Spencer then continued with his description of events. Pamela's eyes seemingly grew wider and wider, and he ended by saying, "I think the word is estranged. That's how I read it. We've managed to drift out of the natural order of family love and react to each other as business adversaries would. I imagine he and Mary will be consumed with trying to salvage Celldesign. I have no idea what's next for the company. I know one thing, though; this was not my objective. I didn't want this to turn out this way."

"Are you going to talk to Alan?"

"It's kind of awkward."

"You should know—I never got 'back together' with him. I just felt confused about you. And the situation you were in. I think I was just holding on to my relatively carefree youth. All you'd have to forgive is one night."

So little, so much.

From Cambridge, Spencer took a train downtown to Alan's office. The receptionist showed him to "Mr. Brown's" office.

Alan stood, smiling broadly. "How does it feel to be an official whistleblower?" He pointed to a chair.

Spencer sat. "Not sure. That's why I'm here. I want to know what it means," he said.

Alan looked at Spencer and felt a change about him. "We need to talk, bro," Alan said. "I fell for Pamela two years ago, man. Thought I was over her. Thought she was over me. Guess what—I was half right. I'll tell you straight up; nothing truly happened between us after she met you. Not that I didn't try, you understand. I mean, boys will be boys. Bottom line: just friends. She's smart as hell, man. And kind. Anyway, if you think that's a conflict, I'll turn the file over, no problem. But I don't see it."

Spencer looked at him closely and concluded Alan was telling the truth, for whatever the truth was worth. Objective reality in a given moment. Subject to change.

"Got to be able to trust you, man," Spencer said.

"That's your call," Alan said, and he waited.

Spencer thought for a moment. Who else was he going to get to be his lawyer at this point? He didn't want any more complications; he looked at Alan and nodded slowly.

"Okay," Alan said. "Got to make an assumption here. Got to assume Celldesign is now officially toast. Gonna file Chapter 11. That will stop the case they filed against you, and all claims for damages get transferred to bankruptcy court. Like, all in one pot. Their claim that you stole their proprietary info isn't going nowhere. On the other hand, your whistleblower claim looks like gold now."

As he left Alan's office, Spencer was troubled. When he'd pressed send, he'd intended that his email would go to Mary, someone he trusted. Instead, the email had sent the entire company on a tailspin that was just beginning to shatter people he loved. Way more than he ever considered possible.

And after all that, he was being told that he'd won.

The problem was that Spencer did not feel like he'd won. Perhaps Alan did because he would be assured of getting paid. Perhaps Pamela did because she wanted him to feel better about himself. Perhaps his mother did because a mother must, under such circumstances. But Spencer himself did not.

He recalled that his mother liked to say, "The proof of the pudding is in the tasting." He considered what his *winning* day looked like—a day alone, watching television or surfing the web aimlessly, a delivered pizza, a few beers, a run—none of that seemed like a win.

There was a bar near Boston University, within running distance, named Peterson's. People were there, he'd bet. There would be conversation. Maybe they were Pats fans, maybe not. But he had to get out of the apartment; it was closing in on him.

Walking into Peterson's in the daytime hurt the eyes. It was dark inside, probably the atmosphere the customers wanted. *Maybe they're all winners like I am*, Spencer thought sardonically.

Spencer was not a regular, so he was greeted cautiously. He ordered a beer on tap and a hot dog with the works, which was what Peterson's was known for.

It didn't take long for the bartender to recognize Spencer— not the person per se but the type, the winner who had lost.

"You're not a student, right?" he asked.

"No," Spencer answered.

"I knew it," the bartender said in a self-satisfied voice. "Put a suit on you and you're one of the guys at the fancy places down the street. We get a lot of students here but mostly at night. There's a difference, you know. Makes me want to know—what you doin' here. If you don't mind my asking."

Spencer wondered how to answer him. "Family business."

"Yeah? What'd you do?"

"High tech."

"Wow. But that don't answer why you're sittin' here."

"I blew the whistle on something I saw."

"On your own family?"

"Yeah."

"Wow. Was it true?"

"I don't know, was it? Narrow little truth, maybe; larger truth, maybe not." And Spencer rattled off a shorthand version of the Celldesign matter.

The bartender listened intently, his elbows on the bar. "We get a lot of law students in here. Pains in the ass. But you can't help but overhear. They all talk about intent. I'm sure there's more to the story, but it don't sound like you intended anything bad. You being a little hard on yourself, maybe?"

"Maybe," he said, to keep the conversation going. *But maybe not*, he thought. "Intent would make it really bad, like go-to-jail bad, go-to-hell bad. But not being ... careful? Where does that leave you? Well, I'll tell you—here."

As soon as those words left his mouth, Spencer wanted to call them back. They were inconsiderate, insulting, disdainful. Where did he get off taking that attitude with the earnest businessman looking back at him?

"Whoa, whoa, whoa," the bartender said. "I got a lot of pride in this place. No reason to knock it, right. Just trying to help, buddy. Here's your hot dog."

The few men in the bar seemed to sense that something had changed, most looked over at Spencer from behind their shoulders, eyes menacing.

Spencer ate his hot dog, paid the bill, leaving a good tip, and headed out before one of the menacing glances turned into something more.

His walk home was lonely. The people milling about the streets only emphasized his isolation, and he regretted the mistake he had made with the bartender. He had been so obviously inconsiderate and callous. Who was he, anyway?

He had no answer.

It was still early enough, so Spencer returned the voice mail from his mother that had pinged into his cell phone. He thought about not answering, putting it off, but he knew she would just call every day until he answered. He knew what they would say to each other. She would tell him that he'd persevered and wound up on the side of truth, ostensibly the winning side. But it was just so much noise. The only thing it meant to him was that his lawyer would get paid—cold comfort when he thought about all of the other consequences, specifically the impact on his parents. Celldesign was either worth much less or worth nothing at all.

"How much will it affect you?" he asked his mother.

"We'll be okay," she lied.

He knew she was lying—a white lie, but how does one get to the truth?

"Is Dad holding up?"

"Sure," she said, another lie. "You know, Spencer, he was just not aware of what that Olga was doing. I think it would have been perfectly fine with your father if they had pulled back and fixed the patch so that it *did* work the way they thought. Sure, it would have delayed that damn IPO, but they would all still be optimistic and feeling good, instead of what he is now—a self-described failure. Kicked off the board. The word *fraud* being bandied about."

"It was my fault. I'm sorry."

"Oh, fiddlesticks. There was a dark place somewhere in Celldesign's history, but it sure as heck wasn't you. Olga's getting the blame, but maybe it goes back to Mary."

"Well, if she had just read my email—"

"Yes, that's true. My point. She just found the spotlight, liked it there, and never checked for the dark place. And that was her job. All these lawsuits are apparently saying that—according to the *Globe*." Mandy paused. "I'm wondering when somebody is going to see the light. When you trace back to Mary, don't stop there. Think of her partner in this, her mentor—the great Mr. Lloyd."

CHAPTER 12

Arthur felt that he had been waiting for the other shoe to drop: the news about the data was not unexpected. Not with the recent disclosures relating to Patty and Olga. It was there to be seen by anyone who cared to add things up. And now it was out in the open. Garrigall had it, and he would pound it to salt. It would be the talk of the town. He couldn't stop fidgeting. Standing up, sitting back down, pacing the room—how had it come to this?

He had no answer.

"Your colleagues know better," Dorothy said, seeing him slumped in his chair at the kitchen table. She knew what that meant, how important his public reputation was to him.

"My colleagues are the same types that waited for Caesar outside the Coliseum," Arthur said dryly.

"You know better than to wallow, dear," she replied. "Self-pity is hardly the way to proceed."

"Dorothy, please," he said, exasperation in his voice. "This news will be followed by a panic. People will think it means more than it does. And I mean our bankers, our creditors. It could go even further. Massive instability. The reality may be that after a simple adjustment to the patch, we'll be up and running again, but the appearance will be that we've had a major stumble. Vultures will come out. Everything is at stake."

One thing Arthur knew was what a business panic looked like; he had been teaching about business panics for years. When he saw Garrigall's article announcing the state lab's action overturning Celldesign's data reporting, he knew full well that a panic would threaten Celldesign to its core. There was no way around it.

And at the end of the panic, there would be the license. Was it already too late? Was Monroe Benjamin already working behind the scenes to revoke it? Arthur had a mental image of Mary flirting with Monroe at his party, something that he did not think much about at the time, but that stayed with him, for some reason. Now it raced back into his mind, so much so that he reached for his phone.

But he could not get through to Mary. The receptionist would not put him through, as she had always done before. "The new regime is here," Arthur murmured into the phone. He was told that she was on the phone, that the phone had been ringing off the hook, that she would have to get back to him. *There's likely some truth to that*, Arthur thought. First it would be the commercial bankers, then the investment bankers, then the first investors, then the clients she had developed, then the representatives of small governments in Africa and Asia, then the lawyers for the bankers—it would be a barrage.

He could picture her. By late morning, she would have sweated through her white blouse and sent one of the few remaining staff (the majority had up and left without notice) out to Bloomingdale's to buy a new one. She would have closed the blinds in her office and would be pacing around the desk (she had the only desk made of real wood—mahogany). Her emotions would be running high, a combination of disillusionment, anger, and sadness. She would look to the high-priced talent, old Charlie, for advice, support, direction, and he would be looking to place blame. Would blame still be directed toward Spencer?

How could that be? Spencer had been proven right; that should exempt him from blame.

No, it would more likely be Arthur himself that old Charlie would now turn against—the man with his hands on the strings, the man who reeled in the license, who set up the financing, who did all the critical things; the grandfather whose grandson had set the whole thing in motion and who now would be seen as responsible for it all.

Mere weeks ago, the picture facing the great Mr. Lloyd would have been unimaginable. The worst seemed to be coalescing, gathering, readying a final blow. The proof of that was looming in plain sight. Everything was being canceled— that's what Mary's phone calls were all about; he knew that much. Hell, Garrigall undoubtedly knew that much. The loans were being called due, the IPO had been put off, and the investment bankers had long since moved on. And the African and Asian governments that Mary had labored over were not only canceling future contracts but were refusing to pay their current obligations. Even the office furniture supplier called to demand payment or else he would drive a truck up to the front door and take everything away. It was a nightmare.

The very next day, Arthur saw it in print. Garrigall's headline was "Panic at Celldesign." And he knew that more was coming their way. It was always a matter of time, nothing more, until the lawyers arrived, seizing the opportunity to get their name in print, calling the *Globe* to announce their intentions, to offer an interview, urging potential clients to act now or lose their place at the table.

The panic was confirmed, officially recognized and in full effect.

I must rise to the moment, he thought. *At long last, it is all upon me.*

With the plague of the morning edition of the *Globe* open before him, Arthur sat for another hour or so, draining most of the pot of coffee Dorothy had made. It was unusually silent in the apartment until he suddenly made a call downstairs to Jimmy. He had been thinking all day and night.

"I'll need the car," he said.

"One twenty-eight?" Jimmy asked.

"No," said Arthur in a slow, unsteady voice. "Things have changed. Please—Rodney's house."

They drove north to Marblehead, an historic and idyllic town on a cove, twenty minutes from Boston, overlooking the bay dotted with sailboats at anchor. Rodney had a huge home built on a foreclosed lot in 1985, with a view out over the boats to the sea. It spoke of old money.

"I have to admit I thought about just staying home today— calling in sick or whatever," Rodney said humorlessly as he got in the car. "But breakfast at the Statler Hilton sounds good. I'm going to have to answer the clients' questions sometime, no matter how distasteful, and so I go to do my duty." There was an unmistakable edge of sarcasm in his comments.

The two of them were virtually unnoticed as they walked into the hotel, blending as they did with all of the other captains of industry. The Statler Hilton was the place to go for a breakfast meeting—quiet, with tables well-spaced, and there was an unspoken agreement among everyone there that what was seen or heard would not be repeated.

The two had been friends for years, often serving on the same boards or as panelists in the same seminars given by the same organizations to which they both belonged. It was Rodney, in fact, who had introduced Arthur to Dorothy after the death of his first wife, Winston's mother, when Arthur was in sad shape.

Both were known to the waitstaff at the Statler and were seated immediately at a remote table.

"I assume you've read Garrigall this morning," Arthur said quietly.

"Unrelenting," Rodney said wearily, looking around the room, obviously checking to make sure they were not overheard.

Arthur paused as a waiter came by and poured coffee. They both ordered eggs and bacon. Arthur continued. "What do you think Apple's approach will be now? He's done this before, you know."

Rodney said, "Apple rubs me the wrong way. He doesn't do things the way we do."

"I'm aware. But one wouldn't expect a lawyer and a banker to see things in the same way."

"But can he succeed with his approach—that control-the-narrative business? That's what I'd like to know. Frankly, I must ask: what has been accomplished since he was retained? He merely tried, unsuccessfully, to ruin your grandson, who, as it turns out, had the decided advantage of the truth on his side. It worries me when someone so successful, like Apple, cares nothing for the truth. When the results came in, shouldn't they have had a joint press conference, declaring that Celldesign's problems were no big deal and that they would get back on track and bring it to market at the right time? Probably should have rehired and promoted him." Rodney leaned toward Arthur, inviting him to share a confidence. "None of this is doing me any good with my board, Arthur. I'm worried about my own position."

"That's why we're here, Rodney. I also am worried; I could be a target. Don't you agree that this whole thing has been a management fiasco?" When Rodney looked surprised, Arthur added, "I don't mean me, Rodney. I'm not in *management* at Celldesign. But I was the founder. They will make something of that."

"Arthur," Rodney said with evident caution, "you may have a point, regrettably. My bank invested largely on your reputation and your position as founder. I doubt we would have gone in solely on Mary's presentation."

That was not the response that Arthur had hoped for, and a long silence followed.

Finally, he said, "The whole thing looks like a fiasco. And the one thing that senior, responsible people like you and me cannot have happen is to be the lead characters in a farce. Which is what we look like right now."

The point hit home to Rodney. "I see your point there, Arthur. What is your recommendation?"

"Mary is the CEO; she is running things. But the smart money always hedges their bets."

"What in God's name does that mean, Arthur?"

"It means that Mary and Charlie and all their strategy and all their persuasiveness may not be enough. Look at your own bank, Rodney. You had your VP and your lawyer on the phone all day yesterday, threatening lawsuits, cutting off the line of credit, leaving the company stranded financially. All the others are doing the same. Employees are standing up from their desks and walking out, for fear that they will not be paid. Panic. That's what it is—panic."

"Now listen here, Arthur," Rodney said, sitting upright. "The bank is required to take these steps to protect the shareholders and depositors. Surely you know that. It's our fiduciary duty."

"Oh, don't get high and mighty with me," Arthur said disdainfully. "You're covering your ass, period. Nobody knows what to do when things seem to go unrelentingly bad, except run to the lawyers." He waited for a response from Rodney, who appeared to be offended but without any retort. So he continued. "Rodney, I think it is perfectly reasonable to act in self-preservation mode. So much so that I think that you and the other banks should do whatever you can to push Celldesign into Chapter 11."

Ending triumphantly, Arthur waited a moment for the impact of what he'd said to register and then added quickly, "Of course, this discussion must never be repeated, not to anyone, nor must you ever confirm it in writing. Do you promise?"

"Yes, of course I promise, but what is on your mind that you want your own company in bankruptcy? It spells death."

"Because death may be the only way to survive. Paradoxically. And you will have an important role in the process. Your bank will be the key creditor. I would hope that you can arrange for all the banks to get in line and support our position. Paraphrasing old Charlie Apple, the truth must become what we say it is. Can you get on board with that?"

After leaving Rodney to walk to his bank's offices downtown, Arthur had Jimmy drive him to 128 to meet with Mary. He had spent the previous night thinking about what he had to say. *This elaborate game of charades must end*, he had decided. *It is no way to manage a panic.*

He went over the words he would use to tell Mary that he

would advise the Overseers to demand that the company be restructured in a Chapter 11 proceeding. And that there were no circumstances under which Mary could remain as CEO.

Arthur expected a tension-filled, daunting meeting, one that would cut all the ties between them, once and for all. She would think that he had betrayed her. There was a sadness to that; it was something he regretted having to do, but he saw no alternative. He tried to steel himself and hoped he could carry it off, for in his heart, he knew that she and the company were one, in some fundamental way, and that a part of her would die if their meeting went as he planned.

Jimmy pulled into the building's parking lot, and Arthur passed by security, as usual, and went upstairs. As he walked into the office space, he was wide-eyed: most of the cubicles were empty, and the receptionist's desk was unmanned. It had become an empty space; what was once busy, active, and optimistic had become sepulchral and dim, manned only by a skeleton crew of young staffers who probably didn't know what to do in this turmoil, except repeat what they had been doing and hope that things would work out. He could see through to Mary, again on the phone, so he waved to let her know he was there and then wandered about unobtrusively, his mind full of anticipation.

As Arthur passed by Olga's old office, he peeked in. There was a yellow ribbon preventing access, presumably marking a potential crime scene. She was dead and buried at her own hand, but her office remained curiously ready for her. All her furniture remained in place, down to a few odd photographs pinned on a bulletin board behind her chair, depicting childhood scenes, presumably in Ukraine. The police apparently had cordoned off her office but had done nothing more. *The police are probably focused on the motel*, Arthur thought. *They probably look at the motel as the primary crime scene, but it's not. The crime happened here; they just don't know that. What took place at the motel was nothing more than afterbirth. Tragic, perhaps, but not the real crime.*

He could not resist; he bent to get under the yellow ribbon and walked in to what he considered the dark heart of Celldesign's demise.

Absently, Arthur opened the middle drawer of her desk, curious to see if she'd left behind any other photos or personal items, anything that would give an insight into her inner life. He saw nothing unusual, and as he moved his hand to the upper right drawer, he recalled the last time he'd seen her, when he unexpectedly walked into her office, and she had pushed a smartphone into that same drawer, as if it were something forbidden, secretive.

Arthur opened the drawer—there it was.

For a moment, he couldn't believe his eyes—an iPhone, by all appearances the same device that he'd watched her secret away, just before she'd killed herself.

Celldesign policy was clear: no personal computing devices of any kind in the workplace, and that surely covered smartphones. But she had disobeyed and done so anyway.

Arthur hadn't thought much about it at the time; after all, Olga had had a senior position, and her loyalty to Mary was unquestioned, so one would expect some latitude to have been earned and probably given. *But still*, Arthur thought as he stood in stunned silence, *it was only a short time later that she killed herself in that ritualistic way.*

In hindsight, everyone knew she had been hiding something, but perhaps no one knew the *extent* of what she was hiding. The accountants would be assigned to figure it all out, but that would take months. Her personal phone, on the other hand, would tell the whole story in her own words, all the darkness, the motivation, the plan, what went wrong. All there.

It was a crossroads for Arthur, like no moment before. Seemingly right versus wrong was at stake: point out his discovery to the authorities or... not. He could not take his eyes off the phone—a little hand-sized device that held within it answers to all he was speculating about. And yet, he thought immediately, if he handed it over to the authorities—or worse, to old Charlie—what would wind up altered or changed or deleted? Who but he himself could be trusted?

Arthur looked up quickly. No one appeared to be looking. He casually went to Olga's cubicle window and turned the wand on the blinds, and they closed. He hoped that his silhouette did not show through. He had a moment. He reached in, grabbed the phone, and stuffed it into his pants pocket. Then he reopened the blinds and walked into the hall, knowing full well that he had crossed a line, that what he was doing at that moment was indistinguishable from what Spencer had done when he'd walked out with the data months before. The phone did not belong to him. It was unquestionably evidence in a crime investigation, and he was taking it.

"What else should a prudent person do?" he asked out loud to the empty room, then shushing himself immediately when his voice seemed to echo the slightest bit. He quickly calculated his options. Olga's phone—her voice from the dead—was in his pocket. No one had noticed; that was crucial—it was his secret at that moment, his alone. Was the risk worth it? The phone could well have important information—emails and texts and electronic files—as well as anything that she wanted to keep private about the whole affair. It could also have information about him, something that might cast him in a bad light. Maybe Mary had said things about him. Maybe he would be giving his new adversary a weapon that she could turn against him. All that just to be "a good boy" and turn over this fantastical discovery that he had stumbled upon. Each second seemed like an eternity. He began sweating.

The phone in the modern world was where people kept their records, their secrets. *Yes*, he thought, *the real story is right here. Do I given them over to someone else, merely because some rule not intended for this situation would suggest that I do? Or do I first confirm what is inside this inscrutable little device?*

He looked around, more carefully this time. The security cameras were dark—they must have been turned off to save cash. The phone was unobtrusively in his pocket. His heart was racing. The temptation to simply walk out and then see what was on the phone was enormous. Too much.

He concluded that, if caught, he would simply say that as a founder of the company, he was merely ensuring the safekeeping of that property, which had been left negligently in plain view for anyone to take. *Yes,* he thought, *that would do quite nicely.*

He wanted to get out quickly; he thought his appearance might betray him. He peeked in to Mary's office—still on the phone. They made eye contact. Arthur signaled with his hand that he was going to leave but would call her. She signaled OK and that she would be tied up on the phone indefinitely. They exchanged wan smiles. And he simply walked to the elevator and went down to the first floor.

At the time, he also did not consider the irony of the fact that he had just done what he had called theft when Spencer had done something similar. Morally, it would be an even exchange at best. His mind was elsewhere; he wanted to see what secrets Olga had, for they would be at the crux of Celldesign's situation, and only he would know about them. *There will be an advantage in that,* he surmised.

He waved to the security officer at the first-floor desk and headed for Jimmy, who was sitting, waiting, in the car.

Arthur moved as quickly as he could, not wanting to be noticeable yet getting away from there as quickly as possible. He was breathing heavily yet wanted no one to notice that fact.

As he approached the car, he could tell from Jimmy's face that he looked different. Jimmy was squinting, as if he were trying to see something, perhaps a new feature in Arthur's face.

"Jimmy," Arthur said from the rear seat, "isn't there someone you know from your ... contacts who is a computer genius *and* can keep a secret?"

Jimmy looked at Arthur in the rearview mirror, his brow knotted.

Arthur saw Jimmy's confusion. "It seems that I've come upon a smartphone—quite by chance—and I'll need the password to open it and then return it to the appropriate person."

Jimmy looked again in the rearview mirror and smiled. "We'll be there in half an hour."

Jimmy drove toward Framingham, a seedy little city west of Boston on the way to the Berkshires. The drive took twenty minutes or so, and for the entire time, Arthur maintained an inner debate: had he or had he not committed a felony?

Jimmy found the neighborhood of small, relatively unkempt homes that he apparently had been looking for, and he pulled into and parked on a cracked asphalt driveway. He got out quickly and walked in front of Arthur in a concerned way, up a set of three wooden steps leading to the front door, which had, at one time, been all white; the paint was now curling off, disclosing an earlier, dark-green color. A middle-aged man answered, whom Jimmy called "Rolls," presumably referring to his waistline, which protruded from under a white T-shirt. They were let into a disheveled living room with the television on—*The Price Is Right.*

At that moment, Arthur thought that he had made a mistake by asking Jimmy for the introduction to Rolls, but it seemed too late to do anything about it.

"What we want, my friend, is to find out the password to this phone, so that we can access the files. It's a long story, but the owner of the phone has died, and the business—my business—needs to see what is on here."

Rolls nodded but seemed indifferent. "Can you leave it overnight?"

Arthur answered quickly. "No. That would be impossible." Arthur thought that if Rolls opened the files, he could do anything with them, including—though this was unlikely—go to the authorities.

Rolls said, "A hundred. Cash."

Jimmy looked at Arthur, who pulled out his wallet, counted out five twenty-dollar bills, and handed them over to Rolls.

Rolls made a grunting noise and sat down at his kitchen table with the phone. He began to click icons with instructions, telling Jimmy and Arthur to "take a load off" as he pointed to a worn and stained sofa.

Within thirty minutes, Rolls looked up and said, "The password is 'outofUk4ever.' There are a lot of files here. For another hundred, I'll forward them to your laptop. They'll be easier to see that way, especially the photos. I can encrypt them. You'll never get caught."

Photos?

"Yes, that sounds like a good idea. A hundred, you say?" Arthur reached for his wallet and drew out another five twenty-dollar bills, nodded at Rolls, and started to leave, but Jimmy caught his arm and said, "Let me help you get down the stairs, Mr.—er, sir. Remember there are three steps, and we don't want to tumble, now do we?"

When he arrived back on Beacon Hill, Arthur went directly to his library, sat at his desk, and opened his laptop, as Rolls had instructed. The first thing he saw was a series of files titled "Cousins," containing numerous photographs, all apparently taken the past summer and all involving a Lloyd. They were crude surveillance photos of Arthur, Winston, Mandy, and Spencer. There was also a recent file on Monroe Benjamin.

It was a dossier, like something from a spy novel.

Looking at the photos felt very much like peering into a window between curtains or under a half-closed shade—not that the photos were salacious, but rather because the subjects, including Arthur, had been tailed without their knowledge. The photos captured moments that the subjects must have thought were private but were not, and instead, something—their conduct, their whereabouts—was being captured without their consent to be used against them all. Arthur thought it was probably illegal even to look at them, and thus, his unlawful conduct was compounding, but he could not drag himself away. There was a file with photos of Mandy with another man, sitting on a bench on Commonwealth Avenue, sharing a light kiss, then entering a brownstone, a look of intimacy passing between them. There was a file with many photos of Spencer walking with a willowy young woman Arthur had not seen before and the young woman leaving his apartment well after the sun had set. There were other pictures of Spencer in running shoes, bounding into an office building downtown, and finally, Spencer's lawyer walking arm in arm with the same willowy young woman. There was a picture of Spencer rushing out of Arthur's building, a look of panic on his face. And there was a new file with pictures of Monroe Benjamin, walking away from Mary's condo building after dusk, with the diminutive doorman watching after him with those reflecting eyes, ones that block out the light in a photograph and look opaque.

Arthur was not exempt. The photographer had caught him coming and going from Beacon Hill but also leaving the building on 128, walking toward the car, his eyes on Jimmy, while Mary was at the large window in the reception area on the fourth floor, looking down, watching, with old Charlie standing next to her. The photo froze in time an eerie moment, ominous and uneasy, like a Hopper painting might. And there were pictures of Arthur and Rodney, huddled over eggs and toast at the Statler, seemingly conspiring.

A man named Dmitri had sent Olga a narrative with the photos, explaining where and when they were taken and who was in them.

Arthur was exhausted. He poured himself a scotch and joined Dorothy in the living room. He felt uncertain, secretive, yet drawn to the dossier like a moth to flame.

Then he stopped, almost dropping his glass. Suppose they were still at it? Freelancing. Had he captured Arthur walking out of the building with the phone in his pocket? Had he followed them to Rolls's place? Was there a photo of Arthur walking down the steps from Rolls's seedy house with the phone in his hand? Had he remembered to keep the phone in his pocket, out of sight?

But Arthur Lloyd was above reproach, wasn't he? He would get the benefit of the doubt.

Dorothy put her hands down on the chair she was sitting in, as if she were ready to jump to his aid. "Arthur! You look like you've seen a ghost! Are you all right?"

He stared at her, but he could not tell her. How could he tell Dorothy Quinn what he was in the middle of? They did not have that kind of sharing relationship. She was a Quinn, and he had possession of a dossier that was certainly illegal. *A step deeper*, he thought.

"Nothing, dear," he managed. "Just a little dizzy for a moment."

"Well, really! You get on the phone tomorrow to Deaconess and get an appointment to check that out. I saw it! You almost fell."

The irony of her use of the past tense of *fall* hit him, and he coughed. But all he could muster was, "Yes, of course. You're right."

It was there on Arthur's computer—emails and notes between Olga and two Ukrainian cousins, Dmitri and Alex, whom she agreed to pay off Celldesign's books for information on people whom she regarded as her adversaries. It also appeared that by the time Spencer sent his email to her, Olga had, for months, been consciously shaping the test results of the patch, moving the data from unfavorable to favorable, first in Kenya and then in a remote outpost in Tanzania.

It saddened Arthur as the story began to come together. Olga simply could not bring herself to tell the objective truth, which was that the patch seemed to have a declining value. She did not know how to end that many plans, that much hope. Her emails to Patty wondered aloud what steps would have to be taken with those who tried the patch and had a gene edited in reliance on the disclosures Celldesign was making, which, she noted, were "incomplete."

But she was left alone. Patty was no help, offering banal prescriptions, such as, "It'll all work out," or "God has a plan."

"Who knows how she expected to extricate herself, ultimately?" Arthur said to himself. "Maybe the thought process stopped before she reached that question." There was a sense in her emails that she felt trapped, like an animal in the wintery fields of her homeland. Perhaps she began feeling responsible for the *results*, not merely the *process*, and she sacrificed the latter for the former, getting in deeper and deeper with each data run, postponing the reckoning until it was too late.

Arthur could see his photo on his laptop screen—his face and all the wrinkles around his eyes and mouth. Dmitri's photographs showed an old man who could barely get into or out of the car without Jimmy's help, who fell asleep on the bench in the university's quadrangle, and who now was reading another person's mail.

He wondered if he could delete his file without detection. Perhaps Jimmy's friend Rolls?

He scrolled back to the shots of Mandy. "Her file, too," he said to no one.

He stepped away from the screen, seeking solace in the kitchen, with its window facing west, overlooking Boston, a view that had always been reassuring but not now. The phone had spoken to him as he thought it would. And now what?

Arthur found it deeply troubling, knowing things—intimate things, in secret—about others, people close to him. Things that others did not know that he knew. It was illegal for a definite reason; it upset the balance of power in human interaction. He knew that he should have turned in the phone and the information on it, but he did not. He argued internally, back and forth, but told himself, "Not every technical wrong is wrong in the fundamental sense; I mean, there are many examples—history and literature are full of them."

Instead, he scheduled lunch with Winston at a small Italian restaurant off Boylston Street. The photos of Mandy were on his mind, even though he told Winston that they were meeting to talk about his thoughts for Celldesign.

Arthur simply did not know what to do about the photos of Mandy in the dossier. He had reached the point where he did not want to know about them. He thought that he should probably do something—but what?

If he were forthright and told Winston, what would that do to their already porous relationship? Likely, Arthur concluded, Winston would feel such a discussion as another humiliation. And that would never do.

If Arthur kept the photos a secret, but Winston somehow found out about them, he would regard it as a betrayal. And that might be worse.

His instinct was to talk to Winston, get a feel for what he knew or didn't know. It was a concrete step; he hoped that it would help clear the fog. Arthur looked across the table. Winston seemed as uncomfortable on the outside as Arthur felt on the inside. "And how is Mandy?" he asked.

How to probe about a photograph, the existence of which he could not disclose?

He asked around the issue in several ways: did they have

any travel plans together? Was she keeping up with Spencer? Winston mentioned that Mandy dropped in on Spencer and met a young woman there. Arthur restrained himself from saying that he knew and that she looked beautiful; instead, he just nodded.

Arthur soon concluded that Winston was totally unaware that Mandy had been unfaithful, and that gave Arthur an insight. The cousins had managed to photograph scenes that Winston was unaware of, scenes that were just before or just after, scenes that were of immense importance, such as Mandy straying. If Winston knew what the cousins had captured on film, it would have permanently affected his marriage, perhaps even his behavior in the Celldesign crisis. But because it was done undercover, the effect was incomplete. The other shoe had not dropped. Wasn't it likely that the same thing was happening in connection with each of the photos? Wasn't that the reason those pictures were selected and retained?

"Did you invite me to talk about Spencer?" Winston asked, but Arthur had become distracted; his mind had moved to the pictures of Monroe leaving Mary's condo. Winston's voice reached him. "Arthur!" he said insistently. "What about Spencer? What do you want to talk about?"

Arthur looked up. Winston was perspiring, nervous, concerned. It looked like his hair had begun thinning again. "Spencer will have to take care of himself. I am now glad that he got himself a lawyer," Arthur said quietly, his mind still distracted.

"Well, for crying out loud. What are you saying, Dad?"

Arthur barely heard him. *What in God's name was Monroe doing at Mary's apartment? In the evening?*

Winston repeated himself. "Dad!" There was alarm in his voice. Winston thought that Arthur was acting erratically. There was something said about Spencer, and he wanted to know what it was all about. He could see that Arthur's mind was racing.

"You accept that Celldesign has gone beyond the point of no return, I assume?" Arthur asked abruptly.

Winston crinkled his forehead.

Arthur continued, as if Winston had asked what he meant. "I mean that I was over at the building yesterday, and it's like a bomb hit. Nobody is there. Mary has circled the wagons and is trying to stave off bankruptcy, but I would not like her odds. Everything is falling off—customers, employees, lenders, subjects who tried the patch. Lawsuits are piling up. I would assume that the *Globe* will send someone to peek in and get another front-page story out of it. And that will be it."

Winston listened with obvious despair. He hadn't touched his pasta dish but motioned to a waiter for another glass of Chianti. "You know what this means to me. My firm and I are unsecured creditors. We stand to lose the entire investment."

"Suppose Mary is playing both sides against the middle? Suppose the image she is allowing us to see—the heroic CEO fighting for these people, all the bankers and creditors and employees—suppose that is all eyewash, a charade, and we're missing the truth, which is that she is positioning herself to land on her feet at any cost?"

"Where is this coming from? What is the evidence?" Winston was obviously not following.

"Don't ask," Arthur replied, his mind wild with the image in the photo of Mary and Charlie looking down as he ran for the car and Jimmy.

Winston brought his Chianti to his lips, peering over the top of the glass, inviting an explanation.

Arthur then outlined his plan, a prepackaged bankruptcy, with all the pieces necessary for court approval lined up in advance, passing by the judge only long enough for him or her to place the stamp of approval on it. Arthur had obviously given the matter his attention. He had also taught the subject at the business school.

It would start with finding a vulture, or willing investor, who would line up financing to pay off the banks, buy the remaining assets cheaply, and then become the chief executive officer of the company that would emerge.

"Replacing Mary?" Winston asked.

"We must choose what we wish to salvage, and I do not have the luxury of salvaging Mary's career at Celldesign. How about you?"

Winston bowed his head. Then said, "Vultures are not known for being nice. Suppose we don't like him, or he doesn't like us?"

"You don't have a wide array of options, Winston. And this is precisely where you come in. You have a contacts file. Use it. Find a vulture, the *right* vulture for Celldesign—and for us."

"What about Mary? She won't just walk away."

"I owe nothing to Mary. None of us does. We all have to adapt to that reality." Arthur spoke those words with a firm—perhaps dramatically firm—resolve.

Winston turned his head to the right and squinted at Arthur, as if to ask, *"What happened?"*

Arthur ignored Winston and continued explaining that the hardest part would be refinancing the debt Celldesign already had amassed.

"You're leaping ahead here, Dad," Winston said.

"I'm sure," Arthur replied. "But it hangs together. As of now, we will stop flailing about and work on putting our own plan together."

Winston seemed overwhelmed and left the restaurant on

the pretense of having a meeting, which both of them knew to be untrue—something he had done since he was a child—but Arthur stayed behind, having another item of business to attend to. He had spent a good part of his adult life dealing with Monroe Benjamin, and it was time to see where things stood.

He reached Monroe on his cell phone.

The voice was the same, no hint of deception. "I'm glad you called, Arthur," he said. "We have things to talk about that cannot wait."

"I told you and the Overseers that I'd report back. I'd like to have called sooner, but the last few days have been packed."

"We're very concerned, Arthur. In fact, Bob Birtsch is recommending that we get out. Revoke the license."

Arthur had expected as much. But now the test. "No doubt, Monroe. And I fully respect your position, as I have for all these years. But give me a listen; can I ask that? By the way, have you spoken to Mary about this?"

There was a silence. Arthur had Dmitri's photo firmly in mind. He waited for Monroe's answer.

"Yes, Arthur. I met with her. She has proposed a plan to salvage Celldesign."

The betrayer was Mary, rather than Monroe.

"All right, old friend. I don't know what she said, but here is what I think." And he outlined his plan, the one he had discussed with Winston, which would certainly be fundamentally different from anything Mary proposed, since it would involve a new CEO.

"A new CEO is, unfortunately, necessary for credibility purposes," Arthur said.

He awkwardly walked the few blocks north from the restaurant to his apartment on Beacon Hill, struggling, at his age, over the cobblestones that had remained in the streets since the days of

Paul Revere. Arthur's mind returned to the dossier—to the photo of Mary and old Charlie standing at the window, watching him below, walking much as he was at that moment, struggling for balance, tiring, and resting. The photo captured a conspiratorial moment, Arthur thought, but not the only one. The picture of Monroe, the lover of antiques, departing from Mary's barren apartment told the same story. "Thank God for the dossier," Arthur murmured. "A picture is worth a thousand words."

The moment that thought flashed through his mind, Arthur caught his breath—he had just congratulated himself for breaking the law.

Sweating from the walk home, Arthur felt overheated. With an iced tea in his hand, he headed to the library to think.

A change had taken place right under his nose. Mary saw Celldesign as being stolen from her, and she was not about to go down with the ship. She had assigned that role to him.

But for the dossier, Arthur would not have fully understood that fact. And from Arthur's photographically enhanced point of view, that meant that the narrative Mary and Charlie were working up would, as a final act, sacrifice him.

Thank goodness for the dossier. It had alerted him. How could he possibly give that up?

He went to his desk and turned the computer on, just to make sure the information was still there, still real. As he looked at the photos, he drifted. They had all been caught—all of them. But he was the only one who knew that fact.

"A fucked-up irony," Arthur noted to himself. "The venture that we thought would change the world is built on surveillance, manipulation of data, and all of the shortcomings that you think you are exempt from. And the kicker is that I cannot answer how I know this to be true."

CHAPTER 13

Arthur got a call from old Charlie—"as a courtesy"—to let him know that the company would file in bankruptcy to reorganize. He said the "panic" had reached the point where the protection of the bankruptcy court had become essential. It would put a halt to all the lawsuits and threats. He also said that the *Globe* would publish an article about Celldesign's filing on the following day, which told Arthur that Mary and Charlie were still trying to control the narrative; she would be the source behind Garrigall's story.

The most important step in Celldesign's history, and Arthur was completely excluded, merely given a courtesy call but no other input whatsoever. *They call it being marginalized*, he mused. It was deflating—more than that: he was angry. He would have called old Charlie out before but now, after he had taken the phone, he dared not do so.

It was obvious that Mary and old Charlie were acting in concert—perhaps they had already formulated a reorganization plan—and they had left him in the dark. Essentially, he knew nothing more than the general public would know in twenty-four hours, when Garrigall was scheduled to print his spoon-fed article.

He, the founder, the source of the first seed money, the one who had introduced the banks for the first round of financing, the one whose name was synonymous with Celldesign. The one with the most to lose.

Thank God for the dossier. Without it, they would have caught him flat-footed. Instead, he too had been working on a reorganization plan, one that did not propose that Mary continue as CEO.

The next day, Arthur opened the *Globe* to Garrigall's headline: "Celldesign to Reorganize." The second line, in slightly smaller print, read, "The Failure behind the Failure."

Citing "informed sources inside the company," Garrigall reported that Celldesign had decided to file papers for Chapter 11 and intended to reorganize itself, defer certain payments, and come out of bankruptcy to complete its God-given mission to "change the world." It was Mary's message; everyone knew that. A note of affirmation in an otherwise dark time. "Controlling the narrative," Arthur said to no-one.

All of that had been expected, but it was the last paragraph that gave Arthur pause. Garrigall wrote in a kind of summary fashion:

> Celldesign's fortunes abruptly changed after an email from the company founder's grandson unexpectedly publicized previously unappreciated irregularities in the data presentation, which the company is confident can be rectified in short order.

"Spoon-fed," Arthur moaned.

A courier arrived later that morning with the Chapter 11 filing, some five inches thick, front to back, listing assets, liabilities, and different classes of creditors. Arthur scanned the papers with merciless speed, looking for two items: the license and the whistleblower claim. Both were buried in the paperwork, but there they were. The license was listed as an asset, and Spencer's whistleblower claim as an unsecured liability.

To Arthur, they were no such thing, neither of them.

A courier had also stopped at Spencer's apartment, dropping off his copy of the petition with a thud on the kitchen table, then standing, distracted, while Spencer signed a receipt, which he handed over while asking, "Why do I get a copy of this?"

The courier answered vaguely. "I'm just doing a job," he said, "but you're probably named in there."

"Shit," Spencer said under his breath.

The courier responded flippantly with the universal insincerity, "Have a nice day," and walked back to his truck, which was double-parked.

After an hour of review, Spencer was convinced that he was only named because of his whistleblower claim. Alan confirmed, but it was a short call; he apparently thought Spencer's concern was more or less juvenile. Plus, he would later concede, no provision had been made for legal fees to be awarded, and that had upset him.

Spencer sat in his empty and dark apartment, looking over five inches worth of legal papers, without the faintest idea what the presence of his name would mean.

And that is when Garrigall called.

"Hey, man," he said, "I'd like to get something from

you—on the record, of course. Pretty big take-down. How do you react to the filing?"

"You want me to have a reaction—I get it. But I really don't have one."

"You got to feel vindicated. Wouldn't be human otherwise."

"Okay, okay, maybe I feel vindicated to the extent that nobody's calling me a thief or an idiot. Okay? But beyond that, I wish none of this had ever happened."

"Come on! You're becoming famous! And wait until you have the trial on the whistleblower claim! When you win that, the sky's the limit. Fame and fortune, my man. You'll replace your grandfather as a celebrity in this town. And I can help you. Everybody's got that vanity, man; everybody I've ever met. Somewhere deep down, everybody wants to be looked up to. They all think it's their God-given right. Can you honestly tell me you don't want that? Huh?"

Spencer raised his eyes from the phone he was holding to the window in his kitchen. He was pale and suddenly looked and felt older than he ever had before.

When Arthur picked up the *Globe* from his front door the next day, he opened the business section and stopped in his tracks. The headline read, "Celldesign Grandson, Now Vindicated, Pursuing Whistleblower Damages."

Arthur had been in the public eye long enough to know a setup when he saw it. The article sounded like it was 90 percent Garrigall and 10 percent Spencer. But still, the flow of events just did not relent. Just then, Dorothy called Arthur to the phone; it was Rodney.

Garrigall had called him for comment. He'd thought nothing

of it until he opened that morning's paper. "What do you think?" he asked Arthur and proceeded to explain that apparently, after pouring over the photos and negatives of Arthur's party, Garrigall had noticed that Rodney and Arthur had stood next to each other most of the evening. On a hunch, he called a friend at Rodney's bank and asked casually if Rodney and Arthur were hanging out together, since the bank was, according to sources, pulling the plug on Celldesign.

His friend said, in effect, "Of course they are! They're not going to let Celldesign merely fade away. That would be far too great a loss in money and emotion. Won't happen. Bet on it. They're talking all the time. That's obviously all I can say."

It was enough. Garrigall told Rodney that the reporting was beginning to focus on the incestuous links and connections among the Lloyd family members. "In fairness," he said, "you should have an opportunity to comment."

"Well, by that time I was fit to be tied," Rodney said. "But I know a trap when I see one."

Arthur was satisfied that Rodney knew enough to end the call peremptorily. But Rodney's true point was valid; it seemed that the Lloyds were under siege.

Garrigall had come out and openly questioned whether the Lloyd family conflicts of interest had a role in the downfall of a company that would otherwise have simply re-worked the data, instead of bankrupting the company. Arthur's connections were all over the picture, including family members, from his grandson to his son and on to his brother-in-law. Garrigall noted that Arthur was not fending off the banks, not pleading to give Celldesign more time, as one might expect. Rather, he seemed to be colluding with them, getting the banks in position to force the issue. Garrigall asked rhetorically if that was the behavior of a fiduciary.

Hunched over the paper, Arthur read and re-read the article. He was under attack.

There was a knock on Spencer's door. He had just gotten back from a long run, still sweaty and unshaven. He opened the door and stood speechless. On the other side of the threshold, Pamela looked at him, making a face that said that his running clothes were gross. "You need a shower," she said.

Spencer looked at her. "I'm a runner."

She walked past him into the apartment and sat at the kitchen table, her head in her hands. "What are we going to do?" she lamented.

"You said I needed a shower. How about helping out, just to make sure I'm clean enough for you?"

The morning was warm and simple; he did not know if they were making up. It was enough that he was looking at her and touching her, and she was smiling and returning his kisses. Spencer wished it could go on forever.

"Maybe we should move to Europe," he said wearily.

She peered over the newspaper that he was holding and saw the headline. "Come on, baby," she said, "You've got to get past it, honey. You're not responsible for the bankruptcy filing. And maybe now it will just blow up, liquidate, and who knows? Maybe we can have an anonymous life again. Let it go."

Spencer looked at Pamela. Her longing for normalcy, for ordinariness, came through as she placed her hands on the table, clasped, and pointed in his direction. He saw the look of a young woman being pushed out of adolescence into an adult life that she was neither prepared for nor attracted to, but there she was, because of him, because of the spark between them.

But, he wondered, would that spark be enough? There were still headlines to come, a bankruptcy that involved them all, and a family coming apart.

As she rinsed the breakfast dishes in the sink, he said, "I think we can make this work. It's all I want. *You* are all I want. When we're together, I feel this sense of wonder—that two people could find so much in each other. Can't we just go with that?"

He knew he warmed her whenever he smiled, so he flashed his best forgive-me look and saw her smile in return.

She said, "Let's do something fun, okay?"

And they decided to go to Haymarket Square, a huge, mostly open-air market downtown. They would walk over for the exercise.

It was a long walk but a brisk day. They each wore fall coats and remarked on the light-green cast to the leaves along Commonwealth Avenue, the first sign of the yellows and golds that would follow.

Spencer said, "Your father must really disapprove of me— of us."

"Not at all," Pamela replied. "He's a professor of philosophy, you know. First thing, when I come home after visiting you, he wants to know everything. Well, not … you know." She blushed. "But he wants to know what you're experiencing. He's into this concept of"—she raised the first two fingers of each hand in air quotes—"'moral choice,' and he thinks that there are intentional moral choices, and then there are accidental moral choices. You fall in there somewhere. And he wants to know what it's like for you. I think he uses your situation in his class. You should probably get a royalty or something."

"I don't think anybody could be more accidentally moral than I," Spencer said.

They walked down into Beacon Hill and merged with the crowds walking through the market. The makeshift stands were full of autumn's bounty—squash, pumpkin, eggplant. The smell of fresh bread was in the air, and fishmongers tried to lure customers. For about half an hour, they were absorbed with buying food for the week.

The walk back was far more laborious, lugging bags of vegetables and fruits. But Pamela returned to their conversation. "My position with Dad has been that we're too young to be caught up in a drama like this. Not ready. I just don't care enough about what's moral, I guess. I just want to make a life. He's been fixated on moral action as a theme for his whole adult life, which, not incidentally, is in total shambles. Divorce, no money, bores all his acquaintances to death so he has no friends, lives vicariously through his daughter." She stopped to take a breath; the bags were heavy. She turned toward Spencer. "Would you do it again?"

"No," he said, "I don't think so. I haven't heard from my grandfather since I crashed his eightieth birthday party!" He smiled, meaning it as a joke. "How many grandsons can say that?" Then his face stiffened. "I can't take credit or blame for much, as I see it. But perspective helps; in the end, what I did may have been accidental, as your Dad would say, but it had to happen. I was just there."

She nodded with a smile. "But you did the right thing. There must be a recognition of that in some way."

But he wondered—although their answers agreed, they agreed for different reasons, she to keep her life uncomplicated and free, and he to take back the pain he had caused, inadvertently, to his loved ones. *Did it matter?*

Walking a step behind her, Spencer watched the sway of her hips and recalled the feel of her skin, smooth and warm. He realized that she could have her choice of most any man. She was not burdened by high-minded moral choices. She could easily play the game she talked incessantly about—to just form a family, just be happy in small things.

When will she take off again? he wondered, wincing as he regripped the paper bags full of food, his arms burning from the weight. "Hey, these are heavy!" he said with a laugh, but she kept on walking.

Arthur wondered if he were becoming paranoid. He loved Jimmy, but they had come to share a secret, and that was a dangerous place for any two people to be. Arthur chastised himself for getting Jimmy involved with Rolls and the phone, and now Jimmy had dangerous knowledge: he knew that Arthur had stolen a phone and paid one hundred dollars to a guy named Rolls to open it up for his use. He also knew there were photos. Jimmy could go to the police and tell his story at any time, without any real concern. He had no skin in the game; he didn't even know who owned the phone, aside from the fact that it was someone from the office on 128. But it would be enough to alert prosecutors and perhaps ruin Arthur.

Allowing Jimmy into such a position was uncharacteristically careless. Arthur was standing on a knife's edge. Jimmy worked for him, but if there were any change, if anything happened that Jimmy did not like, he would have a terrible advantage over Arthur.

How much did Arthur really know about this man who suddenly had leverage over him? Was Jimmy aware of his position? Would he use it?

The next day, Jimmy was waiting in the car, which he had

managed to park on the street in front of Arthur's apartment. When Arthur got in, he asked, "Are there two Jimmys?"

Jimmy turned in the front seat to face Arthur in the back seat. "Not sure what you mean by that, sir."

Arthur smiled. "Relax. I know it's a strange question. But it's a strange world. Perhaps I should ask the question another way. Do you think of yourself as loyal, Jimmy?"

"Oh, indeed, sir. Loyal as the day is long. I've bounced around a bit in my days, and one lesson I've learned is to keep your friends and family close and your enemies closer. They say that, you know. And I believe it!"

"Interesting," Arthur said, smiling thinly. "I think I'll just go over to campus, Jimmy. I have some things to think about."

CHAPTER 14

Arthur was getting irritated. Winston had to come through for the plan to work; he had to get the "vulture" to become Mary's replacement. Without a vulture to swoop in and carry away the company, it would die in bankruptcy and be picked apart by the lawyers for all the creditors, leaving behind nothing but thoughts of what could have been. He paced his campus office. "What is Winston doing?" he asked the empty space. Arthur disliked delays in general, but locking up a vulture was of such high importance that he was particularly anxious. He sat at his desk, tapping his feet, but it was doing no good.

He kept a bottle of scotch locked in his credenza; "If not now," he murmured and poured himself a short drink. It seemed to calm him; the sting of the scotch in his throat invited a deep breath, and from there, a respite for his overactive mind. He recalled that day, years ago now, when his then-student stood before him and talked about changing the world. *And now*, he thought wearily, *I'm planning to replace her with a vulture.*

And she is planning to eliminate me.

A second sip, and he was in a more philosophical place. "How does one justify one's life?" he wondered aloud. "By turning on those you have known and loved, in one sense or another? Tit for tat?" It seemed somewhat petty. But there was the dossier—pictures of the conspiracy against him; Mary with old Charlie, instead of with him. He could not bring himself to step aside and let Mary try to work her way out of Celldesign's collapse, not if it meant trampling him. It was just a measure beyond his capability, like a high note demanded from a baritone.

Arthur's reverie was interrupted by a ping announcing a call on his cell phone.

Winston was terse. "Ronald Storrs," he said.

Arthur's reaction was immediate; to Arthur's way of thinking, it was an excellent choice.

A picture of Storrs bolted into his mind: short and wiry, with curly, thinning, salt-and-pepper hair; darting eyes; and an overall British demeanor that he acquired during his childhood growing up in London, Storrs had been a Bostonian since graduating from Harvard Law twenty years earlier. He knew who Winston was and had an immediate interest in Celldesign. He followed bankruptcies like Spencer followed the Red Sox.

But Storrs had a well-known iron rule in business: he would not go into a deal—any deal—without a predefined advantage. That is how he made his fortune.

And so, when he answered Winston's call, his question was simple: "What is my advantage?"

Winston, Storrs, and Arthur agreed to meet to talk over the deal but not in one of the usual places, such as the Parker House or Locke-Ober—too public, too likely to incite speculation. Also, too likely to be picked up by Garrigall. What a field day he would have with that information.

Instead, Winston suggested his home, just outside the city. "We'll arrange take-out," he said and took orders for sandwiches from a local—and discreet—deli. Arthur had Jimmy pick up

Storrs and bring him to Winston's, where the two of them were waiting.

After everyone sat down around the dining room table, Arthur told Storrs of the original concept for Celldesign, as well as its recent history, beginning with Spencer's email.

Storrs listened carefully, sipping a Poland Spring water from the bottle. "Again, why should I take the risk?" he asked. "I know zero about gene editing, and frankly, making no apologies, I don't care about the developing countries unless I can profit from them. This 'change the world' stuff is B.S. to a man like me."

The sandwiches arrived, and the room was quiet as the paper bags containing the food were placed on the table, with each of the men eyeing the others. Storrs, in particular, seemed nervous, his eyes bouncing from Arthur to Winston, as if he had something to fear from one of them, but he did not know which one.

Arthur said, "I take it that being part of a venture to improve the world is not your cup of tea."

"Let's say I am not moved by it. I don't mind the world getting better, but that is not my goal. And frankly, it worries me when doing good is part of the rationale for a business," Storrs replied. "It shouldn't be."

Arthur was about to speak, but Winston preempted him. "Once the patch is fixed and the data are rerun, everything else will be in place. The manufacture and delivery, contracts, a plan to expand, and the overseas revenues will be taxed favorably, quite favorably. We are dealing with the poorest of countries, and they are not looking to tax us; to the contrary, the tax structure and exchange rates ought to appeal to you. And for icing on the cake, there are possibilities of financing through the governments over there at rates that will bring a smile to your face."

"I believe that is called an advantage," Arthur said gently.

"I don't know," Storrs replied. "The lenders will look at this and want my personal guarantee. Just so much risk."

Arthur leaned toward Storrs. "Perhaps the lead bank can take care of that."

"Well," said Storrs with a smile, "that has the ring of an advantage."

Storrs said he would have his lawyers and accountants start in on the due diligence; he would go that far. "But what's in it for the two of you, and what about the current CEO?"

Arthur's response was mixed. He explained that the banks would be repaid at twenty cents on the dollar, the old shareholders would retain a diluted interest in Celldesign, and Winston would get a fee for brokering the deal. "And we will have a success rather than a failure to explain. At my age, that means a good deal. As for Mary, well … when one rises to the point of running a company, one falls if the company does. It's like getting on in age; it's a process that cannot be stopped."

"A final question," Storrs said. "A statement, really. I understand that your grandson has been listed on the petition as a whistleblower with an unliquidated claim. That could be a non-dischargeable debt of unknown amount; dead weight to the company and of no interest to me. My plan, if there is one, will not provide for payment of whistleblower damages. I will rely on you two to arrange that. He's your problem, after all."

Arthur had Jimmy drive Storrs both ways—his Mercedes was far less conspicuous than Storrs's Bentley—but Arthur decided to stay at Winston's place to talk over what had transpired. Arthur put his hand on Winston's shoulder and said, "I think this just might work."

Winston frowned. "I'm okay with Storrs getting his grubby hands on Celldesign. That's not the part that bothers me. What I don't like is the way he's intentionally putting his boot on our throats about Spencer. We have to screw Spence in order to make the deal. That's hard to swallow. How would I live with that? How would you?" Winston's voice was incredulous.

Arthur considered the point. "He wanted to see if we have guts. Look at it this way: if the deal is made, you get a fee that will set you up again. Important. I get to stay on the Overseers. Important. Spencer loses out on a claim he never had a right to make, merely a windfall. Unimportant."

At that moment, the front door opened. It was Mandy, home a bit earlier than anticipated. Arthur felt trapped. Winston was obviously skittish about the part of the deal that would eliminate Spencer's whistleblower fee, and Arthur did not want to be in the middle of an argument, especially with the photos of Mandy with another man fresh in his mind. But he did not know how to escape.

Mandy walked over to Winston and gave him a peck on the cheek. She must have seen something in Winston's demeanor, because she simply stood there, looking at him.

Without saying a word, she demanded to know what had just happened.

Arthur stood, towering above her, and attempted to explain the terms of the proposed deal with Storrs. Mandy's face was impassive as she listened, turning from Arthur to Winston and back again.

When Arthur finished, Mandy looked directly at him. "So, the great man wants to take away Spencer's claim. The claim that Spencer suffered for, the claim that you, Arthur, denied and denied and have never acknowledged. You now want Spencer to bail you out so that you can continue to appear to be great. Is that about it?" Her voice dripped with sarcasm.

Arthur knew that was merely the beginning, so he held back. But in his mind, he was screaming *"Hypocrite!"* at her. (He had watched carefully when she came home and straightened her hair in front of the hallway mirror.) He gritted his teeth and remained quiet, staring at her intently.

"So," she said, "with all your influence and fame and money, you want your only grandson to bail out your ass. Right?" She turned ten degrees to her right. "And you, Winston. Tell me about what you said. Tell me how you stood up for your son."

Arthur watched the air go out of Winston's chest like a deflating beach ball. He thought for a moment that Winston would break down in tears, and it was clear that Mandy saw it too, because she relented, backing off her verbal attack. Her weight shifted to her right side; her right hand embedded in her auburn hair.

Arthur held back. *It's their fight,* he thought.

Winston said simply, "It's not that easy, Mandy."

"I think you should let *him*"—she pointed to Arthur—"do the dirty work. Don't be an enabler."

"Okay, fine. Let's say I do just that," Winston replied. "How on earth would that help Spencer?"

"At least you won't have blood on your hands," she shot back at him. "You want this deal to happen for your own selfish self—admit it."

"Of course I want the deal to happen. We'll get a big fee and save face. Money and honor. Without this deal, we have other decisions to make. Financially, we're at a crossroads. We put everything into Celldesign."

Mandy was calming down; her face relaxed a bit, and she dropped the edge from her voice. "It just feels wrong to have Spencer bail us out. It's supposed to be the other way around."

"But it's not," Winston said in a resigned voice.

"A part of me wants him to say no and keep the claim, and let all the chips fall where they may, and we'll be clean. Is there any other way for us to ever be clean?"

Winston did not respond. It always ended at that spot. Over and over again.

Arthur heard Jimmy honk the car outside. He had returned from dropping off Storrs; Arthur looked stoically at Mandy, and left.

As it happened, Spencer met with Alan Brown on the same topic—the whistleblower award—at the same time, right after Garrigall's articles on the Celldesign reorganization filing.

"I'll tell you what it means," Brown said in reply to Spencer's asking. "Nothing. That's what it means to you. Why, you ask? Because you will be paid first out of any proceeds. Whether reorganization or liquidation. And that's because you are a whistleblower, and the powers that be shine on you. Besides, we've got to be talking liquidation here. What's there to reorganize? Huh? A patch that doesn't work? I don't see it. So they'll wind up selling off what they've got in hand, which isn't much. This was really a dream machine, man. That's all it was. So, there'll be some proceeds, and you stand to get most of them—and I'm gonna get paid!"

Brown sat back in his chair and folded his arms across his chest.

"Sounds weird," Spencer said. "A couple of months ago, this was headed to be a big IPO, and now it's a zero?"

"That's investments, baby," Alan replied.

"Just because Olga threw out too much data?"

"Just because Olga defrauded everyone. That patch don't work, man."

"Maybe it does, at a certain level, but the level isn't high enough to be deemed effective by the state. Somebody will see that and fix it."

"Maybe, but we still get paid first."

"How much? Who decides?"

"The bankruptcy judge will hold a hearing; he'll decide. But these awards have a *purpose,* man. And the award has to be big enough for that purpose, which is to give dudes like you the courage to do what you did. So, I'm confident we're talking about a good deal of money, money, money."

Spencer seemed far away. "Accidental," he mumbled in a barely audible voice. "Accidental moral acts—ever hear of that? It's different than if you mean to do one. I don't think you're entitled to justify yourself in the same way."

Alan Brown turned his head at an angle, seeming not to have the foggiest idea of what Spencer was trying to say. Then he stood. "I have other clients."

And Spencer wandered out of his office.

CHAPTER 15

As Jimmy drove him back to Beacon Hill, Arthur was quiet, subdued. The afternoon had not gone well, he thought. Storrs put him off with all the questions. Not the number but the direction of them. He didn't sound committed; he didn't sound reliable—he sounded like a snake ready to strike. *And why should that surprise me,* Arthur wondered.

I am sinking, he thought, as a growing sense of impotence began to wash over him. And Mandy's disdain merely highlighted the growing disdain he felt for himself.

What had he gotten himself into?

Even if Storrs went along with the plan, what if he somehow got his hands on Dmitri's files? What if Dmitri tried to sell the files to Storrs? It could all backfire terribly.

Was there any chance that Storrs would protect him, if it came to that? None.

He was really out there, alone on an island of his own making.

He longed for someone to confide in, but he had already gone too far for that. There would be no avoiding the authorities. The story would come out; there would be a scandal. He absently brought his right hand up to his forehead and held it there.

They were all arrayed before him—Mandy, Mary, old Charlie, Storrs. All dangerous. Could they subpoena Rolls?

I'm in it up to my neck, he thought. He had become anxious— he needed to walk. But alone. He couldn't tell Jimmy, as he would want to tag along. Instead, he would wait until Jimmy drove away and then find a bench to sit on and calm himself down.

He was not sure exactly how he got there, but he found himself in front of a Starbucks with a long line, almost out the door. It was easier than walking, so Arthur joined them, feeling just in the right mood for a latte or perhaps one of the caramel coffees that he had always looked at but never ordered. As the line moved inexorably forward, it took him along. And soon he found himself looking at a young man about the age of his students, who wore a tag on his shirt that read *barista,* and who was impatiently asking for his order. He glanced quickly up at the menu of offerings printed on the back wall—so much information. The people behind him were becoming impatient. He froze, unable to decide, feeling the exasperation of the strangers around him.

"Nothing," he said. "Sorry." And he made his way back out to the street, leaving in his wake a soft but audible tittering about the confused old man.

Little do they know, he thought.

Turning to go back home, he went over the logic once more. He had always been a careful man. A judge and the creditors would never accept a reorganization that included Mary reemerging in control. That would go against common sense. And she would never accept anything less.

He could not be on her side. Mary had hired Olga, who had reported to her, and yet, somehow, Olga had managed to set up a fraud without Mary's knowledge—a cardinal sin in the world she had chosen.

By that time, he had walked down by the muddy and dark Charles River, and he stopped to watch the sculls as they glided over the water. He marveled at the youthful men on the oars. They brought Spencer to mind; he had been a member of crew at Tufts. He recalled watching the races when Tufts went against Harvard, and he felt nostalgic. A lump formed in his throat, but he quickly told himself, "Now is not the time to be sentimental." As he continued walking, he said out loud, but to no one in particular, "It's logical for us both to be replaced but on our own terms. In recognition." People walking by heard him but paid no attention.

"Recognition—silly word," he said out loud, shaking his head. "You must be able to stand the light that gets shined on you. He now had a secret, he no longer qualified for recognition—it had become too risky. No longer could he welcome the spotlight. It was all quite exhausting—he spotted a bench along the river, and sat. *What is the way out?* He asked himself.

Arthur felt like he had touched a tar baby. Like Br'er Rabbit. *How to get clear?* he asked. The answer was not to turn in the dossier—that would be insane. Could it be that the answer was just the opposite: more of the dossier, more intelligence, not less. Starting with Mary. What tactics would she deploy? How would she keep control of the company? What if he had something on her—like *they* had tried to get on him and everyone on his side?

Options are narrowing. Looking upon the Charles, his thoughts turned again to the Ukrainian cousins. Their email address was at his fingertips on the stolen phone. *Could they help? Just this one last time.* Then he would bury the phone and destroy the files on his computer with all the major objectives checked off—and he could re-examine things then, when the dust had settled. As part of a plan, his thoughts seemed cooler, less fevered, more reasonable.

He looked about himself; it would be a ten-minute walk back home. Hopefully, nobody would see him.

Once inside his apartment, he hurried to the library, so carefully fashioned to highlight his life story, but he was focused elsewhere. He sat at his desk, noting that Dorothy, thankfully, was out, and clicked on to Olga's files. He typed out a short note:

> I have Olga Numerovski's smartphone, which I intend to turn over to the authorities unless there is some information in your possession that might be worthy of a trade. Discretion required. You must respond without delay. This line of communication will not be open for long.

His computer flashed "message sent," but he only knew that what he typed had gone out to the shadowy figure he knew as Dmitri. He had to admit it would have been an unthinkable step just months earlier. The other end of the message he'd sent was a complete unknown, worse, actually—a dark space, a place he had been unfamiliar with and that threatened everything. That thought began to frightened him, to the point where he felt sweat on the back of his neck, his breathing shortened and his jaws tightened—who was he?

The electronic impulses from Arthur's computer traveled irrevocably to their destination, a laptop in a dingy, cramped room above a laundromat in Jamaica Plain, a small neighborhood on the outskirts of Boston, about as far from Beacon Hill as it was possible to get. The cousins, Dmitri and Alex, had been camped out there since the news hit that Olga was no more.

Arthur, a man who had communicated with cabinet members, had reached two unshaven illegal immigrants from Ukraine who conducted business as they did in Eastern Europe—with one eye always on the back door because that is where they came from in the middle of the night. But the choice was made; and Arthur was riding a wave of events outside his control.

"I knew it," Dmitri said upon reading the email.

Alex nodded.

Dmitri looked triumphant. "I knew someone would find us. I knew the information would be too valuable. I knew it." He shook his head and let out a sigh.

"So, how you respond?" Alex asked.

"Very professional," Dmitri replied, straightening himself up and pacing around the room. "First, to find out who is this and what is wanted."

They did not live in a nice, neat world, and in their world, information was king. They had expected to hear from Mary, "the boss," but this was not Mary. Wrong tone, wrong language.

Dmitri typed: "Identify, please," and pressed send.

Arthur saw the message and imagined the people behind it, the cousins on Olga's phone. He hesitated a moment; if he was ever going to get out of this situation, now was the time. But he typed a response: "Will remain anonymous."

Dmitri read the reply out loud. Alex had a blank look.

Dmitri handled such things. The moment called for caution but not to the point of losing the contact; they needed the work. He typed: "What is wanted?"

The ping of the computer, merely signaling an incoming message, nevertheless jolted Arthur, as if it were unexpected. He read and immediately replied again—there must be more information that is needed. "Confirm identity before we go further."

Dmitri replied immediately: "You say you have phone. Let us stop games."

There was a tone in Dmitri's message that suggested to Arthur that he comply.

He typed, "Interested possibly info on MK reorganization plan for Celldesign."

Dmitri's eyes widened. Who was he speaking to?

He typed: "You want intelligence report?"

Arthur felt a chill. He typed: "Perhaps. Cost, security, safeguards?"

Dmitri felt increasing confidence. "We are professionals. Cash only. Suggest listening device."

Arthur replied: "Need to isolate these communications. Cannot lead back."

Dmitri typed: "We feel same. Will create new file and encrypt. From now on new password needed. Gulagarchipelagousa. You write back, and we set up."

There! He had done it. He stood, thinking that it was a matter of self-defense. Yes, that was a legitimate rationale.

But the night wore on, and as he reexamined what he had done, Arthur became more agitated. It was a large risk, aimed merely at uncovering information about Mary's reorganization plan. He sat back; it seemed insane. Why was he, Arthur Lloyd, a great man, dealing with Ukrainian operatives? It was like being at a gaming table and betting one's entire life on red thirty and then watching the wheel spin around. It went against everything he had been or stood for. He headed for bed and determined that he would call it off in the morning. It was not rational. He would turn in the smartphone, the transcripts, everything and explain himself as simply confirming the role the Ukrainians had played under Mary's regime. It would be a huge risk, but he had to take it.

But morning came, and he never made the call.

It took two weeks, but "gulagarchipelagousa" finally contacted Arthur. An envelope with $50,000 in cash was required to be delivered to a middleman, the Ukrainian owner of a restaurant in downtown Boston that billed itself as Italian, on their promise that a transcript of a conversation held over Bluetooth in Mary's car with old Charlie Apple would then be sent electronically and that it contained potentially damaging information.

"Damn," Arthur said out loud upon reading the Ukrainians' email. Listening in on attorney-client conversations—a larger step than he had anticipated. Yet it was what he wanted. He should disclose and turn over the entire scheme to the authorities immediately. He knew that, but it is not what he did. Transfixed by the prospect of gaining a decisive advantage in the looming battle for Celldesign, he instead arranged to put together the cash (in a way that would not trigger banking regulations) and had Jimmy deliver the money downtown, as instructed.

Ping. Arthur scrambled to open Dmitri's attachment, skimming it first, then reading each word, filling in the inflections, the changes in tone, the intentions behind the words:

Mary was driving out to Wellesley. That was where Monroe Benjamin lived. She dialed up Apple on her voice-activated phone.

"Charlie," the transcript read, "I'm headed to Benjamin's house. I think I can lock up a commitment to recommend that we get the license, and Arthur does not."

"Arthur's not going to like that," Charlie responded, trailing off at the end of his thought.

"It's all passed him by. He can't run Celldesign; only I can! Frankly, I don't know why he doesn't just back off. I'd find some role for him; he should trust that. But that's not him, is it?"

"Listen, I've got to ask: what about you? Why don't you just walk away? You still have your good image. You're young. I'm sure you'd be in demand elsewhere. Doesn't have to be in Boston; could be in New York, San Francisco."

"There's something about Celldesign. Kind of like a first love. You've slept with him and cared for him, and you just can't let him go."

"I can't persuade you to just get out?"

"No, Charlie. Let's figure out how to stay in."

"Okay. Don't say I didn't warn you. Okay, as I've said, we've tracked down Patty in Phoenix. It's only a matter of time before someone else finds her. I'm pretty sure that Garrigall is working on it."

"Why do you say that?"

"You know how I've been massaging him like all get-out, trying to keep the narrative favorable, and I just know he's holding a card back; I feel it. If that happens, she'll say that Olga cleared her actions with you. And that will be a nightmare."

"But it's not true."

"Really? Didn't you check her computer one night just before Olga drank the antifreeze?"

"But it was—"

"Unclear, blah, blah, blah."

A pause. "Okay, you're the lawyer. What can I do?"

"Well, you could pay her a little money. Have her keep traveling until this thing blows over."

"How much would it take?"

"Start at a hundred. But if you get caught, it's bad news. Officially, I have to advise you that it would be wrong. Unofficially, I can have someone I trust make an inquiry."

"There is no alternative. Playing by the rules makes it come out all wrong, not really the way it was."

"What about Arthur?"

"Don't worry. I'll handle Arthur."

"That's a pretty glib assertion."

Mary paused, then said, "Yeah. Well, I know too much."

"Come on now. What's that mean?"

"It's all about Winston. You know, how Arthur funneled the money and used Winston as a figurehead. It was fraudulent. Not enough to stop Arthur but fraudulent, nonetheless. Technically. At least not squeaky clean, which is all that Monroe Benjamin understands. He'll hear about that and start going off about Arthur's fiduciary duty, and Lord knows where it will end, but it will be the end of Arthur."

Old Charlie blew out a chestful of air. "You willing to do that?"

There was some static, but then the transcript picked back up. Mary said, "Listen, Charlie, I'm freaking out about Olga's phone. You and I knew about it, and that's it. Nobody else. I'm sure it was in her desk drawer. I kept meaning to grab it and throw it in the harbor. Damn it to hell. Why didn't I?"

"It's got me concerned too. We probably should have turned it over to the police right after the … funeral."

"No way, Charlie. We'd have had to listen to it all. We couldn't have just turned it over and trusted that everything would be okay. That would have been stupid."

"The damn thing'll turn up at the wrong time and in the wrong hands; you can bet on it. Hope we don't go all this way and get tripped up by a fucking phone."

The transcript paused, noting more static.

"I've staked my argument for the license on my integrity, and Monroe is buying it—even though he looks down my blouse almost the whole time."

"Did ya put on a nice see-through bra for today? Might just help."

"Watch it, Charlie. I don't have a see-through sexy thing. You, of all people, should know that."

Laughter.

"Okay, I'm almost there. How are you doing with the interim financing?"

"I'll give the bank a call. It's still early out there, but I'm optimistic."

Just as I suspected, Arthur thought, with an odd and uncomfortable sense of satisfaction. He looked up from the screen and paused before pressing *print.* All he had to do was put a copy in the mail to Monroe Benjamin, who had spent his life on the straight and narrow.

But how could Arthur do that without exposing himself as the sender, with all that that would imply?

"Another problem every time I turn around," Arthur grumbled to himself. Pushing away from his desk, he hurried over to his gentleman's bar and reached for the scotch. "This must end," he said forcefully.

But before he went to bed that night, Arthur called Jimmy and ordered that his car be swept for bugs. Just in case. Jimmy assured him that there was "a guy" who owned a body shop and knew of such things.

Within an hour, the guy had found a listening device under the front seat, apparently an obvious place. "Whoever planted this," he told Jimmy, "didn't care if he got caught. A rogue. Not law enforcement."

As Jimmy duly reported these facts, Arthur made the obvious mental connections and thought, *why are the Ukrainians bugging me? Who's behind that?* But there was something else—a glint in Jimmy's eye, a slant to his brow, the eye of a coconspirator.

"We're all clean now," Arthur said to Jimmy. "Right?"

Jimmy nodded, silently, the kind of answer Arthur was beginning to understand.

CHAPTER 16

"I'm worried about your state of mind, dear," Dorothy said, her eyes peering at him over her reading glasses. "You seem to be withdrawing into yourself."

Arthur could not admit it, but he felt the same way. Everything in his mind seemed so shaded, nothing was clear. But he could not bring Dorothy into that world, so he dissembled. "Perhaps I have ... been a bit distant. But it shouldn't trouble you." He smiled wanly.

"Dear, anything that troubles you also troubles me. What is it?" Her eyes were clear and selfless, inviting him to speak.

He decided on the middle ground; he could safely (and honestly) discuss one thing. "Dear, I find that I must confront Mary today at the special board meeting they called to approve her bankruptcy plan, something I do not relish. I will be challenging her, and I will be outgunned. Old Charlie will be there, and he treats me like a ragamuffin. But I have to get my point across. I intend to file a competing plan."

"Can they stop you?"

"I suspect so. The company—that is, the board—has certain exclusive rights, and filing a reorganization plan is one of them."

"Is this the business you've been whispering about with Winston?"

In point of fact, Arthur had not been invited to the board meeting, nor was he on the agenda. Old Charlie had accorded him the "courtesy" to inform him that an executive decision had been made that he, as well as Winston, were deemed to be "in conflict of interest" and therefore disqualified.

"Nothing personal, old buddy," Charlie had said.

But Arthur had other thoughts. He decided almost immediately to attend the board meeting, regardless of old Charlie's feelings about the rules on conflict of interest. "Those rules don't apply to someone in my position," he said to Dorothy, who appeared sympathetic. Their little discussion helped them both.

Arthur had always been invited to board meetings, not because he was on the board (he wasn't; that was Winston's role) but because he represented the key interest, the license. The mere fact that Mary was proceeding without him said to Arthur that she had a certain confidence that he was no longer required for that purpose.

And that concerned him above all.

When Arthur walked into the board room of the building on 128 at the appointed time, he was carried along on a burst of adrenaline. As he stood erect, with his enormous height, his presence caused everyone to stop chatting. It was like something supernatural had occurred and demanded everyone's full attention. Arthur's voice, stern and stoic, filled the room. "I'm afraid I can't allow a meeting of this importance to take place outside the presence of the Lloyd family. Bad enough that you have precluded Winston from attending, but I am an ex-officio member of the board, and I will exercise those rights."

He proceeded to sit on an available chair and looked in

Mary's direction, but she had leaned over and was talking energetically in old Charlie's ear.

Old Charlie looked at Mary as if to say, *I'll handle it*, and then intoned, "Arthur, my friend, I'm afraid that's impossible. You're not a voting member of the board, and this is a very important technical requirement for taking the next steps necessary to salvage this company. You can't crash a board meeting as if it were a party."

Arthur looked at old Charlie. "I can, and I will. I intend to stay. I have a power of attorney from Winston, who would be here if he hadn't been improperly asked to step down—and everybody in this room knows it. The Lloyds' agreement to fund Celldesign when it first started specifically says that a Lloyd *will* be on the board and *will* have a vote on all important matters. Mary signed it! Would you like to see it?" Arthur held a document high above his head.

Old Charlie looked at Mary; his jaw slackened. All she could do was nod, eyes wide, her chin set hard.

Old Charlie said, "I need a moment with my client"; he indicated Mary.

Arthur was unrelenting. "We're all your clients, Charlie. Or else *you* have a conflict of interest. I suggest you proceed."

After taking a moment to collect himself, old Charlie did just that. There was soon a single issue for the group. Under ordinary bankruptcy procedure, Mary would have the exclusive right to present a reorganization plan. Multiple plans were allowed only if there were very specific reasons—mismanagement for one; opposition of the creditors for another.

When old Charlie mentioned mismanagement, Arthur shouted out, "Explain Olga!" And when Charlie mentioned the creditors, Arthur shouted, "I have the lead bank's proxy."

Charlie said, "What the hell do you want, Arthur? Do you intend to file a plan?"

Arthur cast his eyes slowly around the room. He calculated that he had many friends there, most of whom he himself had proposed for the board. "I want to reserve that right, sir."

The room was unsettled; nobody knew what to do.

Arthur then stood, put his hands on the table, and leaned forward. "I suggest we amend our papers to the court."

When he finished, Mary's look could have cut him in half. The vote was sharply divided between Lloyd loyalists and Knightbridge loyalists. In the end, Arthur held up Winston's proxy and voted it in favor of multiple plans. Old Charlie was as red as a beet and threatened litigation against everyone there who had gone against his advice (which was to vote for Mary's exclusive right to propose a plan). But that was what was done.

Arthur had achieved his objective. He would submit a competing reorganization plan to the court, where his plan and Mary's would go head-to-head. He left the room with a sure and confident step, feeling a vast satisfaction at having pulled off a victory. He felt that perhaps he had turned a corner.

The Celldesign bankruptcy case was filed in federal court in Boston and assigned to Judge Morris ("Mickey") Greenberg, a man in his mid-sixties. He was of medium height, medium weight, medium skin tone, and a moderate amount of balding. He wore a short-clipped beard, glasses, and the perpetual look of a cat who'd eaten the canary. Arthur had known him for years, well before the time that Mickey was appointed bankruptcy judge, back when he was a Boston attorney representing creditors. Arthur always felt that he and Mickey were kindred spirits when they shared a conference table or a dais, each a cut above the norm. But being a party to a lawsuit, especially a bankruptcy, in front of his old friend was something entirely new to Arthur.

The first step Judge Greenberg took sounded conventional enough. He scheduled a conference in open court to sound out the positions of the parties.

Arthur had been in the courthouse many times as an expert witness. The federal courthouse in Boston was as burnished and impressive as any courthouse anywhere—granite floors, mahogany millwork, chandeliers, fifteen-foot ceilings—most awe-inspiring. The idea, Arthur assumed, was to promote respect for the majesty of the law, and he thought it did just that.

Occupying the entire rectangular third floor of the building, the bankruptcy court was organized around four courtrooms, one in each corner, with a majestic staircase in the center. Judge Greenberg's courtroom and chambers were situated in the northeast corner, almost within sight of the west-facing window in Arthur's library. At nine o'clock sharp on that day, the court clerk called out from his corner desk, "All rise!" Everyone in the courtroom—all the parties, all the lawyers, all the staff, all the visitors—stood as Judge Greenberg entered from his chambers. Black robe flowing, he strode quickly toward the dais and his chair, an engaging smile upon his face, perhaps a trifle sardonic, waving his right hand in a downward motion, as if to say, "Sit, sit."

Arthur watched intently from the first row of pew-like seating behind counsel's table, which was occupied by Mary, old Charlie, and two other lawyers from Charlie's firm—the same two who were at the dinner. Arthur looked around and spotted Garrigall standing near the doorway, with his press badge prominently displayed.

Once seated at the dais several feet above floor level, Judge Greenberg scanned the courtroom, commented that the cost of all the lawyers before him would bankrupt anybody (which he had repeated hundreds of times), and then opened the file and scanned its contents.

Arthur listened absently as Mickey Greenberg gave a brief background on the nature of the case, but his mind was elsewhere—going over the past decade, visualizing the rise and the fall of Celldesign—and he began to feel anxious. He noticed it first as his hands began to sweat.

He heard Judge Greenberg say, "I called this conference to get a feel for this case, so I'd like to hear first from the main parties, the debtor and claimants. First of all, I see that there will be at least two plans filed, and that the debtor, Celldesign, has renounced the exclusive right to file a plan that is provided in the statute. Very unusual. I'd like some light shed on this, Miss Knightbridge. Is this true? Please confirm it for the record." With the light upon him from several enormous chandeliers overhead, and his chair on the dais at least seven feet above the counsels' chairs below, Judge Greenberg had changed the more relaxed atmosphere he'd initially brought into the courtroom in an instant by the tone of his voice, which, because of the height of his dais and the acoustics of the massive courtroom, seemed to echo in a weighty way.

Arthur looked over at Mary, unsure if she would be able to affirm what had happened at the board meeting. He knew it was anathema to her, as caustic as the liquid Olga had forced down.

She stood, however, and said, "Yes, Your Honor, it is true. On behalf of the Celldesign board, I renounce the exclusive right. But I add that I am also confident that I will file the better plan, and this will be a minor sidebar."

There was a murmur throughout the courtroom, as her

statement was a rarity. Underlying tension was out in the open, all within the first five minutes. What was behind it?

Arthur, of course, knew what was behind it. He also knew what Mary's plan was, and he scanned the courtroom until his eyes lit upon his old friend, Monroe Benjamin. Their eyes crossed for a moment, and an awkward smile was exchanged. Arthur again felt his hands moisten with anxiety and wondered if anyone could tell. His stomach was in knots, and a picture of Olga—oddly, he thought—crossed his imagination. It was her darkness that transfixed him.

Even if I win, I lose, he thought.

Arthur saw old Charlie stand to address the court, although he was unsure exactly why. He assumed it probably was something having to do with the exclusive-right business.

Then Arthur watched with some interest as Judge Greenberg cut him off. "Mr. Apple, I've read about your exploits in the press, and I'm duly impressed. But I want to tell you that having two competing plans out there could be a problem for your client. I'm guessing that she will want to stay in the driver's seat, but her record isn't so great. People, including me, will ask why she should have two bites at the apple. No pun intended. It could get very personal on you if you don't watch out."

Arthur swallowed hard as he saw old Charlie sit down. *How easily Mickey handled him.* He looked around, and saw Mary intently whispering in Charlie's ear.

Mickey Greenberg was not finished. Singling out Arthur's lawyer, he said, "Mr. Gordon, I have known you for many years—very competent in business matters—but what about these blatant conflicts of interest involving your client? Did you advise him that he could be both an Overseer and an investor? I cannot believe you would do that. You know fiduciary law as well as anyone. What gives? When we gather here again, I'd like to have a full disclosure of all his financial interconnections."

Arthur's voice went off in his head like a cannon. *What?* It would be tantamount to an investigation targeted against him. *Intolerable.* He would not stand for it!

He happened to glance over. Mary was stealing a look at him, and she seemed to be smirking. Had he seen that look before? Yes—in the dossier photo, the conspiratorial pose, the one with old Charlie, the two of them looking down upon him. He felt overly warm—he wondered if he were sweating through his shirt. *I must maintain my composure, my appearance of strength*, he thought.

Alan Brown thought it was the moment right for some reason and stepped forward. "Judge, we have a valid claim, and we merely want our day in court. Our request is quite simple and should be handled right away."

Judge Greenberg looked at him. "Yes, yes, I understand your claim. I have to say, however, that it looks like your young man just fired off a missile one day that had quite a series of unintended consequences. The law says that I must reward people who bring truth to light, and I am but a servant of the law. So, you will have your day in court, but we all know that a whistleblower trial will cause delay and press coverage that may effectively end any opportunity to reorganize. Have you discussed that with your client?"

Arthur's body temperature was going down, and he felt the perspiration drying on his skin as he looked at Spencer, who was sitting next to Alan Brown, who, in turn, was stammering, obviously having no retort to Judge Greenberg. Arthur's attention, though, was focused on his grandson. He was sitting with good posture, dignified almost. It was the first time in

weeks that he had given Spencer any thought, ever since the
state lab had basically concurred with his email.

Then, inexplicably, given the way the conference was
going, the lawyer for the consortium of banks stood to speak.
Tall and smooth, he had an old Boston accent that he studiously
maintained and brought out for use whenever he was in court
but rarely otherwise. "If it please the court," he said, "my clients
are in quite a different position. We simply loaned money to
the debtor in good faith, with the usual covenants, and those
covenants have clearly been broken. We are entitled to be
repaid. What could be more reasonable?" After a studied pause,
he glanced at Rodney and continued. "Having said that, we
all feel that a change in personnel would be … helpful. If the
business is to reorganize, it is fundamental that the sacrifice
must be shared, including management."

Precisely what Arthur wanted to be said in open court. He
clenched his right fist, which he held in his lap.

Judge Greenberg, however, retorted: "My dear sir,
underneath your bravado, you really don't have much in the
way of collateral, do you? A few accounts payable, some desks
and the like. But the biggie—the license—is revocable at any
time, regardless of its impact on you. If we sell the pieces here,
without the license, what will you have? I can answer that for
you—a substantial loss that your clients will have to report."

Judge Greenberg, who had been leaning forward in his
chair (somewhat aggressively, Arthur thought), sat back and
said to the entire assembled group, "I have a few thoughts.
There is a clear public interest here. This technology should be
given every opportunity to prove itself safe and effective. That
argues in favor of a reorganization. By the same token, the fox
seems to be in the vicinity of the henhouse, and that troubles
me. I want to know what will happen to the license. Who, if

anyone, will get it, and who will provide interim financing to pay for it? Also, gentlemen—and ladies—try to address some of the concerns I raised here today when we meet again in two weeks. At that time, I expect progress. You must try to take in the true perspective of things. This little patch could actually help people. Let's hope so. Hopefully, you all can come together. You are certainly familiar enough with each other. If not, well, it is an odd battle that I foresee and not a happy one."

The hearing had lasted less than an hour, but it seemed to Arthur like weeks. He saw the parties half listen to Mickey Greenberg but focus almost entirely on their own goals. It was quite disconcerting—the Lloyds left not as a family but as strangers, and Arthur and Mary left not as mentor/protegee but as adversaries.

As he was leaving the courtroom, Arthur spotted the small and wiry Ronald Storrs, impeccable in a top-of-the-line handmade suit, standing alone in the back, even though it had been agreed that Storrs would stay away so as to avoid tipping their hand. But it was too late. Arthur also saw Garrigall, standing in the rear and only a few feet away from Storrs, barely suppressing a smile. Arthur knew how much Garrigall envied the stars of the business world, and Storrs certainly qualified. Not only was Garrigall in the presence of a man like Storrs, but Arthur surmised he had deduced the essence of Arthur's reorganization plan at the same time. What else was Ronald Storrs there for? Garrigall would be able to put that together, and Arthur was sure that it would be all over the papers in a day or two. *An excellent stop on his journey to a Pulitzer*, Arthur thought as he joined the crush of people looking for an elevator down.

CHAPTER 17

A rthur opened the business section the following day and saw what he expected. The headline read: "Founders in Conflict," and the article reported not only that Mary agreed at the board meeting to renounce her exclusive right to file a plan but also that there were indications of "bad blood" between her and Arthur that only could have been picked up by someone who was there.

He gets closer to that Pulitzer every day, Arthur thought. He smiled ruefully as he recalled the reporter whom he had called a little man.

Arthur sat still and took a breath. It was no use demeaning Garrigall. He was doing what his nature and his employment commanded. It seems that Arthur had become more tolerant recently—since he picked up the phone and put it in his pocket.

Whenever he thought about the phone, he became anxious, constantly worried about being "found out." His conduct would be unforgivable to a straight arrow like Mickey Greenberg, no matter how Arthur explained it away. *Luckily*, he thought, *it's still my secret alone—mine and Jimmy's. And Rolls's.*

He put his weary head in his hands, raising his eyes just a bit to look into Dorothy's eyes. *She knows something is going on, but she thinks it's just normal business,* he thought. *She would be stunned to know the full extent of where I am.* He turned back to Garrigall's piece, his eye going to the final paragraph:

> The well-known head of several vulture funds, Ronald Storrs, was noted in the rear of the courtroom. It is unlikely that he was a casual observer. But he escaped out the courthouse door before taking any questions that might explain his presence.

By breaking his agreement to stay unidentified as long as possible, Storrs had just declared to the world that he was Mary's true adversary. Plenty of time for old Charlie to dig up something on Storrs, in order to argue that Storrs would be the wrong choice to run the former Celldesign when it emerged from bankruptcy protection. And Arthur knew that there was ammunition to be found; it would be difficult to square Celldesign's self-described purpose of changing the world with the past business practices of a vulture like Storrs. It was a weak point in his plan.

But of greater importance to Arthur was the simple fact that Storrs had ignored their understanding and—worse—that he neither cleared it ahead of time nor explained it afterward. "Has the vulture we brought in turned against us?" Arthur asked himself.

And the unexpressed point lurking just under the surface: how could anyone put any faith in an acknowledged vulture?

It was a tired and humbled Arthur Lloyd that processed that information, a man who feared rather than welcomed the searching eye of a judge, and so he refolded the newspaper and handed it back to Dorothy, who looked at him with sad eyes that he thought he had seen before.

"I think you came out pretty unscathed," Alan said to Spencer as they reviewed what had happened in court, "but he sure was on a tirade."

Spencer nodded. It had been his first time in court. "Nobody is unscathed. All that happened was I lost a little leverage in the game we're playing to get you paid. Maybe now they'll try to buy out my claim, whoever 'they' are."

"Today foreshadowed what's coming down the pike. And I can't figure out what they think they're fighting for."

"It's a bet on the patch being correctable. If they can do that—improve the technology—the stats will follow, and they will all be staring at the original dream—the IPO."

"Hey, man, your grandfather has more money than he could ever spend. How does an IPO motivate the man who already has money?"

"Unanswered question. There is something deep that drives him. Look, this is the only way I can meet my promise to you, that you would get paid if you helped me out. Otherwise, I'd have folded. I'd have withdrawn my claim long ago. And maybe a lot of shit would not have happened. But why my grandfather is doing this—just don't know."

Spencer turned on his side to face Pamela. They had kissed, and she was running her hand softly up and down his arm, and they were both fully content. The sheets felt warm and slightly moist, the light in the room was low, the window was closed to the cold night air that foretold New England winter, and he was with her again. It was his favorite thing in the world.

"It's just too brutal," he said softly.

She turned toward him, eyes searching, waiting.

"It really is brutal," he repeated, even though he knew that talking about Celldesign was not her favorite thing. "I still think that my email started it, you know, the whole process, but I also see that it really had no beginning in terms of a single act you can point to. Not if you're honest about it. Plus, I turned out to be right. So, the guilt level has gone down a little, although it's still heartbreaking to see Dad—and even Grandpa. What I missed until we were in court was the brutality. I didn't realize how brutal the process would be. There is something lost every day out there."

"What do you mean?" she asked.

"The questions in life seem to change. And the consequences of failing on any given day can be that everything is gone. I wouldn't do it again—join Celldesign."

"But then you wouldn't have met me."

He kissed her. "That's true, isn't it."

"Maybe Storrs will put it all back together again. He's supposed to be good at that."

"Does it take a snake?"

"Well, your grandfather is not a snake, right? Or your father."

"True, but they're getting destroyed. Storrs the snake will get the prize—the IPO—if this thing continues as it is. And that would be totally weird."

"Maybe Judge Mickey can keep that from happening. Isn't that what a judge is for?"

"He raked me up and down."

"Not really," Pamela said, pulling the sheets up to cover herself as she sat upright. "So, what are you trying to say?"

"Well, that courtroom is supposed to be the place of truth, right. And the truth will set you free. Somebody said that. But that's not what I'm seeing." He paused to look at her. "Everybody's got an angle. If you wind up in court, that's what it's all about. Everybody has an angle." He noticed that Pamela was looking at him quizzically. "Oh, I get it, if you don't have courts, how do issues get resolved? By brute power? But I have to say, I'm not all that enthralled with what I see. Not sure I want to spend my life in this environment."

"What are you considering?" Pamela asked, lowering her eyes.

"I don't want anything to do with business or technology. I think I'd like to reschool myself. Maybe somewhere out West— not Stanford, too competitive; not Berkeley, too political; maybe some community college."

"Do they even give master's degrees?" Pamela asked quietly, intently, her lips betraying a pout.

But Spencer did not pick up on her cues. "Well, then, how about Chicago? Maybe I can get into Chicago and become a philosopher." He looked over at her and smiled his killer smile. He had not realized or understood the quiet way in which he had just bypassed the dreams of the beautiful, precious, willowy girl lying beside him, cradling his head on her breast.

When Pamela was not around, it was a dark time for Spencer. He was running almost all day long, taking off down Allston Street or up Commonwealth Avenue, extending his route to three miles, then five, then eight, one foot in front of the other, breathing deeply. He barely looked at his surroundings; rather, he looked inside—looking for the rush, the endorphins that he could almost recognize in his blood chemistry as it changed, and he got a kind of high. Without those endorphin escapes, who knows what he would have done?

The endorphin highs allowed him to hide the disillusionment lows, but he was still caught in the grinding wheels of Celldesign, and it was no place for a young man to be.

He had to reach out—and Mandy answered the phone. He asked if she would like to have lunch and catch up.

They met at a little Greek place down the street from his apartment. She swore that she had some Greek blood but had no proof, and it had become a family joke. It was nice to see her, just simply to see her—the familiar smile, a mother's kiss, which would leave a lipstick trace on his cheek that she would carefully rub off with her index finger as she sat, all in one movement. Spencer felt a sense of stability in that. She had done the same thing for many years, looked at him in the same, nurturing way.

He had not seen the dossier, as Arthur had. Instead, Spencer saw the same steadfast smile as always, as they picked at classic Greek salads—tomatoes, onion, feta, black olives, olive oil.

"How is Dad?" he asked. At the time, it was an immense question, not the mere table chatter that such a question would ordinarily constitute.

Mandy tried to evade the issue. "Let's not get on to your father. He's a grown man, and he'll survive. It's just that he's sensitive. I don't know. He sees a conflict in everything. It's all enemies, in every corner. I'm sure you know how much he wants to stick something in Grandpa's face, no matter how much he denies it." She seemed distracted as she spoke, as if different images were called up. "What about you?" she asked abruptly. "Everybody seems to think that you're going to come into some serious money from your claim. Looks like you're a hero."

Spencer ignored her comment. "I'm not really privy to what's going on, but from what I can see, there's a clash between Grandpa and Mary. Who'd have thought that? As for me, I had an accidental role, nothing more. What I do with my claim, such as it is, depends on who prevails with Celldesign. If Dad and Grandfather prevail, I'm going to take only what I need to pay Alan Brown. I don't want anything more. But if Mary prevails, then … I don't know. Haven't decided."

Mandy feigned indignation. "Why, you deserve every penny! What you went through! And as for your grandfather, he doesn't deserve any help whatsoever—from anybody. He didn't help you, now did he? I'll never forget getting down on my knees for some money so you could have a lawyer, and he said no. I swear I'll never forgive him!"

"You have to forgive him, Mom. He's family."

Spencer saw the truth, or so he thought, in his mother's nervous actions, bringing her hand to her head and running it through her hair, not softly but grasping at the end to squeeze her brown, freshly washed curls in a tight grip that buried her garish red fingernails: Winston was spending most of his days camped out in his library at home, drinking more and more heavily. It was how he had always coped: he retreated. Spencer had seen glimpses of that as he grew up. Winston would wear his heart on his sleeve; when business was bad (especially when he had to go to Arthur for more money), he would retreat into a shell of sorts, staring at the television for hours on end, drink in hand, until he had consumed enough to sleep the night through.

That picture of his father was an important factor for Spencer and accounted for his choice of athletics over scotch. He and his father both gravitated to aloneness—Winston drank alone; Spencer ran alone.

In Spencer's mind, it was Arthur's shadow that wore out Winston. Business after business seemed to fall short of his father's expectations. And the role of Celldesign, in part, was to provide for Winston's deliverance. Arthur had been quite clear on that point, and Winston was not blind. He must have seen—and felt—it as well.

But that was old hat. Spencer sensed something different as well. It was there in his mother's reticence, the way she looked away when the subject came up. His father blamed him, had held on to that feeling, and was unable to let it go. And that was eating Winston up. In spite of the fact that he had been proven right, Winston still blamed him—it was an inescapable fact that his email was the starting point for the downfall, the trigger for everything else. But it seemed like an emotional position, something that Winston should be able to work through. But it was taking longer than Spencer would have expected.

If he had known at the time of the demand, jointly made by Arthur and Storrs, that Spencer's whistleblower claim must "go away," and the fact that they expected Winston to be the agent who would make that happen, it would have answered his question.

CHAPTER 18

Arthur hurried up the street among the skyscrapers that had come to identify Boston—the new Boston, not the old one that he was used to. He was searching for the Starbucks where Storrs had set up their meeting. The street seemed busier than usual, more confusing.

Finally, he saw the sign out front, and as he stepped into Starbucks, he immediately saw Storrs at one of the café-style tables near the coffee bar, reading the *Wall Street Journal*. They exchanged pleasantries and immediately moved to the business at hand.

"Arthur," Storrs said, "I have a simple question: why should I continue to deal with you? Why shouldn't I just go after Celldesign without you? There's going to be a crash landing here, and the bankruptcy court will be perfectly happy to deal with me directly. You seem to be little more than an expensive security blanket, and, frankly, I don't need any complications. I mean, Winston wants a fee, Spencer wants a fee—the Lloyds are an expensive group."

Arthur saw nothing in his eyes, just a vast blankness. There was no emotion there, no recognition of right or wrong, no humor, just the business variables, just the balance sheet, just the numbers.

"Look, Ronald," he said, "your reputation precedes you. You've done these turnarounds, and you've obviously been very successful. But you can't do it alone. I will provide credibility; after all, I was the founder. I have the connections. I am essential. It's not going to happen with Mary; she bears too much responsibility for the data fiasco. No investor would go along for a second test drive."

Arthur watched Storrs's eyes, ceaselessly seeking out weakness.

"Okay," Storrs said, "Credibility. I usually find credibility in the balance sheet. So, same question: Why are you or any of the Lloyds necessary?"

Storrs's glare sent a chill down Arthur's spine.

Arthur looked at his watch. It was time to play the game to win, or walk away.

"One reason, my friend," Arthur said, trying to gain a superior position, "is that I could kill the license for you. Then you would have nothing."

Storrs retorted, "From what I hear, I doubt that you have that power anymore."

"What are you willing to bet on that? The Overseers have been my friends for decades. Unless someone vouches for you, you are simply not the type for them. No offense. But I am."

Storrs just stared.

Arthur finished his thought, essentially proposing a compromise, a settlement. "If we get rid of the whistleblower money, you should be quite content. And if you double cross me, I will leave no stone unturned."

Storrs stayed for a few minutes of small talk and then

left, disappearing into the street crowd, nothing agreed upon, nothing resolved.

Arthur stayed inside for a few minutes. The leftover adrenaline from his meeting with Storrs brought to mind the pictures of Monroe Benjamin leaving Mary's condo. Was Storrs suggesting that Mary had seized the license from under his nose? Was it already gone, no longer amounting to leverage against Storrs? And it was unmistakably clear that without leverage, Storrs would discard him with no more than a wave goodbye. After all he had done in life, after all the accolades, all the friendships, he would not be tossed aside like a piece of garbage!

He perspired; there was a sense of desperation. Where to turn? Nobody was left to speak with, no neutral corner for advice. He took a breath and did what he always did; he assessed the situation. True, he knew Benjamin better, well enough to be certain that any suggestion of scandal or ethical issues would turn the entire Board of Overseers against Mary—and that was what the dossier and especially the information from Dmitri would supply—but should he use that information? He knew it would be a huge step, a crossing of a line he had always respected above all else.

He was face-to-face with himself, his actual psychological needs, and not merely with an image that he had created. "I will not be treated this way," he mumbled as he reached for his phone and called Jimmy for a ride home.

Arthur focused on using the leverage he did have; he would use all of it. He would protect himself, but he would every tool at his disposal. That was the nature of the game. *In for a penny, in for a pound.*

That is when Arthur thought of Garrigall.

As soon as he reached Beacon Hill, Arthur took up his phone. His leverage was that Garrigall undoubtedly was still motivated by his dream of a Pulitzer. In Arthur's calculation, that should mean that Pat Garrigall might be more than normally willing to stretch journalistic ethics, if it meant juicing up the story.

Everyone has a price, he thought.

"Hello," Garrigall said cautiously, obviously having seen Arthur's name on caller identification.

"Arthur Lloyd here," he said gruffly. "We should meet."

Garrigall pressed, but Arthur would not discuss anything on the phone. Who knew what phones had been tapped these days? They agreed to meet at the same Starbucks where Arthur had met with Storrs.

Arthur greeted Garrigall, who had arrived first. Arthur held a briefcase in his left hand, offering to shake hands with his right, and as their hands were clasped and before any introductions or other pleasantries, Arthur said, "You must expressly agree upon your soul that whatever we do and say today is totally confidential, that it will never, under any circumstances, be divulged, and that I will remain anonymous, now and forever."

Garrigall mumbled, "Amen," but quickly agreed.

Arthur looked around to make sure nobody that he knew had happened to walk in. Then placed his briefcase on his lap and opened it, taking out Olga's smartphone and placing it on the café table.

Garrigall looked down at the phone, then up at Arthur, as if to ask, *What's this?*

Arthur looked him in the eye and said, "Olga Numerovski's."

Garrigall's eyes fell again to the phone. Arthur could almost see the calculations in his mind. "How?" was all Garrigall could manage.

"Not at liberty," Arthur said as he put the phone back in his briefcase. "And not relevant to our discussion. But there is important information on here. I obtained the password and had all the files transferred to my own computer." He described the hiring of the Ukrainian cousins, the photos, the email correspondence with Patty, and the transcript of Mary and Apple speaking over the bugged phone.

"But that was *after* Olga killed herself," Garrigall exclaimed.

Arthur nodded and shrugged his shoulders. "I tell you this only to vouch for my credibility. I will give you access to what I have, except for the photos. They are just pure dirt, unnecessary, beneath us both. You will be free to write what you will, but on one condition—you do not coordinate this beforehand, in any way, with Mary."

Garrigall was wide-eyed. "That would violate all journalistic ethics. It would be a hit job."

Arthur narrowed his eyes and asked firmly, "What is the absolute minimum that you would have to do?"

Garrigall paused, shaking his head as if in horror at his own conduct. "I'd have to call her, tell her what I propose to say, and ask if she has any comment. And if she does, I'd print it too."

And thus, it was agreed.

Arthur took Garrigall back to his condo, offered his desk, and allowed Garrigall three hours to review Olga's files, except the photos. At all times, however, he kept his computer in his sight. At the end of the time, Garrigall walked over to the large leather chair in which Arthur had sat for the entire three hours without moving.

Arthur looked at Garrigall grimly. "When?" he asked.

"Day after tomorrow," Garrigall said, hurrying out.

The headline was brutal, and Arthur read it with ambivalence: "Celldesign's Underbelly." The article stated that "sources" had given the *Globe* unprecedented access to computer files that disclosed a culture of spying and buying access to the state and knowingly misstating data results.

Garrigall kept his promise and noted in the article, "Ms. Knightbridge was called for comment but referred the matter to counsel."

The next sentences read,

> Charles Apple, attorney for Celldesign, called it a "hit job, unworthy of any person on the planet, an irredeemable act." The materials appear to show a conspiracy between Ms. Knightbridge and Mr. Apple to obstruct justice.

Garrigall paraphrased the conversation between the two but neglected to say that it had been illegally taped.

As he read, Arthur searched his conscience. He had achieved what he set out to do: he had pushed back in a hard, ruthless, powerful way. He had protected himself. Within the circumference of Celldesign. And he would leave the moralizing for another day. But although his tracks had been concealed, he still had to live with himself.

There was a knot in his throat as he looked up from the paper. Dorothy seemed to have a sense for these moments, and he saw her looking at him. He felt it; she knew. Not all of it, obviously, but enough. He felt like screaming, "I did what I had to," but that would leave too much to explain, to the point where she might become a co-conspirator, so he crashed his fist down on the table, stood, and walked purposefully to the library, where he could be alone.

The same mindset accompanied Arthur as he walked into Mickey Greenberg's courtroom. Over the past few days, he had intended to meet again with Storrs but never made it happen. "What will be, will be," he said with an uncharacteristic weariness. Whenever he tried to think it all through, the process inevitably ended with too much scotch. And too little clarity.

When the day of the hearing dawned, Arthur found himself lethargic. He would have preferred to stay home. It was a gray, cold day, and everyone wore an overcoat, which made everyone look the same, at least from the rear—tan or charcoal, buttoned to the top, collar up, same height, same girth. The parties and lawyers assembled, but there was little communication among them. Positions had been taken, and suspicions were rampant; everyone had dug in. Mary ignored Arthur, and vice versa. Winston was there, sweating bullets in spite of the weather. He sat next to Storrs, who was smiling his way through the ordeal, looking very much like he enjoyed the spectacle. Spencer and Alan were off to the side, waiting to see what would happen.

He watched Spencer carefully. He could almost hear Mandy rebuking him again. *Perhaps she was right*, he thought. *Perhaps Spencer is the only hero of this long saga.* He smiled as he noticed that the young man wore boat shoes with no socks, even to such a weighty and formal gathering. It brought to mind the night of his party; no socks there, either. And perhaps he had the best of it that night after all; he belonged and he went, invitation or not. "He has not compromised himself," Arthur whispered, so low that no-one could hear.

At nine o'clock sharp, the clerk stood and pronounced, "All rise!" Judge Greenberg came out, pushing his hands in a downward motion as usual, urging everyone to sit, but on that day, he did not wear his customary smile of goodwill; rather, he seemed more serious than usual.

After the clerk had read the case caption into the record, Judge Greenberg began. "I've received a flurry of correspondence over the past few days from counsel for almost all of the parties, revising and restating their respective positions. I must say that I've been around for too long to be surprised when cases like this sink into the mire, but it is always disappointing. Let me summarize for the record what seems to have happened. Someone threw the former CEO under the bus and covered her with mud, to an extent that she might not recover, by using information that, as Mr. Apple pointed out, could only have been gotten illegally. I am persuaded that is true, but what can I do about it? The bell has been rung, and I cannot un-ring it.

"Was her tenure at Celldesign admirable? Perhaps not, but in this country, how evidence is obtained is important. If it weren't for the First Amendment, I would frankly put Mr. Garrigall under oath and find out who planted that story and see to it that charges were brought against all who participated. But again, I cannot do that.

"Although your privacy appears to have been violated by someone, Ms. Knightbridge, I cannot ignore the facts that have come out. This is not a case where the police invaded your privacy; it likely was someone you know. I have looked at what the surveillance of you shows, and the picture is very bad, possibly amounting to fraud under the securities laws. I am going to admonish you not to speak today because your rights against self-incrimination may very well be involved.

"And Mr. Apple, you were caught up in the same surveillance, and the materials before me show blatant disregard of several standing orders of this court regarding disclosure of evidence. I am therefore revoking the permission you were given to practice before me, pending a hearing."

Judge Greenberg paused, clearly troubled by what he had said to that point. The audience seemed frightened by where the case seemed to be going, and it had just begun.

"Mr. Storrs has submitted a detailed plan. Mr. Storrs is a highly experienced, well-known turn-around specialist, who offers very little for the assets—well below appraised value—and even refuses to pay any judgment on the whistleblower claim, making payment by others a condition of his going forward. Very aggressive! I don't know why that keeps surprising me as these Chapter 11 cases line up before me. Reorganization, getting a second chance is a bold person's game, isn't it?

"I don't know if Mr. Winston Lloyd is aware of the final terms of Mr. Storrs's proposal, which includes an unusually small, almost nonexistent finder's fee of a few hundred dollars, since the letter was sent privately, directly to my chambers." Judge Greenberg looked around the courtroom until he saw Winston, who had turned as white as ashes and was looking at Storrs, who walked out from the row of seats, winding up standing next to his bodyguard.

"I will not rule on that today, but I caution everyone here that my job has to do with equity, fairness, and justice, and from what I am seeing, nobody else seems to be concerned about that. Now, Mr. Arthur Lloyd is a cofounder of this very promising and hopeful venture. My hat is off to him. And he has thrown his weight behind the Storrs proposal. I am not sure why. But there is a letter signed by Ms. Knightbridge that makes some disturbing allegations, having to do with Ms. Numerovski's personal files. So, the cofounders are really destroying each other at this point, in some kind of effort to have the last word. I often wonder how this point ever gets reached.

"But Mr. Lloyd correctly states one thing: all that we have talked about is quite overshadowed by the license. We all know that by definition, a license is revocable at will. And it seems to me that we have not heard from the Overseers. Do they support a plan? No plan? Do they have their own plan? At the end of the day, the Overseers must say what they are going to do. They hold the trump card. Can you provide that guidance, Mr. Benjamin?"

Arthur looked over to his friend and colleague. Monroe stood ramrod straight and addressed the court. "Your Honor, we have met and discussed this extensively, and we have met with the parties. We have read the press reports and tried to educate ourselves and do our due diligence, and we have concluded that technology is progressing at a greater speed than man. What causes the worst to come out? I stand here, troubled and confused. We have offered a great tool that has great promise, but the guiding hand is human, and there is no alternative to that. It is sad, but a great tool like this CRISPR technology is subject to the human hand. Where are the great men and women who are needed to guide this? Thus, we must advise the court that we revoke the license so that it will not be available to either plan."

The entire courtroom made a sound, a kind of gasp but not that, not really. It was the sound of a missed opportunity. Mary and Storrs cast their eyes about, each seemingly in shock. Winston looked ready to tackle someone. Garrigall stood with his mouth open, but quickly recovered and began jotting down notes.

But Arthur reacted differently, having concluded days earlier that they had all destroyed themselves.

And at that moment, Alan Brown stood up. "Your Honor," he said, "we think that our whistleblower claim should have a priority and be paid out of the first assets that are sold."

Judge Greenberg said in a resigned tone, "I understand you want to be paid, Mr. Brown, and we will take up your client's claim as soon as it is reasonable to do so. First, you will have to prove that your client is a whistleblower at all, and then you have to prove that he has been damaged and in what amount. There is a long way to go, sir. However, I will say that, assuming the foregoing, I intend to give your claim priority over the banks' claims. Perhaps you might consider settlement?"

Rodney Quinn fell backward into his pew, jaw slack, crushed. Arthur knew that he stood to be replaced at the bank.

Outside, the November rains had begun in earnest, taking down the last of the autumn leaves from the oaks along Commonwealth Avenue, chasing the rowing crews off the Charles, and capturing the reflection of headlights as cars arrived to pick up the lawyers who had grimly emptied out of the courtroom.

CHAPTER 19

Arthur seemed impassive, as though he had absorbed it all before it even happened. He simply walked out of the courthouse and kept on walking, not looking back, not seeing Spencer watching him, just walking away as if he had another meeting. He reached the parking lot where he had left his car, having given Jimmy the day off, and headed for 128. He knew who else would be there.

He drove through the main entrance and parked in front of the building that had formerly housed Celldesign. The lease had been canceled when the bankruptcy was filed, so the fourth floor was dark. But he noticed a solitary figure highlighted in a window.

He still had his security pass, and for the first time, he showed it willingly to the security officer and then made his way up the elevator. Stepping off, he saw Mary walking numbly around the empty cubicles. The electricity had been turned off for nonpayment, so the only light came through the few windows on the perimeter.

Mary did not appear to have noticed him, so Arthur said, "That didn't go very well, now, did it?"

She turned to see him, all six feet five inches, a father

figure, the man most influential in her life. "You knifed me, didn't you?"

Arthur looked up at the ceiling and replied, "Only at the end. Otherwise, I gave you your career. How that weighs out, I don't know."

"Why didn't you just let go?"

"I'm not really sure. I just couldn't. It would have been like dying, which I wasn't ready for quite then."

A chair and desk had been moved into the hallway in which they were standing, so Arthur sat down. He felt and looked weary.

"I'm sorry," Arthur said. "There was just something in me that took over. I guess that's it. Mickey was pretty rough on both of us, wasn't he?"

"He was. But I still have to wonder how these men in black robes get to speak to us like that—at least without knowing what we tried to do. They only see the results, and they base everything on that. It's kind of brutal." She paused, appearing to have lost her train of thought. "What's going to happen to Celldesign now?"

"It's too promising to just die."

"Storrs would have ruined it."

"I see that—now. But *now* is too late."

She then walked over and pulled another chair from an empty office. "I tried with all my might," she announced. "I really did. It was all Celldesign—and an empty apartment."

"It takes more than furniture," said Arthur. "But I understand your point."

"What happens now?" Mary asked.

"Garrigall will get nominated for a Pulitzer, satisfying both his vanity and his greed. And someone else will get the license."

"Someone else," Mary repeated thoughtfully. "Quite so. But Celldesign will never again be loved the way I loved it." Arthur nodded in agreement.

The call from Monroe Benjamin had come and went into Arthur's voice mail. He wanted to meet and suggested lunch at Locke-Ober. Arthur thought it was the polite and honorable thing to do in an otherwise embarrassing situation.

Monroe arrived first, an old army habit, and he greeted Arthur warmly when he arrived, minutes later. For a brief second, it seemed like the bankruptcy hearing had not actually happened.

But after they exchanged pleasantries and inquired about each other's family, Monroe said, "Arthur, we have a long history together, and I don't want it to end on a sour note. Nothing will ever change what we have been to each other. But there is a matter of duty. I—and the others on the Overseers— have a fiduciary duty, a high duty, to the technology that has been patented and is under our stewardship. I'm sure you agree."

Arthur nodded, the smile of acceptance already on his face.

"Arthur, the Overseers are going to buy out the Celldesign assets. But we're not going to extend the license as part of the bankruptcy. Without the license behind them, the other assets shouldn't cost too much. We're not going to try to run the business; that would be absurd. But we will find someone. Harvard and MIT are still here, and we will find someone."

Arthur listened quietly and said, "I'm glad, Monroe. I am." Arthur understood that there was an unspoken part of Monroe's message; he could see it in Monroe's face: Arthur's time with the Overseers was over. "My time on the Overseers was a highlight of my life."

The two great men averted their eyes. Then Monroe said, "We feel that we have to protect the integrity of the technology, and that means we can't let just anyone get his or her hands on the contracts, the patch itself, or any of the proprietary information that is behind all that. Once we protect the process, we will look for another person to make a reality out of the dream we all had. But we won't get in bed with Ronald Storrs, and, Lord knows, Mary's career has slipped off the tracks— hopefully temporarily, although I've heard bad things about the US Attorney looking into the matter. They've already contacted us, and, confidentially, my friend, they asked questions relating to Mary *and* to you." Monroe raised his eyes from his plate to Arthur. It was an insider's look, a look that suggested that Monroe had already disclosed more than he should have.

That caught Arthur by surprise. *A US attorney?* It was a chilling prospect. Arthur knew enough to be cool, to say little, and he went back to picking at his scampi.

"I hate to tell you, old friend," Monroe said, "but the Overseers would like your resignation as soon as you feel up to it."

The next morning, after a sleepless night of self-reproach and cold analysis, Arthur concluded that nobody knew about Olga's smartphone except him, but if the US Attorney's office were to raid his apartment, they would surely find it; it was in a small safe he had built into his bookcase years ago, behind his copies of *Crime and Punishment* and *Joseph Anton,* the first place anyone would look. He had to erase his footprints. So, he

gathered the copies of the dossier that he had made and burned
them in the fireplace, and he had Jimmy take his computer
out to Framingham to Rolls's house, with instructions to have
the hard drive cleaned. Then, he put Olga's phone back in his
pocket for one last time and got in his car by himself, after
telling Jimmy that it was for his own good. He drove north to a
small lake just over the Vermont border in a tiny ski town. He
drove over a gravel road branching off the highway, marked
with a sign for Lake Raponda. He parked as inconspicuously
as possible, then walked down a pathway that had been cleared
through the trees to a small boat dock that he knew about
because he had rented a house nearby in past summers, when
he needed solitude to finish one of his books.

He reached into his pocket. The water was clear, and he
could watch the phone sink into the muck at the bottom of the
lake. He took a branch that had broken off from one of the sugar
maples and used it to push the phone farther down, under the
leaves and silt, where it would be lost forever, almost losing
his balance as he did so. Finally, it was gone—not really gone
but hidden, buried, eliminated. At that point, it was all that he
could ask for.

As he turned to walk back to the car, he knew that the day
would come when he would be confronted, and he would have
to lie once again about all that had happened. But on this day,
he had done what was necessary.

When he got back to the car, he regretted having left Jimmy
back in Boston. He was very tired and wondered if he would fall
asleep behind the wheel. Perhaps that's where he got the idea
or, better said, where the first thoughts came from.

He managed to drive up and down the mountains rising
between Bennington and Brattleboro until he picked up I-91,
still awake but only because of the anxiety. It had been a long

ride up, almost three hours, and he had taken nothing to eat, so he stopped at a local greasy spoon in Greenfield, which was visible from 91. As he sat down in one of the booths, he almost wept. He was largely *no longer*—no longer a professor, no longer in control of Celldesign, no longer on the Overseers Board, no longer speaking to his son or grandson. His life had gone from full to absent. He had a hamburger and a cup of coffee, which he paid for in cash, just as a precaution. The restaurant apparently was filled with regulars—everybody seemed to know everyone else, except nobody recognized Arthur.

CHAPTER 20

By eleven o'clock opening-day morning, the temperature had gone up a bit, and the risk of snow had faded away, thankfully for Arthur, who took an Uber to Fenway, Gate C, where he had agreed to meet Spencer. Arthur was a few minutes early, a testament to a certain nervousness he felt. He walked about anonymously, with no concern that he would be recognized, not anymore. He had turned that corner, and although it was liberating not to be on display, there was also a loss of self-importance—a big change for person like Arthur—but on the outside, he looked like just another fan, mesmerized by the anticipation of a new season. A sardonic smile even had formed at the corners of his mouth.

He thought a great deal in those days about the people of Celldesign—Mary, Winston, old Charlie—and how they had fared, but most of his thought went in Spencer's direction.

He stood motionless in the swarming crowd, towering above everyone, as usual, an almost eighty-one-year-old man who had been up and down in life, just like a baseball team goes inning by inning, ahead and behind, and arbitrarily in the ninth, the rules end it, no matter if the tide was turning or if the outcome had long since been determined. In the ninth, it was over. He was not enough of a fan to understand extra innings. He hadn't even taken notice of the Carlton Fisk game when it happened and the rest of Boston went crazy.

He was there but in his own world when he felt a hand on his shoulder and heard Spencer's voice behind him, still familiar. "You all right, Grandpa?"

Arthur smiled, noting that Spencer was wearing a Red Sox cap with the visor to the rear. He nodded and let Spencer lead him by the hand toward the hot dog vendor, where Spencer ordered two dogs, loaded, and two Cokes, but deferred to Arthur for payment. They made their way, without talking, to their seats, right above the Red Sox dugout, and settled in.

It was awkward since they hadn't spoken in months, and even at that time, their relationship had suffered under the weight of Celldesign, always going back to the email—the starting point, some thought, but not Arthur, not any longer. He knew better now. The start of it all was at some place much farther back, perhaps somewhere in Mary's DNA, or in Olga's upbringing in far-off Ukraine, or perhaps even farther back than that, on the streets of Brooklyn, where Arthur Lloyd began trying to make something of himself.

The Sox hitters were knocking bullets into the outfield during batting practice, especially Bogaerts. Then Big Papi stepped in and crushed ball after ball into the right field bleachers, where Spencer usually sat but not that day.

The seats Arthur wrangled could hardly have been better. The two of them got to hear the players, see them up close, and feel their sense of optimism about the new season, with the entire season still in front of them. Spencer was captivated; Arthur was waiting.

And across the diamond, the hated Yankees. As they

warmed up, one could see a certain confidence there, the magic
that comes from winning.

At one o'clock sharp, the head umpire shouted, "Play ball!"
and the season was under way. Yet Arthur sat quietly, with
much on his mind, while Spencer joined all the fans in their
agony and ecstasy over each pitch and each swing. By the
fourth inning, the Yankees were ahead, 2–0. A vendor walked
down the stadium stairs with a portable serving tray that hung
from his neck, shouting, "Beer here, beer here." Spencer looked
over at Arthur, who shook his head and instead said, "How are
you doing?"

An earnestness in Arthur's voice made Spencer turn, but
the beer vendor was insistent. Spencer turned quickly to say
no to the beer man, so that he could answer Arthur. "Okay, for
now. I'm getting my résumé together to apply to grad school for
the summer session, now that the whistleblower issue has been
resolved. I have the money to pay my lawyer and my tuition.
Dad's not—I really can't ask him."

"How is he doing?"

"He's better now that they've moved to Georgia, though
he had a breakdown for sure. But they've got him on some
medication, and he's starting to get it together. Mom's a big
help."

*Thank God the dossier never got public. They must never
give up on each other; that's all there is.*

"That's good. Are you headed for Stanford? You know that
I'm friends with the dean there."

"I'm hoping to get into Chicago."

"Economics?"

"No, psychology."

"That's new. Suppose I could get you into Harvard?"

"Think I'll stick with Chicago."

Their conversation drifted along somewhat awkwardly, but the Sox scored three runs on a homer by Mookie Betts with two aboard, and Spencer was drawn back to the game. But he turned back when he heard Arthur say, "I wanted to explain myself."

Spencer heard a new quality in Arthur's voice—not anger, not frustration, nothing demanding; rather, a tone of opening up—and he turned his head and body away from the playing field so that he faced Arthur and could see his eyes.

"You will hear soon enough. The US Attorney's Office has been in contact. They are concerned that I obstructed justice. Somebody apparently saw me throw a cell phone into Lake Raponda, and they claim that the phone was Olga's. Even though she was dead, it still counts as obstruction of justice." Arthur turned his head out toward the right field bleachers, even though there was no action out there. Pedroia was at bat against Severino, grinding out every pitch like he always did.

Spencer remained riveted on Arthur. "Does that mean jail?" he asked with an air of disbelief.

Arthur smiled wanly. "I will not go to jail," he said firmly. "Although more to the point, I am guilty of many things, including not meeting the standards that I … taught and lived by, or so I thought. You know, if you slide off the rails, you need to get back on right away, or things will accumulate. There is temptation, and sometimes that is very strong. Before you know it, you have done something that was unthinkable just moments before. You should remember that."

Spencer felt something. "Well, you'll be around to remind me."

Arthur pursed his lips, an expression of some hard-won inner compromise. "I'm sorry I doubted you."

"I'm sorry I sent the email to Mary instead of consulting with you."

"Mine was the greater sin," Arthur said.

They looked on as one of the Yankees batted against Price, neither of them really watching.

Arthur pressed on. "And how is your father?"

"Grandpa, you just asked that. Better, now that he's moved."

"I mean, what does he say about me?"

"Same as always. What happened in bankruptcy didn't really change much for him. You cast a pretty big shadow. Celldesign was … more of a symbol of that for Dad than anything else. He's taken up painting. Goes to the beach in the morning and paints the waves. It seems better for him than Boston was."

They went back to the game. Price struck out the side. It was time for the seventh inning stretch.

"It was not logical, you know," Arthur said. "It was not logical that you were right."

Spencer didn't know how to take that, so he replied jokingly, "You're right about that! Me against the cubicle squad. Who would have thought?"

But Arthur's eyes were serious. "I mean, you can't be a scientist and falsify the data being reported. It goes against the whole concept. And we hired nothing but scientists."

Spencer looked back at the playing field. "Except me."

"I mean, it was a hard call. Two paths before me—which one to take?"

"Same here. I'm no hero. I would have renounced except for old Charlie and his shenanigans. But then the state lab came out and sort of made the decision for me."

"Hmmm," Arthur said in a kind of agreement. "You were right, at the end of the day. And I was wrong. In good faith, mind you, but wrong. And you kept on being right, and I kept on being wrong, and somewhere in that sequence of things, the good-faith part got lost."

The game started back up. Arthur asked, "What did you say you're doing next?"

"Chicago. Psychology."

"You sure you don't want to go to Harvard?"

Spencer shook his head.

Arthur asked, "Is there anyone in your life?"

Spencer thought how unusual it seemed for Arthur to ask such a question. "Well, there was a girl, a wonderful girl, but it didn't work out. Too much spotlight, too much being on the news. It just wasn't normal, and we kind of fell apart. My fault, I guess."

"I'm sorry to hear that. But don't give up. You may have to tough it out, but sometimes that works out best. Sometimes it doesn't."

They each faced the field. It was the bottom of the eighth inning, with the Yankees still one up.

Spencer, now distracted, snuck a look over at his grandfather; it seemed to be a trigger of sorts.

Arthur said, "You know, son, I painted myself in a certain way—for public consumption. As I walked across Harvard Yard, my vision was focused ahead, sure, but I was simultaneously watching a movie inside my head—a movie of myself as I assumed others saw me, the Arthur Lloyd that I thought others saw: kind of idealized, looking the part, noticeable, 'Hey, there's the great Arthur Lloyd.' And, you know, that inner movie worked for a heck of a long time. It made me feel good; it was so nourishing. But in the end, my life did not hold up to the movie version."

Spencer did not know what to say. He looked down and

noticed Arthur's hand, the one closest to him. It had two brown spots near where the thumb and forefinger meet. Age spots, he was sure; he had heard his mother complain about them often, but he had never paid much attention to them. He had never noticed them before. He moved his own hand over until it rested on his grandfather's and covered the brown spots. It seemed to be enough, somehow.

There was a pause. The Red Sox were down to their last out. Arthur looked tired, so Spencer said, "It's late in the game. The outcome is already determined. Why don't we head on home?"

They walked up the concrete steps and then down the walkway, out to the street. "I feel better," Arthur said as he looked hard at Spencer.

Spencer smiled and said, "You all right to get home?"

They parted, as they had on the courthouse steps, but this time facing each other in the middle of the sea of humanity pouring out of the stadium. On ordinary days, the two of them would have been jostled and pushed and talked to irately for having stopped and stood still in such a place. But it was opening day, and camaraderie was in the air. Spencer would chalk it up to that. A new year, a year (for them) in which Celldesign, having been broken down into assets and sold, would become someone else's dream. Spencer thought that the odds of that working out were approximately the same as the Red Sox winning the World Series. He smiled to himself and gave Arthur a hug. To Spencer, it all seemed perfectly fine—a feeling so bittersweet that it would stay with him for all his remaining years.

Arthur hailed a cab and headed not directly home to his apartment but to his parking garage. Getting out of the cab, he searched for the key fob and walked in. It was dark, with no natural light. Any illumination came from ceiling-mounted fluorescent lights encased in filmy plastic that always seemed to be marked by the shadows of dead insects. His steps echoed. The contrast between Fenway and the parking garage could not have been starker, yet he felt that he would have been as alone in Fenway as here, if not for Spencer. He got into his graphite-colored Benz 550 with tinted windows, the point of which he had never before appreciated as much as on that evening. He turned the radio off and headed west, out Route 9, and, as planned, took the cloverleaf-shaped exit for the Mass Pike. Then, pushing down on the accelerator, wheels screeching as he began the turn and then pressing his foot down harder on the accelerator, harder, bouncing left, the driver's side gave in to centrifugal force, wheels losing contact, rolling twice and hitting a lamppost, square in the middle of the car, driver's side, crushing Arthur. And he slipped into a dream. He was walking across Harvard Yard, head high, a tartan scarf around his neck to ward off the cold, just like his movie. And he stayed there for eternity.

Arthur's name carried weight. There was a reputation involved, an image built up over the years. It was often, as Spencer considered the matter, a backward-looking creation of those who were not really close to him. But Spencer thought that Arthur would have foreseen that and accounted for it. It would have been as much on his mind as choosing the exit ramp that he knew he could not navigate at that speed. He would have taken the process farther, to the next step. That would have been his nature.

THE GREAT MR. LLOYD

As Spencer sat in the nondenominational church in Harvard Yard, he felt a certain pain, not just from Arthur's passing—that pain was evident elsewhere. He looked over at his father and saw a mixture of sadness and relief that Arthur was gone. Winston was orphaned, but he was finally wealthy. It was all there on his face. Dorothy's face. Mandy's face—the same.

Spencer felt something different, perhaps because he was the last one to see Arthur alive and because he knew that Arthur had planned for that fact. *What*, Spencer asked himself, *did Arthur mean by that? What?*

Why on earth did he spend his last moments at Fenway, a place he'd disdained for decades?

When Dorothy called him, she said, "Accident."

Who is she kidding? he thought.

Yet everyone seemed to accept it as fact.

It was more of an agreement, Spencer thought. Like a nondisclosure agreement. But unspoken. In short, everyone knew it was untrue, that it was not an accident, but everyone went along with the story. It was credible—enough. And it avoided any more questions. And it ended Celldesign. Finally and forever.

Thus, it was a bewildered young man who sat in the corner spot in the first pew.

The service was a somber affair. Dorothy insisted on a closed casket, but the nondenominational church was open to guests and dignitaries, all of whom looked serious and sad, as if scripted, just in case there was a cameraman hidden nearby, just in case a photo would wind up on the six o'clock news.

But it was a charade, Spencer thought, everyone pretending that the last two years never happened, when, as Arthur himself knew best, they had.

The viewing followed script, except for the closed casket.

Dignitaries, former students, old friends—they all walked past the casket with somber faces. But Spencer was thinking about the curse of the Bambino. The story was that the Red Sox had bowed to a false god almost one hundred years before. They traded the Bambino, the great Babe Ruth, to New York for a pocketful of money, and they spent the next eighty-six years without a World Series, as divine punishment. He recalled a day, many years before, when he, as a young boy, tried to explain the curse to his grandfather and was told with a tolerant smile that it was merely a superstition. At the time, a crushing blow.

But Spencer continued to believe in the curse nevertheless; it was part of being a Red Sox fan.

And at that moment, he felt that was all he had—the sum total. A Red Sox fan with a dead famous grandfather.

Spencer glanced over at Winston and Mandy, sitting together expressionlessly. *Arthur would have foreseen that*, Spencer thought.

The state police had found Olga's phone, but it had been effectively destroyed by the muck and lake water, and so, what was on it would never be revealed—lost with Arthur, as he wanted it.

Mary had gone to Garrigall, expounding on how that was proof of Arthur's criminality, and of course there were follow-up articles in the *Globe*, speculating about what had happened. Meanwhile, Mary was put under house arrest by the U.S. Attorney's office, to await trial on security fraud charges. She had asked for Alan's firm to be appointed her counsel.

Rodney was a no-show. At some quiet level, that enraged Spencer.

Jimmy walked by the coffin, drunk as a coot, helped along by the next in line.

Then something caught Spencer's eye. In a plain black dress, holding flowers in two hands clasped together, a willowy girl with dark hair and Joan Baez eyes, turned down just a touch at the corners, where a tear appeared ready to drop. She was looking straight ahead, but when she reached the casket, she searched the cavernous church, and their eyes met, again.

CPSIA information can be obtained
at www.ICGtesting.com
Printed in the USA
LVHW090402150220
647082LV00001B/36